About the Author

MITCH ALBOM is the author of numerous books of fiction and nonfiction, which have collectively sold more than forty-one million copies in forty-seven languages worldwide. He has written eight number one *New York Times* bestsellers—including *Tuesdays with Morrie*, the bestselling memoir of all time—award-winning TV films, stage plays, screenplays, a nationally syndicated newspaper column, and a musical.

Through his work at the *Detroit Free Press*, he was inducted into both the National Sports Media Association and Michigan Sports halls of fame and is the recipient of the 2010 Red Smith Award for lifetime achievement.

Albom founded and oversees SAY Detroit, a consortium of nine different charitable operations in his hometown, along with a nonprofit dessert shop and food product line to fund programs for Detroit's most underserved citizens. Since 2010, he has operated an orphanage in Port-au-Prince, Haiti, which he visits monthly. He lives with his wife, Janine, in Michigan.

www.mitchalbom.com
www.saydetroit.org
www.havefaithhaiti.org

The Little Liar

The Little Liar

Mitch Albom

SPHERE

SPHERE

First published in the United States in 2023 by Harper,
an imprint of HarperCollins Publishers
First published in Great Britain in 2023 by Sphere

1 3 5 7 9 10 8 6 4 2

Copyright © by ASOP, Inc.

The moral right of the author has been asserted.

A CIP catalogue record for this book is available from the British Library.

ISBN 978-0-7515-8457-8

Printed and bound in Great Britain by
Clays Ltd, Elcograf S.p.A

Papers used by Sphere are from well-managed forests
and other responsible sources.

Sphere
An imprint of
Little, Brown Book Group
Carmelite House
50 Victoria Embankment
London EC4Y 0DZ

An Hachette UK Company
www.hachette.co.uk

www.littlebrown.co.uk

For Eva and Solomon Nesser, and others who wore the numbers on their arms, and for all who still mourn them.

It is not your memories which haunt you.
It is not what you have written down.
It is what you have forgotten, what you must forget.
What you must go on forgetting all your life.

—JAMES FENTON, "A German Requiem"

Everything's gonna change, everything but the truth.

—LUCINDA WILLIAMS

Part I

—

1943

"It's a lie."

The large man's voice was deep and hoarse.

"What's a lie?" someone whispered.

"Where we're going."

"They're taking us north."

"They're taking us to die."

"Not true!"

"It is true," the large man said. "They'll kill us once we get there."

"No! We're being resettled! To new homes! You heard the boy on the platform!"

"To new homes!" another voice added.

"There are no new homes," the large man said.

A shriek of train wheels silenced the conversation. The large man studied the metal grate that covered the only window in this lightless wagon, which was intended to carry cows, not humans. There were no seats. No food or water. Nearly a hundred others were crammed inside, a solid block of human beings. Old men in suits. Children in their sleeping clothes. A young mother cupping an infant to her chest. Only one person was sitting, a teenaged girl with her dress hiked up over a tin bucket the passengers were given to relieve themselves. She hid her face in her hands.

The large man had seen enough. He wiped sweat from his forehead then pushed through the bodies toward the window.

"Hey!"

"Watch it!"

"Where are you going!"

He reached the grate and jammed his thick fingers through the holes. He grunted loudly. With his face contorting, he began to pull.

Everyone in the cattle car went silent. *What is he doing? What if the guards come?* In the corner, a lanky boy named Sebastian stood against the wall, watching all this unfold. Next to him was most of his family, his mother, his father, his grandparents, his two younger sisters. But when he saw the man pulling at the window grate, his focus turned to a thin dark-haired girl a few feet away.

Her name was Fannie. Before all the trouble began, before the tanks and the soldiers and the barking dogs and the midnight door-pounding and the rounding up of all the Jewish people in his home city of Salonika, Sebastian believed that he loved this girl, if there is such a thing as love when you are fourteen years old.

He had never shared this feeling, not with her or anyone else. But now, for some reason, he felt swollen with it, and he focused on her as the large man wiggled the grate until it loosened from the wall. With a last mighty pull, he ripped it free

4

and let it drop. Air rushed through the open rectangle, and a springtime sky was visible for all to see.

The large man wasted no time. He pulled himself up, but the opening was too small. His thick midsection could not fit through.

He dropped down, cursing. A murmur went through the train car.

"Someone smaller," a voice said.

Parents clutched their children. For a moment, nobody moved. Sebastian squeezed his eyes shut, took a deep breath, then grabbed Fannie by the shoulders and pushed her forward.

"She can fit."

"Sebastian, no!" Fannie yelled.

"Where are her parents?" someone asked.

"Dead," someone answered.

"Come, child."

"Hurry, child!"

The passengers shuffled Fannie through the scrum of bodies, touching her back as if sealing wishes upon it. She reached the large man, who hoisted her to the window.

"Legs first," he instructed. "When you land, curl up and roll."

"Wait—"

"We can't wait! You must go now!"

Fannie spun toward Sebastian. Tears filled his eyes. *I will see you again*, he said, but he said it to himself. A bearded man who had been mumbling prayers edged forward to whisper in Fannie's ear.

"Be a good person," he said. "Tell the world what happened here."

Her mouth went to form a question, but before she could, the large man pushed her through the opening, and she was gone.

Wind whooshed through the window. For a moment, the passengers seemed paralyzed, as if waiting for Fannie to come crawling back. When that didn't happen, they began pushing forward. Ripples of hope spread through the boxcar. *We can get out! We can leave!* They crushed up against one another.

And then.

BANG! A gunshot. Then several more. As the train screeched its brakes, passengers scrambled to put the grate back over the window. No luck. It wouldn't hold. When the car stopped moving, the doors yanked open, and a short German officer stood in blinding sunlight, his pistol held high.

"HALT!" he screamed.

Sebastian watched the hands fall away from the window like dead leaves dropping from a shaken branch. He looked at the officer, looked at the passengers, looked at the teenage girl crying on the waste bucket, and he knew their last hope had just been extinguished. At that moment, he cursed the one missing member of his family, his younger brother, Nico, and he swore he would find him one day, make him pay for all this, and never, ever, forgive him.

Let Me Tell You Who I Am

You can trust the story you are about to hear. You can trust it because I am telling it to you, and I am the only thing in this world you can trust.

Some would say you can trust nature, but I disagree. Nature is fickle; species thrive then flame out. Others suggest you can trust faith. Which faith? I ask.

As for humans? Well. Humans can be trusted only to watch out for themselves. When threatened, they will destroy anything to survive, especially me.

But I am the shadow you cannot outrun, the mirror that holds your final reflection. You may duck my gaze for all your days on earth, but let me assure you, I get the last look.

I am Truth.

And this is a story about a boy who tried to break me.

For years, he hid, during the Holocaust and after it, changing names, changing lives. But in the end, he must have known I would find him.

Who could spot a little liar better than me?

"Such a beautiful boy!"

Let me introduce you to him, before all the lying began. Stare at this page until your eyes drift into cloudy subconscious. Ah. There he is. Little Nico Krispis, playing in the streets of Salonika, Greece—also known as Thessaloniki—a city by the Aegean Sea that dates back to 300 BCE. Here the ruins of ancient bathhouses mix with streetcars and horse-drawn wagons, the olive oil market bustles, and street vendors sell their fruits, fish, and spices taken off the morning boats from the harbor.

The year is 1936. The summer sun is heating the cobblestone by the famous White Tower, a fifteenth-century fortress built to protect Salonika's shores. In a nearby park, children shriek happily in a game called *abariza*, where two teams draw chalk boxes then chase one another between them. If they are caught, they must stand in the box until they are "freed" by a teammate.

Nico Krispis is the last one left from his team. He is being chased by an older boy named Giorgos. The captured children shout "Look out, Nico!" whenever Giorgos gets too close.

Nico grins. He is fast for his age. He dashes to a streetlamp, grabs hold, then spins around, launching himself like a sling-shot. Giorgos pumps his arms. It's a footrace now. Nico's toe touches the edge of the chalk box just as the older boy slaps his shoulder.

"*Abariza!*" Nico yells as the children scatter. "*Liberté! Freedom!*"

"No, no! I got you, Nico!" Giorgos declares. "I tagged you before you touched!"

The children freeze. They turn to Nico. What's it going to be? He looks at his sandal. He looks at Giorgos.

"He's right," Nico says. "He got me."

His teammates groan. They stomp away.

"Oh, Nico," one laments, "why do you always have to tell the truth?"

I know why.

I can always spot an admirer.

∞

Now, perhaps you ask: Why focus on this one little boy? Of what interest can he be? Are there not billions of lives that Truth could share, baring the intimate accounts of their time on earth?

The answer is yes. But with Nico, I offer you a story of consequence, one that heretofore has never been told. It concerns deception, great deception, but also great truth, and heartbreak and war and family and revenge and love, the kind of love that is tested over and over. Before the story ends, there is even a moment of magic, set against an endless tapestry of human frailty.

When we finish this story, you may say, "That was impossible." But here is the funny thing about truth: the less real something seems, the more people want to believe it.

So consider this about Nico Krispis:

Until he was eleven years old, he never told a lie.

That will get you noticed, at least by me. If Nico snuck a sweet roll from the kitchen, he would admit it the moment he was questioned. If his mother said, "Are you tired, Nico?" he would confess he was, even if it got him sent to bed early.

In school, if Nico was unable to answer a teacher's question, he would willingly share that he had not read his homework. The other students laughed at his honesty. But Nico's grandfather, Lazarre, whom Nico adored, had taught him early on of my precious value. When Nico was only five years old, they were sitting near the harbor, staring over the gulf at the majestic Mount Olympus.

"My friend told me the gods live up there," Nico said.

"There is only one God, Nico," Lazarre replied. "And he does not live on a mountain."

Nico frowned. "Then why did my friend say it?"

"People say many things. Some are true. Some are lies. Sometimes, if you say a lie long enough, people believe it's the truth.

"Never be the one to tell lies, Nico."

"I won't, Nano."

"God is always watching."

Three things to know about Nico Krispis.

1. He had a remarkable facility for languages.
2. He could draw almost anything.
3. He was an attractive child.

The third item will prove significant as we go on. Nico was blessed with the best features of his tall, muscular father, a tobacco merchant, and his fair-haired mother, who volunteered at a local theater in hopes of taking the stage. I claim no credit for a person's physical features, but I can tell you that whatever countenance you were born with, Truth will enhance it.

I have a look.

Nico wore that look on a face that was so pleasing, even strangers stopped to admire him. "Such a beautiful child," they would say, touching his cheeks or his chin. They would sometimes add, "He does not look Jewish." This, during the war, would also be significant.

But what strangers were mostly drawn to with Nico, beyond the wavy blond hair, the sparkly blue eyes, or the full lips that spread over prominent white teeth, was his pure heart. There was no guile anywhere.

He was a boy to be believed.

Over time, people in his neighborhood began calling him Chioni—the Greek word for "snow"—because he seemed so untouched by earthly deceit. How could I not take note of such a creature? In a world full of lies, honesty glimmers like silver foil reflecting the sun.

The Rest of the Cast

Now, to fully tell you Nico's story, I must include three other people, who will intertwine constantly over the course of his unusual life.

The first is his brother, Sebastian, whom you've met already on the train. Three years older, dark-haired, and considerably more serious, Sebastian tried to be a good son while quietly harboring an older brother's envy of his pampered younger sibling.

"Why do we have to go to bed now?" Sebastian would moan.

Translation: *Why does Nico get to stay up as late as me?*

"Why do I have to finish my soup?"

Translation: *Why doesn't Nico have to finish his?*

The older brother was bony where the younger was lithe, and self-conscious where the younger was at ease. Many a time when Nico was entertaining the family with comic imitations, Sebastian would be curled up near the window, a book in his lap, a frown on his face.

Was Sebastian as truthful as Nico? Sadly, no. He lied about the usual things, brushing his teeth, taking coins from his father's drawer, whether he'd paid attention at synagogue, and, once he reached adolescence, why he was taking so long in the bathroom.

Still, the older boy was fiercely devoted to his family, his mother, Tanna, his father, Lev, his grandparents Lazarre and Eva, his twin baby sisters, Elisabet and Anna, and yes, when pressed, even his younger brother, Nico, who was his rival in racing through the olive oil market, or swimming off the city's east side beaches.

But Sebastian saved his greatest devotion for the girl named Fannie.

Fannie is the third person in the little liar's tale. Before the train ride that changed her life forever, Fannie had been a shy twelve-year-old on the cusp of young womanhood, her features in midbloom, flashing olive eyes, generous lips, a shy smile, a slim, budding figure. Her raven corkscrew hair covered her narrow shoulders.

Fannie's father, a widower named Shimon Nahmias, owned an apothecary on Egnatia Street, and Fannie, his only child, would help him organize the shelves. Sebastian would often visit the shop on the pretense that he needed something for his mother, but he was privately hoping for time alone with Fannie. Although they had known each other all their lives, and had played together as children, things had changed in recent months. Sebastian felt a rumble in his stomach whenever she looked at him. His hands began to sweat.

Sadly, Fannie did not share this attraction. Being younger, she was actually in Nico's class in school, where her seat was just in back of his. The day after her twelfth birthday, she wore a new dress that her father had purchased as a present, and Nico, forever honest, smiled at her and said, "You look pretty today, Fannie."

From that moment, her heart was set on him.

I said I had a look.

But all right. To complete the introductions, let us return to that train, which in the summer of 1943 was barreling from Salonika up through central Europe. Many today are unaware that the Nazis, in their efforts to conquer the continent, invaded Greece and claimed that hot country as their own. Or that Salonika, prior to the war, was the only city in Europe with a Jewish majority population—which made it a ripe target for the Nazis and their Schutzstaffel, or SS, troops. They did there what they did in Poland, Hungary, France, and elsewhere: rounded up the Jewish citizens and led them to their slaughter.

The final destination of that train from Salonika was a death camp, the one called Auschwitz-Birkenau. The large man had been right. Not that it did him any good.

"HALT!" the German officer repeated, as he pushed his way through the passengers and reached the window. He was squat and thick-lipped, his face tightly cut, as if there were no spare skin to soften his jutting chin or bulging cheekbones. He waved his gun at the grate on the floor.

"Who did this?" he asked.

Heads looked down. No one spoke. The German lifted the grate and examined its sharp edges, then gazed up at the bearded man, the one who'd told Fannie to "be a good person" and "tell the world what happened here."

"Was it you, sir?" the German whispered.

Before the bearded man could answer, the German swung the grate into his face, ripping the skin from his nose and cheeks. The bearded man shrieked in pain.

"I'll ask again. Was it you?"

"He didn't do it!" a woman screamed.

The German followed her eyes to the large man standing silently by the window hole.

"Thank you," the German said.

He raised his pistol and shot the large man in the head.

Blood splattered the train wall as the large man collapsed. The gunshot's echo froze the passengers in their shoes. The truth was (and I should know) there were enough people in that car to overwhelm the German officer and put him down. But at that moment they could not see me. They could only see what the German wanted them to see. That he, not them, was the minister of their fate.

"You want to go out this window?" he announced. "Very well. I will let one of you go. Who should it be?"

He turned his head left and right, considering the haggard faces before him. He stopped on the young woman clutching her baby.

"You. Go."

The woman's eyes shot back and forth. She edged toward the opening.

"Wait. First give me your child."

The woman froze. She pulled the infant closer.

"Did you hear what I said?"

He pointed his gun at her nose and grabbed the baby with his free hand.

"Now you can go. Hurry up. Through the window."

"No, no, please, please," the mother stammered. "I don't want to go, I don't want to go . . ."

"I'm giving you the chance to leave. Isn't that why you destroyed my window grate?"

"Please, no, please, *please*, my baby, my baby."

The woman collapsed into the legs of her fellow captives. The officer shook his head.

"What is it with you Jews? You say you want something, then you don't."

He sighed. "Well. I said one of you can go. I must keep my word."

He stepped to the window, and, with a swift swing of his arm, tossed the baby through the opening. As the mother howled and the prisoners trembled, only Sebastian made eye contact with the officer, long enough to see him smile.

His name was Udo Graf.

He is the fourth person in this story.

A Parable

When God was about to create Man, He gathered all the top angels to debate the merits of the idea. Should it happen? Yes or no?

The Angel of Mercy said, "Yes, let Man be created, for he will do merciful deeds."

The Angel of Righteousness said, "Yes, let Man be created, for he will do righteous acts."

Only the Angel of Truth disagreed. "No, let Man not be created, for he will be false and tell lies."

So what did the Lord do? He considered all that was said. Then He cast Truth out of heaven and threw him to the depths of the earth.

Well, as your young people say: that hurts.

The story is accurate. How else could I be here, talking to you?

But was I wrong to warn God that Man would be deceitful? Clearly, I was not. Humans lie constantly, especially to their Maker.

Still, the reasons for my heavenly expulsion are hotly debated. Some suggest I was buried beneath the ground to rise when mankind was elevated to its best nature. Others say I was being hidden on purpose, as my virtue is beyond your capacity.

I have my own theory. I believe I was hurled to earth to smash into billions of pieces, each of which finds its way into a human heart.

And there I thrive.

Or die.

Three Moments

But enough of that. Back to our tale. Life changed quickly for our four protagonists during the tumultuous years of the 1930s and 1940s, when war was brewing, then stewing, then everywhere.

Let me present three specific moments.

You will see what I mean.

We are in 1938.

A festive night on Venizelou Street in Salonika. Inside a busy café, a "crowning ceremony" is taking place. In the Jewish faith, this marks the day parents marry off their final child. Food is spread across two long tables, fishes, meats, plates of cheeses and peppers. Cigarette smoke hangs in the air. A small band of musicians plays guitars and Greek bouzoukis.

The dancing is energized and sweaty. The bride's name is Bibi, and her proud mother and father are Lazarre and Eva Krispis, Nico's grandparents, who have been together for so long their hair is turning gray simultaneously. They are hoisted on wooden chairs and danced around the room. Eva grips her chair's levered back, afraid of falling. But Lazarre is enjoying himself. He raises his hands in an "up, up, up" motion.

Little Nico is seven years old. He stomps his feet to the music.

"Higher, Nano!" he yells. "Go higher!"

Later, around a table, the family cuts pieces of baklava and walnut cake soaked in syrup. They drink dark coffee, smoke cigarettes, and converse in multiple languages, Greek, Hebrew, or Ladino, a Judeo-Spanish spoken commonly in their community. The children have already finished their dessert, and some of them play on the floor.

"Whoo, I am so tired," Bibi says, taking a seat.

Bibi is the last of her parents' three children to reach the altar. She is hot from all the dancing and wipes the sweat from her forehead.

"Why did you wear that thing over your face?" Nico asks.

"It's called a veil," his grandfather interjects, "and she wore it because her mother wore one, and her mother's mother wore one, and all the women going back to the ancient days wore one. When we do something today they did thousands of years ago, do you know what that makes us, Nico?"

"Old?" the boy says.

Everyone laughs.

"Connected," Lazarre says. "Tradition is how you know who you are."

"I know who I am!" the boy declares, pointing his thumbs at his chest. "I'm Nico!"

"You are a Jew," his grandfather says.

"And a Greek."

"A Jew first."

Bibi taps the hand of her new husband, Tedros.

"Happy?" she asks.

"Happy," he says.

Lazarre slaps the table, smiling broadly.

"Next, a grandchild!"

"Oh, *Papa*," Bibi says, "let me get out of the wedding dress first."

"That's usually how it happens," Lazarre says, winking.

Bibi blushes. Lazarre lifts Nico and places him on his lap. He cups his cheeks.

"How about another one like this?" he says. "Such a beautiful boy."

Across the table, Sebastian watches, tapping his fork, silently absorbing the fact that his brother, not him, is the one his grandfather desires to replicate.

Later that night, the family walks along the esplanade. The night air is warm and a soft breeze comes off the water. Fannie and her father are there, too, and Fannie shuffles beside Nico and Sebastian, taking turns kicking a rock along the cobblestone. Nico's mother, Tanna, pushes her sleeping twin daughters in a stroller. Up ahead she sees the majestic White Tower, looking out over the Thermaic Gulf.

"Such a nice night," she says.

They pass a closed shop with newspapers in the window. Lev scans the headlines. He nudges his father.

"Papa," he says, his voice low, "have you read what's happening in Germany?"

"That man is crazy," Lazarre says. "They will get rid of him soon."

"Or it could spread."

"You mean here? We're a long way from Germany. Besides, Salonika is a Jewish city."

"Not as much as it used to be."

"Lev, you worry too much." He points to the shop window. "Look at how many Jewish newspapers there are. Look at how many synagogues we have. No one can destroy such things."

Lev looks back at his children kicking the rock. He hopes his father is right. The family walks on in the moonlight, their conversations echoing over the water.

We are in 1941.

The door swings open. Lev stumbles in wearing a soldier's uniform filthy with dirt. The children rush to hug his legs and waist, as he moves stiffly to the couch. Three years have passed since that night on the esplanade, but Lev looks ten years older. His face is gaunt and wind-burned, his dark hair dotted with silver flecks. His once powerful arms are now thin and scarred. His left hand is wrapped in fraying bandages, which are caked with dried blood.

"Let your father sit," Tanna says, kissing his shoulder. "Oh, dear God, dear God, thank you for bringing him home."

Lev exhales as if he just climbed a mountain. He drops into the couch. He rubs his face hard. Lazarre sits down next to him. Tears fill his eyes. He puts a hand on his son's thigh. Lev winces.

Six months earlier, Lev left his tobacco business and joined the war against Italy, which had invaded Greece shortly after blowing up a Greek cruiser. Although the Italian dictator, Mussolini, had wanted to show the Germans he was their equal, the Greeks fought back hard, and resisted his invasion. Their newspapers carried one-word headlines:

"OCHI!" (NO!)

No, the nation would not be oppressed by the Italians—or anyone else! Greece would fight for its honor! Men from everywhere volunteered, including many Jews from Salonika, despite doubts from older members of that community.

"This is not your fight," Lazarre told his son.

"It's my country," Lev protested.

"Your country, not your people."

"If I don't fight for my country, what will happen to my people?"

Lev signed up the next day, joining a tram full of Jewish men, all in a hurry to fight. I have witnessed this countless times throughout history, men pumped with the adrenaline of war. It rarely ends well.

The Greek offensive was, at first, highly successful. Their dogged efforts pushed the Italians backward. But as winter descended and conditions grew harsh, the Greek resources dwindled. There were not enough men. Not enough supplies. The Italians eventually sought the help of the powerful

German army, and for the Greek soldiers, this was the end. They were like horses who'd galloped into an open field, only to discover it was full of lions.

"What happened?" Lazarre asks his son.

"Our guns, our tanks, they were so old," Lev says, his voice hoarse. "We went through everything. We were hungry. Freezing."

He looks up, his eyes pleading.

"Papa, in the end, we didn't even have *bullets*."

Lazarre asks about others they knew, Jewish men who'd signed up to fight as Lev had. Lev shakes his head at each name. Tanna puts her hand over her mouth.

Sebastian watches his father from across the room. Something about seeing him so weak keeps the boy from speaking. But Nico is unaffected. He approaches his father and hands him some drawings he made to welcome him home. Lev takes them and forces a smile.

"Were you a good boy while I was gone, Nico?"

"Not all the time," Nico says. "Sometimes I didn't listen to Mama. I didn't finish all my food. And the teacher says I talk too much."

Lev nods wearily. "You just keep being honest like that. The truth is important."

"God is always watching," Nico says.

"That's right."

"Did we win the war, Papa?"

Lev breaks his own advice and lies.

"Of course, Nico."

"I told you, Sebastian," Nico says, smiling at his brother.

Tanna leads her son away. "Come, Nico, time for bed." She looks at her husband, fighting her tears.

Lazarre rises to the window and pulls back the curtains.

"Papa," Lev says, his voice barely audible, "it's going to happen. The Germans. They are coming."

Lazarre pulls the curtains closed.

"They're not coming," he says. "They're here."

We are in 1942.

A hot Saturday morning in Liberty Square, Salonika's main gathering center. It's been more than a year since Lev's return from the war. Shortly after that, the German army invaded the city with tanks, motorcycles, rows of soldiers, and a musical band. Ever since then, food has grown scarce. Services are closed. Nazi soldiers roam the streets and life for Jewish families is horribly restricted. Signs hang in shops and restaurant windows. NO JEWS PERMITTED. Everyone is afraid.

Today the July sun is baking. There are no clouds. The scene in the square is bizarre, almost surreal. It is jammed with lines of Jewish men, shoulder to shoulder, nine thousand of them, standing just inches apart. They were commanded to gather by the Nazi forces who now control the city.

"UP, DOWN! UP, DOWN!" officers scream. The Jewish men hold their hands out and squat, then rise, then squat, then rise again. It looks like calisthenics, except there is no end to them; if a man stops, rests, or falls over exhausted, he is beaten, kicked, and attacked by dogs.

Lev is among the men rounded up here. He is determined

not to break. Sweat soaks his skin as he goes down, up, down, up. He glances to a balcony that overlooks the square. Young German women are taking photographs and laughing. *How can they be laughing?* He looks away. He thinks of the war. He thinks of what he endured in the winter cold. He can handle this, he tells himself. How he wishes for cold right now.

"UP, DOWN! UP, DOWN!"

Lev sees an older man fall to his knees. A German officer yanks on his beard, pulls out a knife, and slices the hair from his face. The man screams. Lev turns away. Another man who has fallen down is kicked in the stomach, then dragged to the street. A bucket of water is tossed on him and he is left there, groaning in pain. Bystanders do nothing.

"UP, DOWN! UP, DOWN!"

It will come to be known as "the Black Sabbath," chosen deliberately by the Germans to violate the Jewish holy day, forcing men who would otherwise be praying in synagogue to be humiliated in public for no apparent purpose.

But there is always a purpose to cruelty. The Germans wanted to change me. They wanted the Jews of Salonika to accept a new version of Truth, one in which there was no freedom, no faith, and no hope. Only Nazi rule.

Lev tells himself he will not succumb. His muscles are so exhausted, they are quivering. He feels nauseated, but he dare not throw up. He thinks of his children, the girls, Elisabet and Anna, the boys, Sebastian and Nico. They keep him going.

"UP, DOWN! UP, DOWN!"

Lev does not know that at this moment, Nico is approaching the scene. He is used to roaming freely around the neighborhood, something his mother has warned against doing. But he slips out anyhow and follows the noise that can be heard blocks away.

When he reaches the edge of Liberty Square, he lifts on his toes to see over the crowd. A German guard spots him.

"Come here, boy. You want a better look?"

Nico smiles and the guard lifts him up.

"See what happens to the filthy Jews?"

Nico is confused. He knows he is Jewish. The guard, fooled by Nico's blond hair and lack of fear, assumed otherwise.

"What are they doing?" Nico asks.

"Whatever we tell them to do." The guard smiles. "Don't worry. They will all be gone soon."

Nico wants to ask where they are going, but the guard suddenly snaps to attention. A transport carrying a short officer in the passenger seat is approaching. It is Udo Graf. He is in charge of this operation.

The guard raises his arm in a salute. Udo nods. Then, in their first but hardly last encounter, Udo sees Nico. He winks. Nico tries to wink back.

The transport moves on, cruising past the rows of exhausted men, rising and dropping under the blazing sun.

How a Lie Grows

Sometimes, I watch people eat. I find it interesting. Food is the substance that keeps you alive, so I would think you would choose the kind that does you the most good. Instead, you choose what pleases the palate. I see you at buffet restaurants, slapping on some of this, some of that, ignoring the rest, even if you know it is more healthful.

I notice this, because it is what you do with me. You choose a sliver of Truth here, a sliver there. You disregard the parts that displease you, and soon your plate is full. But just as ignoring proper food will ultimately decay your body, so will handpicking the Truth eventually rot your soul.

Take a boy, born in 1889, to a large Austrian family. His father beats him constantly, his teachers berate him, his mother, the only person who seems to care for him, dies when he is eighteen. He becomes sullen, withdrawn. He drifts, thinking himself a painter, but finds no acceptance in the art world. Over time, he evolves into a loner. He refers to himself as "Wolf." He develops a penchant for blame. *It's their fault, not mine.* A pattern of self-deception begins.

When war calls, the Wolf volunteers. He likes the clarity of combat, and its chosen truths, for all truths in war are chosen. The only real truth of war is that no one should engage in it.

The conflict ends badly. As his country surrenders, the Wolf lays wounded in the hospital, burning with mustard gas and humiliation. He cannot accept this defeat. To him it means weakness, something he despises, mostly because he has so much weakness inside him. When his country's leaders agree to a peace treaty, he vows to overthrow them one day.

That day arrives soon enough.

He joins a political party. He storms to the top of it. He fires a gun into a ceiling and declares, "The revolution has begun!"

He climbs to power on the back of lies. He starts by blaming his nation's woes on its Jews, and the more he points at them, the higher he rises. *They are the problem! They are the reason for our humiliation!* He accuses Jews of wielding secret powers, hidden influence, of creating a lie so big that no one would question it, an accusation stunningly true of himself. Jews are "a disease," he declares, that must be eradicated to restore German health.

Such falsehoods bring the Wolf power, great power, and crowds of people cheer his speeches. He elevates to chancellor then president then supreme leader. He executes his enemies. He feels his inferiority fading with each new rub of success. He stacks his plate high with lies sizzled in hate, then feeds them to his armies. The armies grow. They follow him over the border, hoping to squash their neighbors under the seductive banner of *Deutschland über alles,* "Germany over all."

Why do they do the Wolf's bidding? Deep down, all humans

know that being cruel to others—torturing them, killing them—is neither good nor righteous. How can they permit it?

Because they tell themselves a story. They create an alternate version of who I am, and swing it like an axe. Why do you think I argued with those other angels? Righteousness? Mercy? I tried to warn them. Those who abuse me will run roughshod over all the other virtues—and convince themselves they are high-minded in the process.

The Wolf's deceptions grow more powerful. He creates words to blanket his evil. This is an old trick. If you want to get away with lying, first change the language.

So he uses the phrase "The Law to Relieve the Distress of the People" to give himself legal authority. He uses the phrase "Living Space" to justify taking land. He uses phrases like "dispatched" or "removed" as kinder words for murder. And he uses the phrase "Final Solution" as a euphemism for his ultimate plan: to wipe Jews off the face of the continent.

He finds loyal followers among the resentful, the alienated, the angry, and the ambitious, in adults who happily turn on their neighbors and in youths who enjoy pushing others to the ground with impunity.

He finds them in bitter, lost souls like Udo Graf, whose mother left his father for a Jewish man, and whose father subsequently took his own life with a blade and a bathtub.

Udo, who studies science at a German university, becomes a loner like the Wolf, a miscreant with no friends. When he is twenty-four, he hears the Wolf speak in a public square. He hears him talk about a new Reich, an empire of German domination that will last a thousand years. He feels as if he's been

given a personal invitation: fol.
of his own miserable existence.

So Udo joins the Wolf's forces. F.
rises in the ranks and, in time, reaches t.
sturmführer, a midlevel commander in the ɪ

Then, in the summer of 1942, the Wolf proɪ.   .nd
sends him to Salonika to execute a horrifying ɩ   .o rid
the city of every Jewish citizen. Which brings us to Liberty
Square that hot July morning. This is how Udo first encoun-
ters Nico Krispis and winks at him, as if all will be well.

It will not be, of course. The end of a lie is always darkness.
But we are far from the end of this story.

A True and Loving Kindness

One Sunday, in the fall of 1942, Lazarre takes Nico, Fannie, and Sebastian to where his parents are buried, just outside the city gates in the eastern section of Salonika. It is, at the time, the largest Jewish cemetery in the world, and some of the graves go back hundreds of years.

"Nano," Nico asks as they climb a hill, "who is the oldest person buried here?"

"Not anyone I knew," Lazarre says.

"There are graves here from the 1600s," Sebastian says.

"Really?" Fannie says.

"It's true, I read it," Sebastian says.

"I don't want to be buried anywhere," Nico says.

"We could throw you in the ocean," Sebastian says.

"That's not nice," Fannie says.

Nico smiles at her.

"I was just joking," Sebastian says. He feels himself go hot with a blush.

They move through the brick and stone markers, which are large and closely placed and cover the ground as far as they can see. Finally, they find the graves of Lazarre's parents. Lazarre takes a deep breath and closes his eyes. He bends slightly and begins to pray, stroking his beard and muttering the Hebrew to himself.

Nico watches. Then he, too, closes his eyes and sways back and forth.

"He doesn't even know the words," Sebastian whispers to Fannie.

"Then why is he doing it?"

"I don't know. He's like that."

When he finishes, Lazarre gets down on his knees and removes a rag from his pocket. He has a small canteen of water, and he wets the rag and begins wiping the tombstone.

"Nano, why are you doing that?" Nico asks.

"Out of respect for your great-grandfather and great-grandmother."

"Can I help?"

Lazarre rips off a piece of the rag. Nico takes it and squats before the stone. Fannie squats next to him and Sebastian does, too. Soon all four are wiping dirt from the markers.

"This," Lazarre says, softly, "is what we call *chesed shel emet*. A true and loving kindness. You know what a true and loving kindness is? Eh? Children? Look at me."

They stop their wiping.

"When you do something for someone that can never be repaid. Like cleaning the graves of the dead. That is a true and loving kindness."

He lowers his voice. "It's easy to be nice when you get something in return. It's harder when nobody knows the good you are doing except yourself."

The children resume their wiping. When they've cleaned the two graves, Nico gets up and walks to another.

"Come on," he says, looking back.

"Where?" Sebastian says.

"We should do theirs, too."

Sebastian rises. Fannie rises, too. Soon the three of them are dipping rags in the water and wiping the facades of strangers' tombstones, one after another. Lazarre closes his eyes and mumbles a prayer of thanks.

Later they walk home in a spray of autumn sunshine. Nico holds his grandfather's hand. Fannie sings a melody. Sebastian hums along. It will be the last time any of them visit that cemetery. Three months later, the entire place will be destroyed.

First, They Take Your Business . . .

Nico loved the smell of his father's smoke shop, which was on the ground floor beneath the offices of the family's tobacco export business. Nico would run there after school, pull the door open, and immerse himself in the sweet, woody aroma. For the rest of his life, he would associate that scent with his father.

One day, in January of 1943, Lev was putting a new box of cigars on a shelf when two men entered the shop. Nico was in the corner drawing cartoons on a notepad. Sebastian was sweeping behind the cash register.

"Good afternoon," Lev said.

The men were Greek, one tall, the other short and fat. Lev recognized the tall one as an occasional customer who bought expensive tobacco for his pipe. The two visitors looked at each other, confused.

"Is there a problem?" Lev asked.

"Sorry," the tall man said, "it's just . . . we are surprised to see you here."

"Why would you be surprised? It's my shop."

The short man held up a piece of paper.

"But no, you see," he said, "it isn't."

Lev stepped forward and examined the sheet. As he read the words, he felt a sickening chill.

Service for the Disposal of Jewish Property

We announce to you that the shop on Votsi Street at No. 10 of the Jew Lev Krispis is ceded to you. You are asked to come to the above service within the day in order to receive the shop mentioned above.

Lev read the words again. He didn't know which stung him more—the usurping of his shop, or the fact that foreign forces were referring to him as "the Jew Lev Krispis."

"We thought you had left," the man said.

Lev scowled. "Why would I leave my own shop?"

"Papa?" Nico said.

Lev stepped toward the men. "Look, I opened this store. I built my business upstairs. Everything you see here, the tobacco, the cigars, the pipes, all this, I paid for."

"Perhaps we should come back tomorrow," the short man stammered.

His partner cleared his throat. "But as you can see, Mr. Krispis, the store has been given to us. It is clearly written—"

"I don't care what is written!" Lev yelled, grabbing the paper. "Do you have no shame? This is *my* shop!"

Nico's mouth dropped. Sebastian gripped his broom. Just then, a transport pulled up and two Nazi officers stepped out.

Lev looked at the paper in his hands, and pushed it back to the strangers.

Ten minutes later, Lev, Nico, and Sebastian were marched to the door and shoved out from behind. That would be the last time they set foot in the tobacco shop. They weren't even allowed to take their coats.

. . . Next They Take Your Worship

The following Saturday, Lazarre, Nico, and Sebastian were walking to synagogue for morning services. Lazarre insisted on taking the boys every Sabbath, ensuring they followed all the rituals and learned to read the texts in Hebrew.

Nico wore a vest over his short-sleeved shirt. Sebastian wore a jacket, tie, suspenders, and, because he had already passed the bar mitzvah age, he carried his own tallit bag, like his grandfather. It was sunny, and the boys walked competitively, hopping from one block of pavement to the next, trying not to land on the cracks between them.

"You missed," Sebastian said.

"So did you," Nico replied.

"No, I didn't."

Nico looked up.

"Hey, there's Fannie!"

Sebastian glanced across the street to see Fannie and her father, also on their way to synagogue. When Fannie waved to them, Nico waved back, but Sebastian looked down.

"You want to kiss her," Nico whispered.

"I do not."

"Yes, you do."

"I do NOT!"

"Who's kissing who?" Lazarre said.

"Nico's lying," Sebastian said.

"He doesn't lie," Lazarre said.

"I'm not lying. You want to kiss her. You told me."

"You're not supposed to say anything!" Sebastian said. His face was red. Nico looked at Lazarre, who wagged a finger.

"If he told you a secret, you should keep it."

"I'm sorry, Nano."

"Say sorry to your brother."

"Sorry, Sebastian."

Sebastian pressed his lips together.

"Race you?" Nico said.

A smile crept across Sebastian's face. He knew he was faster than his baby brother. He knew Fannie would see them run.

"Go!" he yelled, breaking into a sprint.

Nico chased, yelling "Hey!" but Sebastian was far ahead and laughing and Nico started laughing, too. Sebastian reached the corner, hoping Fannie's admiring eyes were on him. He heard Nico's footsteps as he made the turn.

Suddenly, Sebastian pulled to a stop, and Nico ran into him from behind, almost knocking him over. There, standing in the synagogue doorway, were three Nazi soldiers, rifles on their shoulders. They were smoking cigarettes. One of them noticed Sebastian's tallit.

"No church today, Jew," he said.

Sebastian swallowed. He stepped backward. He saw other Germans exiting the synagogue carrying boxes.

Nico edged forward. "But we always go on Saturday."

The soldier eyed the blond-haired boy.

"Why would *you* go here, boy? You're not a Jew pig like him, are you?"

Nico glanced at Sebastian, who shook his head, wanting Nico to say no.

"I'm a Greek and a Jew," Nico said. "But not a pig."

"Where did you get that blond hair?" The soldier grinned. "Maybe your mama liked Germans?"

"Yes," another added. "Maybe she visited Berlin about ten years ago?"

They laughed, but Nico didn't understand why. Before he could respond, he felt two hands on his shoulders. He looked up to see his grandfather.

"Come, boys," he whispered.

He led them around the corner, where they intersected with Fannie and her father, who listened as Lazarre whispered that, as of now, the synagogue, like so many other things in Salonika, was no longer theirs.

"Are we going home, Nano?" Nico asked.

"Not before we pray."

"But the *keliá* is closed."

"We don't need a building."

The five of them walked to the harbor. Finding an empty stretch of pavement along the water, Lazarre took out his prayer book and began to chant, and the others, following his lead, swayed back and forth with him. Fannie stood near the boys, while her father kept a wary eye out for German soldiers. They did this for half an hour, as birds swooped overhead and curious onlookers gawked. When Nico whispered, "What should we be praying for?" Lazarre, with his eyes still closed, answered, "Give thanks to the Lord for all the good in the world."

He paused.

"And pray for this war to end."

. . . Then They Take Your Home

Until he was eleven, Nico knew only one home. It was a two-story rowhouse at No. 3 Kleisouras Street, with white plaster walls, a wooden door, and brown shutters on every window. An acacia tree planted long ago sat out front; come springtime, its leaves turned white.

Inside there was a kitchen, a dining room, and two bedrooms on the main floor, and two rooms in the flat above where Nico's grandparents lived. Large windows looked out to the street. The tobacco business was robust, and Lev, who worked hard and saved his money, was able to keep the house nicely appointed, with a comfortable couch and a grandfather clock. A few years earlier he'd purchased a new set of porcelain dishes for his wife, which she displayed proudly in a wooden hutch.

The house was in a desirable area near the city center, close to the Ladadika olive oil market and within a few blocks of a church, a mosque, and a synagogue, reflecting a Salonika where for many decades Jews, Christians, and Muslims lived together so harmoniously that the city observed three bank holidays a week, Friday, Saturday, and Sunday.

But harmony and humankind make a short marriage. Something always seems to happen.

Which brings us to a rainy Sunday, February 28, 1943.

On that morning, a group of youngsters carrying bulky sacks arrived at Nico's house. Under the Wolf's reign, Jews in Salonika were no longer permitted to attend schools or ride public transportation. Everything they owned had to be declared, including their pets. All their radios were confiscated. Even their food had to be turned over—wheat, butter, cheese, oil, olives, fruits, the fish they caught in the gulf—all of it taken by the Germans for their war effort. Jewish men were ripped from their homes and sent far away for labor projects, forced to work long hours in the hot sun. The men who survived returned only when Salonika's Jewish community gave two billion drachmas to the Germans as ransom for their temporary freedom.

Resistance to this treatment was risky. The Germans controlled almost all aspects of daily life in Salonika. They shut down the Jewish newspapers. They plowed their libraries. They forced every Jewish person to wear a yellow star on their clothing. With the shocking blessing of the local government, they even ransacked the ancient Jewish cemetery that Lazarre and the children had visited a few months earlier, destroying three hundred thousand graves, picking through the bones, searching for gold teeth, as Jewish families wept among the remains of their dead. If there were an honest word for such disregard of other human beings, I would share it. There is not. The Nazis even sold the Jewish tombstones for building material, and some of those tombstones went into street pavements or the walls of churches.

Still, perhaps the most stinging blow to the Jewish community was the closing of the schools to their children. "We have no future if we stop learning," the elders lamented. So they began secret classes in one another's houses. They moved locations to avoid Nazi suspicion.

On this particular morning, it was the Krispis family's turn to host. The sacks the children carried were filled with books, and those books were now spread across the kitchen table. Lev directed the students to their seats. He called for his sons. "Nico! Sebastian!"

At that moment, Nico was hiding in his favorite place in the house: a crawl space beneath the stairs leading up to his grandparents' rooms. The crawl space had no handle; you had to pry the door open with your fingers. Nico would often tuck inside, arms around his knees, listening to the bustling of life outside, his mother chopping food in the kitchen, his aunts gossiping, his grandfather and father arguing over the wages of tobacco workers. He felt secure curled up in the dark. He would wait until he heard his mother or father yell, "Nico! Dinner!" Sometimes he would wait an extra moment, just to hear his name yelled twice.

Meanwhile, at the same time, Sebastian stood by a mirror in his parents' bedroom and checked his reflection. He knew Fannie was out there with the other kids, and he'd spent extra time pulling on his suspenders and pushing his dark hair this way and that, hoping to make himself more presentable.

His primping was interrupted by the sudden sound of banging doors and heavy footsteps. He heard strange male voices. He heard his mother yelling. He opened the door and saw the unmistakable black and brown uniforms of German soldiers moving about the furniture and barking orders in a language he didn't understand. A mustached man who'd entered with them—Sebastian recognized him as Mr. Pinto, a member of the Jewish police—translated the screaming into Ladino.

"Get your things! Five minutes! You must be gone in five minutes!"

What followed was a cacophony of confusion and terror, played out in short, incongruous sentences.

"Where are we going?"

"Five minutes!"

"Tanna, grab what you can!"

"Children, you must all go home now!"

"Five minutes!"

"Where is Nico?"

"Sebastian!"

"Where are we going?"

"Four minutes!"

"Nico!"

"The bread. Take the bread!"

"Do you have money?"

"Shoes for the girls!"

"Sebastian, find your brother!"

"He's not here, Papa!"

"Three minutes!"

"Lev, I can't carry this!"

"Where are we going?"

"Take something to cook with!"

"Two minutes!"

"Where are we going?"

Before they knew it, they were outside on the pavement, as a light rain drizzled on their heads. Lev carried a suitcase and a bag. Sebastian had his clothes in his arms. Tanna held her daughters' hands and pleaded with the officers.

"Our son!" she yelled. "We have another son! We need to find him!"

The Germans were indifferent. Up and down the blocks, other Jewish families were being evicted. They huddled together at the foot of their homes, holding their possessions as if a fire had chased them out. Except there was no fire, only Nazi soldiers smoking cigarettes, some of them chuckling, amused by the confusion. They raised clubs and rifles and pushed the Jews toward Egnatia Street.

"Walk!" a German soldier barked at the Krispis family. Tanna was crying. "Nico!" The soldier again hollered, "Walk!" and Lev shouted, "Please! Let us find our son!" Another soldier slammed his rifle into Lev's chest, knocking him to the sidewalk.

Sebastian lunged to help his father, but Tanna pulled him away. As Lev struggled to his feet, Sebastian looked back at their now-abandoned home. Through the second-story window, he caught a flash of movement. The curtains opened. Peeking out were two faces: Nico and Fannie.

A shiver shot through Sebastian's body. He should have

been happy seeing his brother alive. He should have yelled to his mother, "He's safe! He's in there!" Part of him wanted to. But another part—which felt that if anyone should be protecting Fannie it should be him—trembled in silent rage.

So he did not say a word. And with that silence, he changed his brother's life forever.

Sometimes, it is the truths we don't speak that echo the loudest.

∞

The Jewish families were marched through the streets, carrying their possessions like vagabonds, past the Alcazar Cinema and past the Vienna Hotel and past the many shops and apartments along Egnatia Street. Residents stood on their balconies watching. Lev looked up to see some of them cheering or waving goodbye sarcastically. He looked away.

When they reached Vardaris Square, the families were marched toward the sea and into a run-down neighborhood by the railway station known as the Baron Hirsch quarter, built for the homeless after the great fire of 1917. It was mostly decrepit one-story structures or huts.

The Germans barked out names. They somehow had lists of all the Jews in Salonika, how many members per family, who was male, who was female, their ages, their sizes, details that left the victims mystified. Families were ordered to enter this or that building.

"You will receive more instructions in the coming days!" an SS officer hollered. "Do not attempt to leave or there will be consequences!"

That night, the Krispis family slept in their new "home," a dirty, one-floor flat with no bathroom, no beds, and no sink. They shared this space with two other families, fourteen people overall, their hastily packed possessions now stacked against the wall. It was all that remained of the life they'd known that morning.

Tanna didn't care about her lost kitchen, bedroom, or the hutch with her beloved dishes. She kept crying for her son. "You have to find Nico, Lev! We can't leave him out there!"

So Lev went to search the streets, only to discover that all of Baron Hirsch had been enclosed by wooden walls and barbed wire. He spotted a man he knew from the tobacco business, a squat, bearded merchant named Josef, who was staring at the barricade, as if examining a math problem.

"How do we get out?" Lev asked.

Josef turned.

"Didn't you hear? The Germans said any Jew trying to reach the outside will be shot on sight."

Udo Finds a Place to Stay

As evening fell on Kleisouras Street, the temperature dropped and the rain turned to light snow. A transport pulled up to the Krispis family's now empty rowhouse, and Udo Graf stepped out. He ordered a soldier to fetch his valise. He paused at the acacia tree and ran a finger under its budding white leaves. Then he entered the stairway to the main level, passing Pinto, his translator, who held the door open for him.

Udo looked around. He had wanted a place near the city center and the Nazi headquarters nearby. This would do nicely.

"Find the biggest bedroom and put my things there," he told Pinto. He was claiming the Krispis house for his own, the way all the desirable Jewish homes had been claimed by German officers—and all possessions within them usurped. The Nazi soldiers even wore the suits that were found in the closets and sent the nice dresses home to their wives.

Udo saw nothing wrong with this. Quite the opposite. It all seemed rather pathetic to him, the way these Jews surrendered what they had so meekly, like mice being chased out of a hole. To him, it proved they didn't deserve such things in the first place.

He plopped down on the couch and bounced a few times. If he had to be stuck in this country, the least he could expect was a comfortable couch at the end of the day. He was happy to have earned his large assignment from the Wolf, to oversee the deportation of the entire Jewish community of Salonika— *fifty thousand of them!*—but he privately wished it were closer to home and the cooler skies of his motherland. He did not like anything about Greece, not its summer heat or its noisy people. He couldn't understand their multiple languages. And the food here was strange and oily.

As he pressed into the cushions, he glanced at the remnants of the family who had lived here this morning. Some toys in the corner. An old green tablecloth. Porcelain plates in a hutch. A framed photograph of a family at a wedding.

"What time is it, Pinto?" Udo asked.

"Just past eight, sir."

"See if they have any brandy in this house. Or whiskey. Or anything."

"Yes, sir."

Udo leaned back in the couch and removed a small notebook from his uniform pocket. He made notes at the end of each day, his accomplishments, his thoughts, the names of his collaborators. Having read the Wolf's story in a book, he felt his own existence might be chronicled one day. He wanted the details to be accurate.

As he wrote, he felt his gun press against his thigh. It occurred to him that he had not shot it since yesterday. *A good soldier should fire his pistol at least once a day,* a senior officer had once told him, *like emptying your bowels.*

So Udo reached for his luger and dragged it slowly across his line of vision, looking for a target. He settled on the framed photograph. He pulled the trigger and fired, blowing the frame off the table, shattering the glass, flipping it wildly before it landed on the floor.

Which is when Udo heard a thumping sound. He rose, curious, and went to the stairs. He dug a fingernail into the frame of a crawl space door. When it pulled open, he peeked inside, coming face-to-face with a blond-haired boy whose blue eyes were bulging.

"Well, now," he asked Nico, "what do we have here?"

Acceptance

Of all the lies you tell yourself, perhaps the most common is that, if you only do this or that, you will be accepted. It affects your behavior with classmates, neighbors, colleagues, lovers. Humans do a great deal to be liked. They are needier than I can comprehend.

I will tell you this much: it is often futile. The truth is (there I go, referencing myself) people ultimately see through efforts to impress them. Sometimes faster, sometimes slower, but they do.

The person trying to impress Udo Graf was a Jewish dockworker named Yakki Pinto, an individual who, for most of his life, had longed for acceptance. Mustached, reed thin, never married, fifty-three years old, Pinto lived in the eastern end of the city and walked an hour to the docks every morning. He had few friends and little education. He spoke with a stutter. Before the war, he mostly kept to the boat he worked on and the filtered cigarettes he smoked.

But Pinto's grandmother was born in Hamburg. She had lived with his family when Pinto was growing up, and he'd learned the German language from her.

When the Nazis entered Salonika, they created something called the Judenrat. The word itself translates to "Jewish Council," but I have spoken about the power of twisting language. There was no "council" being sought, just a sham to pretend that Jews had some control over their fate. Those who joined the Judenrat were charged by the Germans with implementing their orders, as were the Jewish "police" established under their control. And while some in these positions tried to stave off the harshest Nazi indignities, most were viewed by fellow Jews as collaborators not to be trusted.

Pinto had volunteered for the Judenrat almost immediately, and Udo Graf had determined his German skills could be useful. He could translate the gibberish these Greek Jews were speaking.

"Your task is simple," Udo had told him. "You translate what I say, and you tell me exactly what they are saying. No lies. No deviations."

Pinto agreed. He actually smiled when he received his official papers with the Nazi stamp on the bottom. He believed working beside the enemy would protect him from their wrath.

Silly thought. Would a lamb be protected from a wolf simply by walking alongside it?

∞

"His name is Nico, but they call him Chioni," Pinto said, as the boy stood against the living room wall, tugging nervously on his clothes.

"What does *chioni* mean?" Udo asked.

"Snow."

"Why snow?"

"Because . . ." Pinto fumbled with the German word for "pure." "Because he doesn't lie."

"Doesn't lie?" Udo was intrigued. He turned to Nico. "Tell me, boy who doesn't lie, have we met before?"

Pinto translated. Nico answered.

"I saw you at the square once. You were in a truck."

Udo remembered. The boy who tried to wink.

"How old are you?"

"Eleven. Almost twelve."

"Why don't you lie?"

"My grandfather says it is a sin."

"I see." Udo paused. "Tell me, Nico, are you Jewish?"

"Yes."

"Do you believe in God?"

"Yes."

"Do you pray in a synagogue?"

"Not anymore. Someone took it."

Udo grinned.

"But before that, Nico. Did you attend?"

"I used to go every Saturday." He rubbed his nose. "And also, I ask the questions at the Passover seder, even though my sisters are younger. The youngest is supposed to ask them, but they don't talk yet, so I do it."

Udo studied the boy's face. His blue eyes were perfectly distanced. He had good teeth, soft cheeks, a delicate chin, blond hair, and a nose that did not look Jewish in any way.

Had the child not confessed his heritage, Udo might have regarded him as a fine example of Aryan youth.

He decided to test him further.

"Why were you hiding under the stairs?"

"There was a lot of noise. Everyone sounded scared. So I stayed inside."

"Were you hiding by yourself?"

"No."

Udo's eyes widened. "Who else was with you?"

"Fannie."

"Who is Fannie?"

"She's in my class. My brother likes her. He wants to kiss her."

Udo laughed. Pinto laughed with him.

"And where is Fannie now?"

"She went home."

Udo stood up.

"Do you know who I am, Nico?"

"No. But you have the black coat. My mother says I should stay away from the men in the black coats."

"Why?"

"I don't know. That's what she says."

Udo scratched his chin. He felt the mother's fear in the boy's voice.

"Can I go be with my family now?" Nico said.

Udo walked to the window. He pulled back the curtain. He saw, in the lamplight, a dusting of snow covering Kleisouras Street.

Snow, he thought. *And they call this boy "Snow."* Was it some kind of sign? Udo believed in signs. Perhaps he was meant to move into this house, find this boy, use him for some purpose.

"I have an idea, Nico. How you can be a hero to your family. Would you like that?"

Nico started to cry. The weight of this encounter was taking its toll. He missed his papa. He missed his mama. It was already dark outside.

"Can they come back to the house?" he asked.

"I'll tell you what," Udo said, smacking his lips. "If you do what I ask, you can all be together again."

He leaned over, his chin just a few inches from Nico's eyes.

"Now, will you help me?"

Nico felt himself swallow. He wondered if Fannie had gotten home. He wished he had left with her.

Wait. What happened to Fannie?

We last saw her peeking through the window curtains with Nico. But what was she doing there?

Well. Remember that children are still children. Even under the most dire circumstances, they will create moments to be exactly their age.

Fannie, at twelve, was of the age when her thoughts were often about boys, how they looked and how they looked at her, and one boy in particular, Nico, who, as mentioned, sat in the desk in front of her at school. He was less severe-looking than some of the older boys, with their pimples and newly sprouted hairs above their lips. Nico was almost . . . pretty.

During class, Fannie would stare at him from behind, seeing how his thick blond hair came to a point just above the collar of his white shirt, how sometimes it was wet in the morning when he first sat down. She imagined reaching over and running her hand through it.

On the day Fannie and the other students arrived at the Krispis home, she looked for Nico but did not see him. She went to the stairs, where she noticed the crawl space door nudged open. She saw Nico peeking out. He smiled but pulled the door back closed. Fannie knocked.

"What are you doing in there?"

Nico eased the door open.

"This is where I stay sometimes."

"Can I see it?"

"It's pretty dark."

"That's OK. I still want to see it."

"All right."

He let her crawl inside. She pulled the door shut behind her. Nico was right. It was dark, and there wasn't much room. She felt funny being this near to him without seeing his face—a bit dizzy, a bit warm, but happy.

"How long do you stay in here?" she whispered.

"It depends," he whispered back. "Sometimes I listen to what they're saying outside."

"Isn't that like spying?"

"I don't know. Maybe. Do you think I shouldn't do it?"

Fannie smiled in the darkness, happy that he sought her opinion. "I think it's OK. It's not really spying if you don't mean to."

Fannie heard the other children talking and pulling out chairs. She knew at any moment they would be called for school. She hoped it wouldn't happen before she got to ask Nico a question, a question she had been practicing in her head for a while. The question was: "Nico, do you like me?"

She didn't get to ask it. There was a loud noise, then the sound of heavy footsteps and German voices hollering orders and things being moved about. Frightened, Fannie found Nico's arm and slid her hand down to his wrist and fingers.

Outside, they could hear things being dragged across the floor. Doors opened. Doors closed. They heard Nico's mother yelling his name, but both of them were too scared to move.

"What should we do?" Fannie whispered.

"My father says if the Germans come, you hide," Nico said.

"So we should stay here?"

"I think so."

Fannie felt her knees trembling. She squeezed Nico's hand. They stayed that way for several minutes. Finally, not hearing any noise outside, Nico eased open the crawl space door. The house was empty. They tiptoed to the windows, pulled the curtains, and looked down to see Nico's family surrounded by soldiers. Nico pulled the curtains closed and they hurried back into the crawl space.

Fannie was crying. She wiped the tears with her palms.

"I'm really scared," she whispered.

"Don't be," Nico said. "My papa is strong. He won the war. He'll come back for us."

"Can I hold your hand again?"

"OK."

They fumbled in the dark until their grips locked.

"I'm sorry my fingers are wet," Fannie said.

"It's OK."

"Where do you think they are going?"

"I don't know. Maybe to that place where you have to answer questions and then they let you come home."

"I hate the Germans. Don't you hate the Germans?"

"You're not supposed to hate people."

"You can hate them. It's different."

"You're supposed to like people."

Fannie exhaled. It was the wrong time to ask the question, but doing so made her feel less frightened.

"Nico?"

"What?"

"Do you like me?"

He took a moment to respond. Fannie felt a knot in her throat.

"Yes, I like you, Fannie," he whispered.

∞◇∞

An hour later, they inched the door open. The house remained deserted but now so were the streets. Nico went to a closet and gave Fannie his brother's raincoat.

"Put this over your head so they don't see who you are," he said.

"All right."

"Where will you go now?"

"To my father's shop. He'll be there. He's always there."

"Good."

"If he's not there, can I come back?"

"Yes."

"Thank you, Nico."

Suddenly, without thinking, Fannie lurched forward and hooked her arms around Nico's neck, pushing her face alongside his. She brushed her lips across his cheek and ever so briefly made contact with his mouth.

"Bye," she mumbled.

Nico blinked.

"Bye," he said, hoarsely.

She slipped out the door and into the street.

∞

Her father's apothecary was to the west, less than a mile down Egnatia Street. Fannie wore the raincoat Nico had given her, which was too big for her skinny frame. She yanked the collar up to her ears.

As she walked along the slickened cobblestone, she thought about how they had kissed. It was a kiss, wasn't it? She had never kissed a boy before. And while she would have preferred that he initiated it, it still counted in her mind, and the fact that he didn't seem to object and maybe even liked it made her light-headed. Already she was thinking about when she would see him again.

That brought a lightness to Fannie's step, and she carried that lightness for the length of her journey, right until the moment she turned a corner and froze in her tracks.

The street was jammed with a procession of Jews walking slowly in the drizzle, their heads down. They carried boxes or suitcases. Some pushed carts. They, too, were being exiled from their homes and led like cattle to the Baron Hirsch neighborhood.

Fannie heard her father's voice in the distance.

"Please! It will only take a minute!"

She spotted him in front of his apothecary, pleading with a German soldier who was gripping a rifle.

"It's medicine, don't you see?" Fannie's father said. "People must have medicine. What if they fall ill, or have an accident, or cut themselves? You can see that, right? Just let me go inside and fill a bag with medicines. I will come right back out and we can be on our way."

Fannie allowed herself a breath. Her father was a good talker. His shop, because of the medicine it dispensed, had been allowed to stay open when other Jewish shops were shuttered. Fannie had no doubt her father would work his way inside. Once he did, she would go to the rear entrance and join him. She watched as the soldier who had been shaking his head looked to the sky, seemingly exasperated. Finally, he stepped aside.

"Thank you," her father said. "I won't be a minute."

He moved past the soldier, heading for the door.

What happened next, in Fannie's mind, seemed to take place in watery slow motion. As her father went to enter the apothecary, another Nazi pushed the first one out of the way, raised his pistol, and shot Fannie's father twice in the back. He died with his hand on the doorknob.

Fannie screamed, but she could not hear her own voice. Everything in her brain was a throbbing boom, as if a bomb had exploded inches away and sucked all sound out of the atmosphere. She couldn't move. She couldn't breathe. The last thing she remembered before blacking out was the feel of two arms under her own, and her body falling in line with the others, in a long, dragging march to the ghetto.

Sebastian could barely sleep.

The poor boy was fraught with guilt over not telling his parents about Nico. He spent the first night in their newly assigned dwelling lying on the floor with a stomachache. The more he looked at his mother's face, the worse he felt. The more he thought about Fannie, the worse he felt. He had a bad dream about Nico yelling from inside a fire, and when he woke up sweating, Sebastian decided to come clean.

As fate would have it, he didn't have to. Just before 8:00 A.M., there was a soft knocking from outside a window. Sebastian, still wearing his clothes from the day before, was the first to hear it. He dragged himself to the door, and when he opened it, his heart skipped. An old woman he recognized as the baker's wife, Mrs. Paliti, was standing in the doorway. Next to her, wearing his raincoat, was Fannie.

"Where is your father and mother?" Mrs. Paliti said.

Before he could answer, he heard them rushing to the door. He tried to get Fannie's attention, but her look was vacant and far away, as if she'd fallen asleep with her eyes open.

When Lev and Tanna appeared, the woman said, "Fannie has news about your son."

She nudged Fannie.

"We were in your house," the girl mumbled. "Under the stairs. We were hiding."

"Oh, dear God," Tanna said, clutching her hands. "Is he all right? Where is he now? Is he safe?"

"He was when I left."

"Why did you leave? Why did you leave him?"

"I went to find my father."

"Did your father go and get him?"

The baker's wife caught Tanna's eye and shook her head slightly.

"He's with the Lord now," she said.

"Oh, no," Lev mumbled.

"Oh, Fannie," Tanna moaned. "Oh, Fannie, come here." Tears dripped down Fannie's face. She leaned into Tanna as if her legs were tied together.

Sebastian didn't know what to do. He had a deep yearning to put his arm around Fannie, to feel her hair against his shoulder, to whisper something comforting in her ear.

But all he said was, "You can keep my raincoat."

Nico Dreams of the White Tower

Salonika is a city of great beauty and history and many stories connect the two. On his first lonely night away from his family, Nico lay in bed, fighting tears, remembering one such story. It brought him comfort, and he fell asleep embracing it.

The story concerned the majestic White Tower, a fortress constructed in the fifteenth century to protect Salonika from attack. It was a proud landmark for everyone in the city, and Nico's grandfather Lazarre had taken Nico, Sebastian, and Fannie there to celebrate Nico's eighth birthday. After a special lunch of beef stew, rice with pine nuts, and Turkish pudding for dessert, Lazarre and the children walked the promenade by the gulf. They passed the old hotels and the outdoor cafés with their small tables and colorful awnings shielding patrons from the sun. Soon they reached the tower, and saw the pavilion, restaurant, and grassy park that encircled it.

"I have a surprise," Lazarre said. "Wait here."

Nico, Fannie, and Sebastian watched as Lazarre approached a guard, and the two of them spoke under a pine tree. Lazarre slipped the man some money. Then he nodded for the kids to hurry over.

"Where are we going, Nano?" Nico asked.

Lazarre grinned. "Up."

Nico slapped his brother's arm, and Sebastian smiled back. Fannie actually jumped in the air. Soon the three of them were ascending the many steps that wound inside the fortress, peeking out through the occasional tiny window covered with metal grates. It felt, to the youngsters, as if they were climbing for hours. Finally, they passed through an arched doorway and stepped out to the roof, where the blue sky smacked their faces and the whole of Salonika was laid out beneath them.

The view was unlike anything they had ever seen. To the west were the city's rooftops and the harbor, to the north the hillside and the ancient citadel, to the east the rich mansions with their manicured gardens, and to the south the gulf and the North Aegean Sea, with snowcapped Mount Olympus as clear as a painting.

"Now, I want to tell you all a story," Lazarre said. "Do you know why they call this the White Tower?"

The children shrugged.

"This used to be a prison. It was dirty and dark and there were bloodstains on the outside from inmates who had been killed. There were so many executions here, they called it the Blood Tower.

"One day, the people in charge decided to clean it up. But it was expensive and difficult. No one wanted the job.

"Finally, a prisoner spoke up. He volunteered to paint the entire tower white, all by himself, on one condition: they forgive his crime and let him go free."

"The whole tower?" Nico asked.

"The whole tower," Lazarre said.

"Did he do it?"

"Yes. It took a long time, more than a year, but he finished the job, all by himself. And, as promised, they let him go. From then on, we called it the White Tower."

"Do you know who the man was?" Sebastian asked.

"Not many remember," Lazarre said, "but I do. His name was Nathan Guidili." He paused. "He was a Jew, just like us."

The children looked at one another. The sun was setting and the horizon was turning orange. Lazarre took his grandsons' hands.

"There is a lesson in that story," he said. "Do you know what it is?"

The boys waited as Lazarre looked out to sea.

"A man, to be forgiven, will do anything," he said.

Another Parable

Once, in earlier times, the Angel of Truth decided to walk among the people and share its message of positive power. Alas, the people turned away whenever Truth got close. They covered their eyes. They ran in the other direction.

Truth grew despondent and went to hide in an alley. That's when Parable, who had been watching all this unfold, came to Truth's side.

"What's wrong?" Parable asked.

"Everyone hates me. They turn away as soon as they see me coming."

"Well, look at you," Parable said. "You're stark naked. Of course, they run. They're scared of you."

Parable, who was decked in many colorful robes, removed one and handed it over.

"Here. Put this on and try again."

Truth did as it was told. And sure enough, covered in new and pleasing colors, Truth was welcomed warmly—by the same people who had once run away.

So what do we learn from that?

Some say it's the reason parables teach humans what raw truth cannot. Personally, I don't know what you're all so afraid of.
But then.
It may explain what happens next.

The Lie of Resettlement

I have spoken already of the great lies in this story. How the Wolf twisted language to disguise his evil. How his Nazi minions followed suit, and created endless lists, forms, and official-looking paperwork, all designed to whitewash their brutality.

In Salonika, the lies were everywhere, some as small as the phony pink receipts Jews were given for turning in their radios, some as large as the promise that their homes would not be disturbed after they vacated them, when, in truth, officers moved in hours later and ripped up the floorboards searching for hidden money.

Still, the biggest falsehood was the one the Nazis saved for last.

The Lie of Resettlement concerned a mythical "homeland" where Jews would be "resettled" to live, work, raise their families, and be left alone. The Wolf knew you can only push a people so far; if they know they are doomed, they may fight to the death. He had already degraded and weakened his targets, starved them, taken their livelihoods, driven them to their knees. But even in run-down ghettos like Baron Hirsch, they remained in public view. And in public view, the Wolf could not achieve his darkest impulse, the one he directed his generals to shape during a meeting in a villa overlooking a lake in Wannsee, Germany, in the summer of 1942.

It was there that a final decision was made concerning not only Nico, Sebastian, Fannie, and the others in our story, but every one of eleven million Jews from the shorelines of the British Isles to the mountains of the Soviet Union. That decision, reached in less than two hours over snacks, cognac, and cigarettes, could be summed up in a single sentence:

Kill them all.

Of course, this meant concealment. Evil seeks the dark. Not because it is ashamed. Darkness is simply more efficient. Fewer complications. Less outrage. The Wolf had already built the sites for his final horror—death camps in places like Auschwitz, Treblinka, Dachau. But there remained a logistical challenge: How could he get his victims there? What cover story could fool that many people on a trip to their own massacre?

He needed a mirage. A robe distracting enough to blot me out completely.

The Lie of Resettlement was born.

Lev first heard this lie on his second night in the Baron Hirsch ghetto. He and several other men were warming themselves around a small barrel fire. A young fisherman named Batrous approached and said he'd overheard a Nazi officer talking to his subordinates. The officer said that the Salonika Jews were to be resettled someplace north where they would live and work. Maybe Poland.

"Poland?" Lev said. "Why Poland?"

"Who knows?" Batrous said. "At least we will be safe."

"But it's so far from here. And closer to Germany. If they hate us so much, why would they bring us closer?"

"Maybe to control us?" another man said.

"That makes sense," added another.

"It doesn't, really," Lev said.

"It's better than staying here."

"How can you say that? This is your home."

"Not anymore."

"I'm not going!"

"And if we stay, what is here for us? Our stores are gone. Our houses are gone. You want to keep living in this garbage dump?"

"Better than Poland."

"How do you know?"

The men argued a while longer, then dispersed without agreement. But the Lie of Resettlement went home with them and spread through the ghetto like a wind blowing through a wheat field.

Udo Needed a Ruse

He dragged on his cigarette and stared at his desk. The paperwork was endless. Lists. Manifests. And train schedules to the death camps. So many of them! Every stop detailed to the minute. The Wolf's instructions were clear. Nothing could interfere with rail efficiency.

Udo privately wondered about his leader's obsession with trains. Was it their imposing size? Their intimidating roar? Whatever the reason, he knew the consequences if any hiccups occurred. He'd heard of an incident in France where Jews on the platforms had revolted and fled. In the confusion, two German soldiers were killed. The Wolf had been furious.

Udo wanted no part of that. He needed to ensure the Jews under his control would board those trains without protest. He already had the Lie of Resettlement. But having his officers bark that out in German hardly seemed reassuring. Udo needed someone to sell the Jews on the idea. In their own language.

Which was where Nico Krispis came in.

The boy had been staying with Udo in the house on Kleisouras Street. He truly was, as Pinto had said, honest to a fault, answering every one of Udo's questions without hesitation. A shame that he didn't have more useful information, like where the Jews who had fled to the mountains were hiding, or where gold and jewelry might be hidden in the neighbors' houses.

Still, Udo had grown convinced that the boy could serve a purpose. He seemed to know many people in the Jewish community, where his family was apparently quite active. If he could help ensure things moved smoothly on the railway platform, it would be worth the trouble of keeping him alive.

Nico had never been inside a train station.

Two weeks after his family had been taken away, he got his first look. The exterior resembled a large house, with slanted rooflines and large first-floor windows. The entrance was rimmed with five glass panes, two long ones and three short ones. On the pale front walls, the Nazis had hung giant Vs, symbols for Victory.

Nico entered the building and gazed up to the ceiling. Udo was on one side. Pinto was on the other.

"Are you certain we can trust this boy?" Udo asked in German.

"Look at him," Pinto answered. "He thinks he's on an adventure."

Nico may have seemed distracted, but he was actually listening intently, absorbing the German language the two men spoke. His ear for different tongues, and his ability to already speak Greek, Ladino, French, Hebrew, and some English, accelerated the process.

"Today I am going to show you your job, Nico," Udo said, nodding at Pinto for translation. "Did you ever have a job before?"

"Not a real one," Nico answered.

"Well, this will be your first. And if you do it well, do you know what you get?"

"A yellow star?"

Udo stifled a laugh. "Yes. I'll give you a yellow star."

"And my family gets to come home?"

"If you do your job well."

"My papa says I am a good worker. But my brother works harder than me. He always sweeps the store. I'm a bad sweeper."

Udo shook his head. The boy never stopped offering information.

They paused in the middle of the hall. By Udo's order, the station had been emptied of personnel, so it was just the three of them inside.

"All right, Nico. Listen to me." He pointed through the doors to the platform. "Tomorrow when you come, there will be many people out there. And there will be a train. The people will not be sure where the train is going. Some of them might be confused. Maybe even scared."

"Why would they be scared?"

"Well, aren't you scared if you don't know where you are going?"

"Sometimes."

"Your job is to help them. You will tell them where the train is going so they won't be so scared. Can you do that?"

"I think so."

"Good. Now, if you see anyone you know, they might wonder where you have been. You will tell them you have been hiding. And you heard a very important German say that the trains are going north to Poland. And everyone will have a job there."

"But I'm not really hiding."

"You were hiding when I found you, weren't you?"

"Yes."

"So, it's the truth."

Nico frowned. "I guess so."

"Good. Now. Let's test you." Udo crossed his arms. "What will you tell the people?"

"The trains are going north."

"And what else?"

"There will be jobs there."

"And how do you know?"

"I heard you say it."

"Correct. You can also say that all Jewish families will be back together."

"All Jewish families will be back together."

"Good boy." He motioned to the platform door. "Now go on out there and practice."

Nico's eyes widened. Even in the shadow of manipulation, children can be curious, and the boy, who had never taken a train ride in his life, was genuinely excited to see the tracks firsthand. He burst out the door.

"Now, say it loudly, Nico!" Udo hollered. "The trains are going to Poland!"

"The trains are going to Poland!" Nico yelled.

"We will have new homes there!"

"We will have new homes there!"

"And the Jewish families will be together!"

"The families will be together!"

Nico stopped and cocked his head, as if watching his voice echo its way toward the Pieria mountains in the distance.

I watched, too. I witnessed this boy, so loyal to me all his life, seduced away by a heartless deceiver. The parable says that Truth was crestfallen when God cast it down to earth. Perhaps. But when Nico Krispis shouted the first lie of his life on those railroad tracks, I wept. I wept like a baby abandoned in the woods.

One Very Large Wedding

The night before the first train departed, dozens of Jews in the Baron Hirsch ghetto gathered outside a shack. It was chilly and damp and they huddled together, rubbing each other's shoulders to keep warm. Every few minutes, a small group was ushered through the doors.

Earlier that day, the Germans had announced that all Jews should prepare to leave the next morning, and to have one bag packed of a certain weight and size. Beyond that, the people knew nothing. Only rumors, including a curious one about the rules upon their arrival:

Married couples will be given priority for their own flats.

Where this started, no one could say. But what if it were true? Realizing there would be no chance to change status later, families quickly arranged marriages. Compatibility did not matter. Age did not matter. Weddings forged in love are about planning for the future; weddings forged in fear are about surviving it.

That night, a rabbi gathered five couples at a time in the shack. By candlelight, he led them in brief rituals that would bind them as wed. Some were older men matched with widows from the war with Italy. Others were teenagers. They repeated a string of Hebrew words, mumbling them flatly and quickly. There was no backslapping. No dancing. No cake. They exchanged rings, sometimes made of rounded paper clips, then exited, making room for the next wave.

When the final group was called, Sebastian shuffled in the back. He clenched his jaw to keep himself from crying. He had just passed his fifteenth birthday, which his family marked with an extra portion of bread and a piece of hard candy. Now he stood beside a plump sixteen-year-old girl named Rivka, whom he barely knew, other than she had a brother who used to push Sebastian around in school. In his hand was a ring his grandmother had given him. He squeezed it so hard it left a mark on his palm.

Sebastian had strongly protested this idea. He told his parents he was too young to be married, and he didn't even like the girl. They insisted it was about security, that when this terrible ordeal was over he could undo it somehow, but for now he must do as they say. Sebastian ran off, red-faced and furious, screaming that he didn't want "a stupid flat." He raced to the barricades and stared at the barbed wire, tears burning his eyes.

I felt for the poor boy. But he was not being truthful. The real reason he did not want to marry the girl named Rivka was because his heart was set on Fannie. A marriage to someone else, he feared, would soil him, mark him as taken, forever lock him away from her. In the weeks that had passed since their relocation, Sebastian and Fannie had spent some time together in the ghetto, playing card games with the other children, or reading whatever books they could find. Fannie, still stunned from the loss of her father, didn't speak much. Still, for Sebastian, those moments felt like the only light in an endless gray day.

Now, standing among a group of soon-to-be-newlyweds, Sebastian thought again of Fannie's face, and he prayed she would never learn of what he was about to do. He placed the ring on Rivka's finger with his eyes averted. At fifteen, Sebastian Krispis became a husband without looking at his new wife, as if not witnessing something could make it disappear.

Three Betrayals

When the Lord was handing out qualities, Trust was freely distributed. Humans and animals each got a share. But betrayal?

That went to mankind alone.

Which brings us to a date:

August 10, 1943

This was the day of three betrayals in our story. All of them took place on the platform of the Baron Hirsch rail station, late in the morning, as the final train left Salonika for the death camps at Auschwitz.

There had been eighteen transports in the previous months. By Udo Graf's judgment, they had gone quite well. On schedule. No incidents. Udo had implemented small deceptions to smooth the process, such as telling the Jews to convert their money to Polish zlotys and handing them credit slips that would never be cashed. Udo watched in amusement as these starving fools willingly handed over the very last currency they had, still trusting that the Nazis would treat them right in the end. He even had guards load the luggage as if they were porters.

His best trick, however, was Nico Krispis. That, he told himself, was a small stroke of genius. The boy had done exactly as instructed, weaving through the platform crowds, whispering promises of jobs, homes, and "Resettlement!" This planted in the passengers' anxious minds that last ounce of trust needed to get them through the train doors.

Nico, wearing the yellow star Udo had given him, was so convincing in his tale of overhearing a German officer say families would be reunited, that some departing passengers actually hugged him in gratitude. Many knew Nico from the neighborhoods or the synagogue—they called him Chioni—and seeing he was alive brightened them just enough to believe his story. Udo was proud of devising this lying-Jew tactic and decided that in his next conversation with the Wolf, he would share it, and perhaps they would talk military strategy.

Udo had let the boy sleep in his old room during this process. That seemed to calm him. At the dinner table Udo watched him gulping bread and meat.

"Slow," Udo said. "You must chew and then swallow."

"*Aber ich bin hungrig sehr*," Nico said, trying his German.

"*Sehr hungrig*," Udo corrected. "Very hungry. *Very* goes before the word."

"*Sehr hungrig*," Nico repeated.

Udo caught himself watching the boy sometimes, curious at how he filled the idle hours, reading dictionaries, playing with the odd toy, or staring out the window. Udo had no children of his own. He'd never married. After the war was won, he told himself, he would find a proper German woman, of good character and excellent features. His stature as a senior officer would provide a wide choice of potential brides, of that he was certain. Children would surely follow.

Meanwhile, he was taken aback by Nico's innocence. After all, the boy was now twelve. When Udo was that age, he'd already smoked his first cigarette, drunk his first beer, and gotten into plenty of trouble fighting older boys from his Berlin neighborhood.

But this kid was different. One night, when Udo complained of a headache, Nico knocked on his bedroom door and offered a towel soaked in hot water. Another night, when Udo was drinking brandy, Nico approached with a German book and held it out.

"You want me to read this?"

Nico nodded.

"To you?"

"*Ja.*"

Udo was taken aback. He knew he had more important things to do than read to a little Jew. But he soon found himself turning the pages, even inflecting his voice.

As Udo narrated, Nico leaned in, wedging against Udo's shoulder. The contact surprised Udo, who had never had a child this close to him. I would like to tell you it melted the man's heart in some way, and softened his future actions. But I am bound to accuracy.

It didn't change him at all.

∞

The day arrived for the final train, a hot, sticky morning with rain in the air. There had been over fifty thousand Jews in Salonika when the war started; by the time this train left the station, forty-six thousand would have been deported. The Nazis intended to vacuum the city of every Jewish crumb.

Shortly after 10:00 A.M., Lev, Tanna, Eva, Lazarre, Sebastian, the twin girls, Bibi and Tedros, Fannie, and the baker's wife stepped into the street and joined a slow march to the train station. For some reason that no one could explain, they had been left in the Baron Hirsch ghetto for months, even as other families came and left.

The twins held hands. The adults held one bag apiece. Lev put his arm around Tanna, who wept at the idea of leaving the city with no knowledge of her youngest son's whereabouts. Sebastian dragged behind, but kept a step ahead of Rivka and her family, who would also be taking the train with him. Rivka smiled. Sebastian looked away.

At the train station, Pinto inspected the luggage car.

This final transport had him excited. Udo Graf had mentioned plans to return to Germany after "the Jew problem" in

Salonika had been addressed. Pinto secretly hoped he could then sneak away to Athens, to wait out the war in relative safety.

He showed no remorse for the tens of thousands he'd helped deport. He needed to survive; that's what he told himself. But I knew the deeper truth. Pinto couldn't wait for this final transport because he couldn't stand to see any more hopeless faces staring back at him as the cattle cars bolted shut. Those sunken eyes. Those down-turned mouths. Such a small distance between the living and the dead, he thought. A few inches, really. The width of a door.

Fifty yards away, Nico stretched his legs.

He knew nothing of the schedule, Udo's and Pinto's plans, or the fact that this was the last train to Auschwitz. He only knew he had missed another Friday. Before the war, on a morning like this, his mother would be in the kitchen preparing for the Sabbath, taking out the good plates and the candlesticks, stirring the food, preparing the *pan azeite y asucar*, bread sprinkled with oil and sugar, Nico's favorite.

He missed his family most of all on Friday nights, the noise, the singing, the sounds of his grandfather clearing his throat before praying, or the way his brother would kick him under the table when they were laughing during a blessing. Sometimes, when Udo Graf was out, Nico walked through his old kitchen, opened the cabinets, and said the Sabbath prayers over the bread, wine, and candles, just so he wouldn't forget the words.

At 10:30 A.M., Nico saw the crowd entering the station. As in previous days, they swarmed quickly, filling the platform, German officers herding them along, forcing them up the ramps and into the boxcars. Nico waded into the pandemonium. He took a deep breath. He didn't like squeezing among people, seeing their sad faces, watching them surrender their suitcases or gaze toward the mountains as if saying goodbye to something forever. He didn't understand why they looked so worried, since they were going to new jobs and houses, maybe even nicer ones than here.

But he did his job, as Herr Graf had instructed. He did it to bring his family home. He pictured the day they would all be reunited, and how his mother would thank him for being a good boy and how his grandfather would rub his head and nod his approval. Nico couldn't wait for that moment. Every night, when he saw Udo Graf sleeping in his parents' bedroom, he felt that he had been plucked from one life and dropped into a new one. He wanted the old one back.

Udo watched from inside the station door.

Less than an hour now, and he would be done. He could file his final papers and escape this city with its dirty harbor and smelly fish market. He wanted to go home to Germany. Cooler, cleaner Germany. Meet with the Wolf. Discuss a new assignment with more strategic responsibilities.

Less than an hour now, he told himself, *as long as everything goes as planned.*

And then, something didn't go as planned. Udo looked

up to see two German couriers hurrying his way, their boots clacking on the station floor. They saluted and handed him an envelope.

Udo recognized the insignia when he removed the contents. It was from the *Oberführer*, his senior officer. The instructions were terse and direct.

> *You will travel with the transport to Auschwitz.*
> *Your new orders will await you there.*

Udo was stunned. He flipped the paper to see if there was anything more. Just like that? They were sending him to a camp? On the train? This was not right. This was not what he deserved. More time spent around these loathsome Jews? Why?

Suspicion took over his body. His breathing accelerated. A heat radiated at the back of his neck.

Somebody has it out for me.

The first betrayal.

∞

Udo's anger propelled him out the door and onto the platform, bumping through the gaunt and exhausted Jewish passengers, a bent old woman with gray hair, a fat, bearded man wheezing breath, two young mustached men, obviously brothers, holding up a weeping woman in a kerchief.

"Get away from me!" Udo barked, disgusted. He grabbed two of his soldiers and told them to hurry to No. 3 Kleisouras

Street and fetch all his belongings. They raced off. As he passed through the crowd, Udo barked out orders in frustration. *"Faster! You are taking too long! Move it, you filthy pigs!"* The passengers huddled closer together, avoiding his gaze.

From a distance, Pinto saw Udo approaching. He pushed up a smile and walked forward. Not knowing what had just transpired, he thought he would ask about the German's plans after this train departed.

His timing could not have been worse.

"My plans?" Udo snapped. "My plans have changed! And so have yours!"

Udo spotted one of his officers. He pointed at Pinto and yelled, "This one goes, too!"

Pinto froze. *What did he just hear?* He was bumped by a tall passenger and almost fell over. A man in a hat slammed against his arm. By the time Pinto regained his balance, Udo had turned his back and was moving down the platform.

"Wait! Herr Graf!"

The next thing Pinto knew, a German guard was nudging a rifle into his shoulder blades, pushing him toward a ramp.

"No! No!" Pinto screamed. "I am with the *Hauptsturm-führer*! I am with Herr Graf!"

Those were the last words he spoke as a member of the protected class. He was shoved into the cattle car and swallowed by the crowd, becoming one of the desperate faces he had so wanted to escape.

The door bolted shut.

The second betrayal.

∞

"The train is going north," Nico whispered as he moved between bodies. "It's all right. Don't be scared."

Faces turned his way. Anxious eyes. Trembling lips.

"What did you say?"

"I heard it from a German officer. They are sending us to Poland. We will have new homes. And jobs."

"Jobs?"

"Yes. And our families will be together again."

Wherever Nico went, murmurs followed behind him. *Did you hear? We will have jobs. It's not so bad.* You might ask why these captive travelers would believe him. But in desperate moments people hear what they want to hear, despite what they might see right in front of them.

Nico kept moving, weaving through the crowd. Some faces looked familiar. He spotted the baker's wife, who burst into tears when she saw him.

"Chioni! You are alive!"

"Yes, Mrs. Paliti! We are being resettled! Don't be afraid."

"Nico, no—"

Before she could continue, a guard shoved her forward. Nico moved on. The platform noise was deafening, so many people crying, yelling questions, guards shouting orders.

"Families will be reunited," Nico whispered. He put a hand to the side of his mouth as if sharing a secret. "There will be jobs. I heard it from a German officer!"

He felt sweat dripping under his arms. There seemed to be

more people today than any other boarding. He wished he could finish and go back to his house.

And then Nico saw Fannie.

She was holding on to the arm of a woman in front of her. Her head was down. Her raven hair was tucked under a cap. Nico pushed forward until he was close enough to call her name.

"Fannie!"

She looked up and reacted slowly, as if something had to be peeled from her mouth before she could move it.

"Fannie! It's OK! We will all be together! They're taking us someplace safe!"

Fannie cocked her head. She smiled. Then her expression changed and her gaze lifted to someone behind Nico—which is when the boy felt two thick hands grab him under the arms and raise him off the ground.

"Stop telling people that!" a deep voice grumbled. "It's a lie. They're taking us to die."

Nico was dropped. His shoes smacked the platform and he tumbled over. He looked up to see a large man glaring at him as he boarded the train and disappeared. Gathering himself, wiping his palms, Nico tried to find Fannie, but she, too, had been swallowed by the crowd.

Nico felt a burning in his stomach. Until that point, he was merely doing what he was told to do, certain it was the right thing. Why would that man say that to him? *It's a lie?* Nico thought of his grandfather. *Never be the one to tell lies, Nico. God is always watching.* No. It couldn't be. *They're taking us to die?* Not true! Herr Graf had promised they would all be getting jobs. Reuniting families. The large man was the liar! He had to be!

Nico spun, searching for the *Hauptsturmführer*, desperate to ask him this question, but there were too many people. The words of the large man kept repeating in his ears. For a few moments, they were all he could hear.

Then Nico heard something else.

Something he'd been yearning to hear since the morning he hid in that crawl space under the steps.

His mother's voice.

"Nico!"

It was unmistakable, even in the din of a thousand other voices. The boy turned and his eyes widened. There was his mama, maybe forty feet down the platform. There was his papa, standing beside her. There was his grandfather and his grandmother and his aunt and uncle and his older brother and his two younger sisters, all staring at him in disbelief.

"Mama!" he shrieked.

Suddenly they were all hollering his name, as if the whole of their language had been shrunk to a single word: *Nico!* Tears filled his eyes. He felt his legs running without even thinking. He saw his mother running, too.

And then, in an instant, he couldn't see her anymore. Three bodies in gray uniforms stepped in front and accosted her.

"NO!" he heard his mother scream. Nico felt someone grab him from behind, and a forearm shoot across his neck.

Udo Graf.

"My family!" Nico yelled.

"I said you would see them."

"I want to go with them! Let me go with them!"

Udo tensed his jaw. *I should let him go*, he told himself. *Be done with him.* That would be protocol. But he knew certain death awaited Nico where this train was going. And in that moment, feeling betrayed by his own superiors, Udo struck back against the rules.

"No," he said. "You stay here."

By this point, Nico's entire family had been shoved inside the wooden boxcar. Nico couldn't see them anymore. He began crying hysterically and writhing under the German's grip.

"Let me go!"

"Easy, Nico."

"You promised! You promised!"

"Nico—"

"I want to go to Poland! I want to go to our new homes—"

"There are no new homes, *you stupid Jew*!"

Nico froze. His mouth dropped. His eyes bulged.

"But . . . I told everybody . . ."

Udo snorted. Something about the child's face, so stunned, so shattered, made him look away.

"You were a good little liar," he said. "Be grateful you're alive."

Steam hissed. The train engines roared to life. Udo

motioned to a Nazi soldier, who swiftly pulled Nico away. Then, without another look at the child he'd broken in half, Udo strode to the front car, angry that he had to get on this transport, angry that his contributions weren't being recognized, angry that this petulant child didn't appreciate how he'd just saved his life.

Minutes later, the train pulled out. The soldier holding Nico, uninterested in playing babysitter, let go and headed for a cigarette. Nico raced down the platform and jumped onto the tracks. He stumbled hard and broke his fall with his hands. He rose and kept running, ignoring the scraped skin of his palms and knees. Three German troops watching from the platform began to laugh.

"You missed your train, boy!" one of them yelled.

"You'll be late for work!" yelled another.

Nico ran. He ran beyond the platform and out into the open spaces where the tracks were surrounded by gravel. He pumped his arms and churned his legs, between the stock rails and past the switch rails, his feet slapping hard on the horizontal wooden planks. Under the hot morning sun, he chased that disappearing train until he couldn't breathe and he couldn't run and he couldn't see it anymore. Then he collapsed in a sobbing heap. His chest was burning. His soles were bleeding inside his shoes.

The boy would survive. But Nico Krispis would die that afternoon and his name would never be used again. It was a death by betrayal, on a day of many betrayals, three on a train platform, and countless more inside those suffocating cattle cars, now heading to hell.

Part II

The Pivots

Truth is a straight line, but human life is a flexible experience. You exit the womb curling into a new world, and from that moment forward, you bend and adjust.

I have promised you a story with many twists and turns. So let me share the following pivot points that happen to three of our four characters in a single week, each of which changes their lives forever.

We begin with Fannie, who falls from the train.

She is hiding by a river now, in a thicket of brush. She dips her hands in the cool water and spills it over her left leg and elbow, which look like they have been scraped with a rake. Her wounds moisten, and Fannie winces.

She has been on the move since the previous morning. She is hungry and exhausted. She wonders if she is even in Greece anymore. She studies the trees by the riverbank, and the dark soil surrounding them. Are they Greek trees? What is a Greek tree? How can she tell?

Her escape from the train comes back to her in flashes: the

fast drop from the boxcar window, the impact with the ground that knocks the wind from her lungs, the sudden flipping, the hard, wild sensation, sky/dirt/sky/dirt, until she finally comes to a halt, flat on her back, gasping for breath. She lays there as pain shoots through her body and the sound of the train grows dim. Then she hears a distant screeching, which means the train is braking.

Someone has seen her escape.

She pushes to her feet, her body so sore it feels as if a bag of glass is being lifted and all its contents shifting. She hears a gunshot. Then another.

She runs.

She runs until her lungs are bursting. Then she stumbles. Then she runs some more. She continues this way for hours, through vast open grass, not a soul in sight, until finally, as the sun begins to set, she finds this thicket of woods framing a winding river. She gulps down handfuls of water, then curls by the trunk of a large tree and hides, fearing the sound of Nazi guards at any moment.

When she can no longer stay awake, Fannie falls into a churning sleep. In her dreams she sees Nico at the train station, calling her name, but she cannot respond. Then he disappears, replaced by Sebastian, grabbing her in the boxcar, pushing her forward. *Take her!*

She awakes with a gasp. Sunlight spills through the branches and she hears chirping sounds. The image of Sebastian is still in her mind and she feels a burn of anger. *Why had he done it? Why had he separated her from the others?* She didn't want to go out that window. She didn't want to be chased like an animal, or sleep by a river with dirt on her forehead and small stones sticking to her neck. Wherever that train was going, it had to be better than this.

She squints in the sunlight. She hears her own breath. She feels a choking loneliness, growing larger as she grows smaller, until every chirring insect, every gurgle of the river, is screaming the words *"Alone, Fannie! You are all alone!"*

She shuts her eyes against a new flood of tears. A moment later, she is startled by the sound of a female voice.

"Zsido?"

She spins to see an older woman with a basket of clothes. The woman wears a long tan skirt and a brown waistcoat over a white cotton blouse with the sleeves rolled up.

"Zsido?" the woman repeats.

Fannie's heart is pounding. She doesn't understand this woman's language, which means she is no longer in Greece.

"Zsido?" the woman says once more, this time pointing at Fannie's chest. Fannie looks down. The woman is pointing at the yellow star on her sweater. The language is Hungarian.

The word means "Jew."

Now to Sebastian's pivot, as the train reaches its true destination.

The doors slide open and passengers shield their eyes from the blasting sunlight. For a moment, all is silent. Then German soldiers in long dark coats are screaming at them.

"Move! Move! Out! MOVE!"

Sebastian, Lev, and the rest of the family are huddled near

the back. It feels like someone is jostling them from a deep sleep. After eight days in this boxcar, their limbs are rubbery and their thought processes groggy. They have eaten only crumbs of bread and small pieces of sausage. They've had almost no water. Their throats burn. The metal bucket to collect their waste was filled by the first day; after that, people relieved themselves in the corners and the stench fouls every particle of air inside the train.

It takes time for the passengers to disembark, because many have perished. The living must stumble through the dead, stepping gingerly over their lifeless husks, as if trying not to wake them. As they move toward the sunlight, Lev glances down to see the bearded man who had whispered to Fannie, "Be a good person," and whose face had been slashed with the grate by the German officer. He is lying on his side, no breath left inside of him, his nose and cheeks a shredded mess of dried blood and pus.

"Sebastian," Lev says, "we cannot leave him here. He is a rabbi. Take his legs."

They lift him together and stagger down the ramp, Tanna and the girls behind them, Lazarre and Eva next, Bibi and Tedros following. Their feet make contact with the muddy earth. Nazi soldiers are everywhere.

"We stay together, no matter what!" Lev yells. "You understand? We stay together!"

What happens next is a bombardment of sights and sounds, absorbed by a fifteen-year-old Sebastian like a violent storm, as if lightning, wind, rain, and thunder all hit at once. First comes the screaming. Officers shouting commands in German, and passengers shrieking the Jewish names of their loved ones. *Aron! Luna! Ida!* Dogs bark and bare their teeth, straining against their leashes. The dead rabbi is ripped from Sebastian's grasp by two soldiers who are piling corpses near the tracks. More screaming. *Rosa! Isak!* A Nazi yells, "Women over here!" and Sebastian sees wives being pulled from husbands, mothers pulled from children, their hands grasping empty air. *No! My babies!* He turns to see his own mother, aunt, and grandmother being pulled away, yelling for their husbands to help them. Sebastian runs in their direction, gets three steps in, and feels a whack across his head that staggers him; a guard has just rapped him with a wooden pole. He has never before been hit in the skull. His eyes go blurry as he reaches for the back of his neck. He feels the warm ooze of blood, making his fingers sticky. Then his father is yanking him backward, yelling, "Stay with me, Sebby! Stay right beside me!" He tries to locate his mother, but she has disappeared into the hundreds of other faces being raced from here to there. Running. Why is everybody running?

Wait. *His sisters! Where are his baby sisters?* He's lost track of them. The dogs howl wildly. There are so many guards, so many rifles, and all these skinny people in striped uniforms, scurrying through the yard like crazed ants. Sebastian glances back at the train; he sees suitcases being thrown into a pile.

More screaming. *Yafa! Elie! Josef!* More orders. *Move! All of you!* The men are broken into lines of five and marched forward, past Nazi officers in various uniforms, some sharply pressed with black tunic collars. When these men point, prisoners are ripped from the line and taken away. It seems that the older and weaker ones are being selected, but it's hard to tell. When Sebastian passes, an inspecting officer looks him up and down, as if studying a piece of furniture. He looks away and Sebastian stumbles forward, holding on to the back of his father's jacket, being tugged along in foggy confusion, still not knowing what country he is in, what air he is breathing, or even having the moment it takes to ask the obvious question: Why is this happening? To him? To his parents? To the rest of his family and everyone on that train?

There is no time to think about his brother.

Nico pivots on the railroad tracks.

Hours after that last transport departed, he is still stumbling along the rails, hoping to see the train reappear. He continues walking west, eventually reaching the Gallikos river, and a metal bridge that crosses it. When night falls, he plops down near that bridge and falls into an exhausted sleep.

He is awakened by a rifle poking him in the chest. He squints into the glaring sun and sees the face of a Nazi soldier, who yells in German:

"What are you doing out here, boy? On your feet!"

Nico rubs his muddy face. His legs ache when he tries to stand. He feels somehow different this morning. Almost numb. He speaks to the soldier in the soldier's native tongue.

"The train," Nico says. "Where did it go?"

"You speak German?" The soldier is taken aback. "Who taught you this?"

"I work for Hauptsturmführer Graf," Nico says.

The soldier's look changes.

"Graf? . . . Udo Graf? . . ." he stammers. "If that's true, why aren't you with him?"

The soldier doesn't seem much older than Sebastian. Nico shuffles his feet and pushes up on his toes, trying to make himself taller.

"Where did the train go?" Nico says again, imitating the tone he often heard Herr Graf use when speaking to his men. "The one from yesterday? With all the Jewish people? Tell me."

The soldier cocks his head, wondering if this boy is being clever or just plain stupid. Maybe it is a test?

"The camps," he replies.

"Camps?" Nico doesn't know that word in German. "What camps?"

"I think they call it Auschwitz-Birkenau. In Poland."

"And what do they do at the camps?"

The man runs two fingers across his throat, as if slitting it.

A shiver shoots through Nico's body. In his mind he sees his mother yelling his name, running toward him on the platform. He sees his father and grandparents and little sisters, calling out for him. Tears begin to stream down his cheeks. The large man had been right.

Nico was the liar.

The weight of all this slumps the boy's shoulders. His head drops like a heavy rock. He doesn't care what this soldier does with him. His family is gone.

What have I done?

The soldier, confused by the boy's demeanor and his strange knowledge of German, decides he isn't worth the risk. If he shoots him, and he truly works for the *Hauptsturmführer*, it could cost him his position. If he lets the kid go, who would know?

He glances down the riverbank. He looks up the road. "Listen, boy," he says. "Do you have any money?"

Nico shakes his head no. The soldier reaches in his pocket and hands over a small wad of bills.

"You tell Herr Graf that Sturmmann Erich Alman helped you. Erich Alman. You hear? Tell him to remember me. Erich Alman."

Nico takes the money and watches the soldier go. He stays by the tracks until nightfall. Finally, in the dark, he begins to walk back to Salonika. He follows the tracks until they reach the Baron Hirsch station. From there, he finds his way to Kleisouras Street. It is well past midnight when he climbs the steps of his family's house. He goes to his parents' bedroom. He looks around. In a drawer, he finds some of his father's old cigars from the shop. He sniffs them and begins to cry. He crawls into the bed where his mama and papa used to sleep. He curls under the blanket, wishing he could wake up and everything would be a year ago.

Instead, when morning comes, the house seems emptier than ever. Even Herr Graf's possessions are gone.

Nico walks down the stairs. He sees his beloved crawl space. He pries the door open. Inside, he sees a brown leather bag, sitting by itself. He pulls it out.

The bag belongs to Udo Graf, who had hidden it there for safekeeping. The soldiers, in their haste, had not looked inside the crawl space. Nico unzips his discovery to find inside, among other things, a good deal of Greek and German money, assorted papers and documents, and a small box with several Nazi badges.

Nico stares at them for a long time. He thinks about what he has done. As the clock strikes ten in the morning, he makes a decision. Like many decisions that change a life, it comes silently, without fanfare.

Nico finds a clean shirt and pins one of the badges to his chest. He hides some of the money in his shoes. He gathers as much food as he can fit in the leather bag and walks out the door, heading back to the train station, where he purchases a ticket on the next train going north, the direction of Poland.

When the curious ticket seller asks his name, Nico does not hesitate. He lies with perfect German enunciation.

"My name," he says, "is Erich Alman."

A World of Light and Dark

I sometimes think about the angels in heaven, what they are saying about me, and what they make of this hard baked world. If you wonder whether certain periods here on earth make me wish I was still there, the answer is yes.

The months that followed were one such period. It was a time of madmen, Nazis drunk on power and bathing in their own cruelty. Much of the world looked the other way. I could not. Truth was forced to acknowledge every act of torture and humiliation, every prisoner made to crawl in the mud like an animal, every new boxcar of victims arriving at the camps, their hands clawing through the planks, begging for mercy when none was given.

It was a time in human history where the world was cleaved in two, those doing nothing about the horror and those trying to stop it. A world of light and dark.

So yes, there were moments where I wished myself in heaven. But there were other moments as well, moments of tenderness and unexpected warmth:

Fannie, as it happened, was not turned in by the woman

near the river, but instead was taken to the woman's home and given a bowl of soup with pieces of lamb and carrots.

Sebastian did not perish that first night at Auschwitz; he curled up against his father in a filthy bunk, and in the darkness, Lev squeezed an arm around his son to keep the boy from shaking.

Nico rode the trains for several days, learning how to pay for his own meals and how to present his tickets without suspicion. A porter one day noticed his impressive Nazi badge and asked where he was going.

"To see my family," Nico said.

A world of light and dark. The greatest cruelty, the greatest courage. It was a strange time to be in the truth business. Yet there I was, unable to turn away.

Twelve Months Later

"Hit him!" the guard yelled.

Sebastian flicked the small whip onto the man's back.

"Harder!"

Sebastian complied. The man did not move. He had collapsed minutes earlier on a work detail and lay on the ground until the guard spotted him. His face was blotchy with dark red spots, and his mouth was open in the mud, as if taking a bite of the earth.

"Are you so weak you can't wake him up?" the guard said, lighting a cigarette.

Sebastian exhaled. He hated inflicting pain. But if the man did not respond, he would be judged as dead, and his body would be burned in the red brick crematorium. At that point, whether he was still alive wouldn't matter.

"Stop daydreaming," the guard growled.

This task, flicking an ox sinew to see if prisoners had expired, was Sebastian's latest job at the camp known by its German name as Konzentrationslager Auschwitz. In the year since his arrival, Sebastian had endured many assignments, always running from task to task (walking was forbidden), removing his cap and lowering his eyes whenever an SS officer approached. He worked all day and had only a portion of bread and some foul-tasting soup to eat at night. Sometimes the guards would throw a chunk of meat into the crowd of prisoners and watch them fight like dogs to grab it, the winner stuffing it down his gullet, the losers crawling away.

Being young and strong like Sebastian carried a bittersweet consequence at Auschwitz; you avoided being gassed to death the day you arrived. Instead, your body withered week by week, starved, beaten, frozen, its ailments ignored, until, like this man in the snow, you dropped.

"Hit him harder," the guard snapped, "or I'll hit you."

Sebastian flicked the whip. He didn't recognize this prisoner, who looked to be in his early fifties. Perhaps he'd just arrived on the train and, like the others disembarking here, had been stripped of his clothes, shaved of every hair on his body, left to stand all night in a shower room, his bare feet soaking in cold, dripping water, only to be rubbed down in the morning with harsh disinfectant, then run naked through the yard to get his striped prisoner clothes and cap. Perhaps this was his very first day of forced labor, and he had already dropped like an exhausted fly.

Or maybe he'd been here for years.

"Again!"

Sebastian did as he was told. For some reason, the jobs he'd been given here were particularly gruesome. While others made bricks or dug trenches, Sebastian had to wheel corpses, or lift the dead bodies of those who did not survive the train journey.

"Once more, then we're done," the guard said.

Sebastian flicked the whip hard. The man's eyes opened slightly.

"He's alive," Sebastian said.

"Damn it. Get up, Jew. Now!"

Sebastian watched the man's face. His eyes were like those of a fish on its side, glassy, lifeless. Sebastian wondered if he could even hear the instructions, let alone comprehend their implications. Did he realize this was the deciding moment between staying in this world or being burned off to the next?

"I said, get up, Jew!"

Despite having taught himself not to care, Sebastian felt his blood rising. *Come on, Mister. Whoever you are, remember it. Don't let them win. Get up.*

"I'm giving you five seconds!" the guard yelled.

The man's head rolled slightly upward, until he was looking straight at Sebastian. He made a high-pitched wheeze, like a rusty squeak. It was a noise Sebastian had never heard from another human being. For a brief moment, the two of them shared a gaze. Then the man's eyes closed.

"No, no," Sebastian mumbled. He whacked the whip, again and again, as if to beat the man back into consciousness.

"Enough," the guard said. "We're wasting time."

He signaled for two other prisoners, who raced over, lifted the man, and took him to the crematorium, with no concern for whether there was breath still within him. As they carried the body away, they didn't even glance at the tall, emaciated dark-haired boy hunched on his knees, staring at his whip, unwittingly playing the angel of death.

He was sixteen.

∞◇∞

That night, in the block where he, his father, and his grandfather slept, Sebastian refused to take part in any prayers. It was a ritual they had established, at the urging of Lazarre, not to forget their past, their faith, their God. Lying in their filthy bunks, they mumbled the words softly in the darkness while a fellow prisoner coughed purposely to prevent the guards from hearing them. When they finished, Lazarre, now a skeletal version of his old thick self, would ask everyone to recite one thing they were grateful for that day.

"I had an extra spoonful of soup," one man said.

"My rotted tooth finally fell out," said another.

"I wasn't beaten."

"My foot stopped bleeding."

"I slept through the night."

"The guard that was torturing me got switched to another block."

"I saw a bird."

Sebastian had nothing to offer. He listened silently as his father and grandfather mumbled the kaddish prayer for his grandmother Eva, who, on her first day here, was deemed by the Nazis as too old to be useful, and was gassed to death. They said kaddish for the twin girls, Anna and Elisabet, who were taken by Nazi doctors for experiments, the details of which were mercifully unknown. They said kaddish for Bibi and Tedros, who didn't survive the first winter. And finally, they said kaddish for Tanna, who died in her fifth month here, after contracting typhus. The women in her block tried to conceal the rash of her sickness, covering her in hay when they went out to work. But a Nazi guard discovered her shivering in her bunk, and she was put to death that afternoon, nothing to bury but ashes from the black smoke spewing out of the crematorium chimney.

After their prayers were finished, Lazarre and Lev huddled close to Sebastian. The older men had taken a protective posture toward the teenager, perhaps because he now represented the last of the children.

"What is it, Sebby?"

"I don't feel like praying."

"We pray even when we don't feel like it."

"What for?"

"For an end to this."

Sebastian shook his head. "It won't end until we die."

"Don't talk like that."

"It's true."

Sebastian looked away. "A man today. He was alive, for a minute. I tried to get him back. But they burned him anyhow."

Lazarre looked at Lev. What was there to say?

"Offer a prayer for that man's soul," Lazarre whispered.

Sebastian was silent.

"And pray for your brother," added Lev.

"Why should I do that?"

"Because we want God to watch over him."

"Like he watched over us?"

"Seb—"

"Nico was working for the Nazis, Papa."

"We don't know what he was doing."

"He was tricking us. He was lying!"

"He never lies," Lazarre said. "They must have done something to him."

"Why do you always stand *up* for him?"

"Seb, lower your voice," his father whispered. He touched his son's shoulder. "You must forgive your brother. You know this."

"No. I'll pray if you want. But not for him. I'll pray for something else."

Lev sighed. "All right. Pray for something good."

Sebastian thought about all the good things he could pray for, all the good things he wanted but could no longer have. A hot meal. A day of sleep. The freedom to walk out the gates of this hellhole and never look back.

In the end, as young men often do, he prayed for his heart's desire.

He prayed to see Fannie one more time.

Nights of Hay

The woman who found Fannie by the river was a plump Hungarian seamstress named Gizella, whose husband, Sandor, had been killed two years earlier in combat.

Hungary had loosely aligned with the Wolf, so it was ostensibly the Nazi cause that Sandor had been fighting for. But Gizella had already learned a hard truth of war: grief does not take sides. Sandor died. His body was sent home. She was left a widow in her thirties, sleeping in an empty bed. The cause made no difference.

When she spotted Fannie hiding by the river, Gizella knew she was a Jew, which made her a refugee from tragedy. It was something they had in common.

So they waited together until nightfall. Then Gizella snuck Fannie back to the hillside village where she lived. She gave the girl a bowl of soup, which the child devoured in seconds, and made a sleeping space in the small chicken coop behind her house. She provided Fannie with some old clothes and took her dress with the yellow star and burned it in the fireplace. She wanted to tell her it was better this way, because many of her Hungarian neighbors considered Jews the same menace as the Nazis did, and if they found out she was harboring one, both of them could be killed. But the woman and the girl had not a single word in common. They spoke at each other, not to each other, using their hands to try and make their points.

Gizella, in Hungarian, tapped the ground and said: "Here. You need to stay here. Here. In this place."

Fannie, in Greek, responded: "Thank you for the food."

Gizella: "It's not safe outside."

Fannie: "I was on a train. I escaped."

Gizella: "The people here, they don't like Jews. For me, it makes no difference. We are all children of God."

Fannie: "Do you know where the train was going?"

Gizella: "Here. You must stay here. Understand?"

Fannie: "They killed my father."

Gizella: "Soup? Do you like soup?"

Fannie: "I don't understand you. I'm sorry."

Gizella: "I don't understand you. I'm sorry."

Gizella sighed, then reached out and took Fannie's hand. She brought it to her chest.

"Gizella," she said softly.

Fannie repeated the gesture.

"Fannie," she said.

For the first night, that was enough. Gizella shut the wooden door behind her, and Fannie fell into a dreamless sleep on a large pile of hay.

∞

In the months that followed, Gizella and Fannie forged a rhythm to their days. Fannie would wake before sunrise and enter the house, where she and Gizella would share a breakfast of oatcakes and jam, and trade words in Hungarian. Later, while Gizella made the rounds of the village, picking up clothes for laundering or tailoring, Fannie hid in the chicken coop. When the sun set, she would rejoin Gizella for a supper of whatever they could scrounge together, potatoes, leeks, bread soup. Once in a great while, Gizella would make dumplings from yeast flour with a small bit of curd cheese inside. Fannie would help her roll the dough.

On Sundays, Gizella went to Catholic church and said a silent prayer for the girl's survival. She took a pouch of red rosary beads with her and clasped them as she spoke to God.

Over time, a relationship developed. Their vocabulary grew. Fannie and Gizella were able to share details of their families, and found themselves united by the losses they had suffered. Gizella explained that the chicken coop had once been a barn for a horse she'd had to sell after her husband died. Fannie told of being thrown from the moving train, rolling along the hard grass, running when she heard gunshots.

Gizella shook her head. "When this war ends, you won't have to run anymore. Until then, you cannot trust anyone, understand? Not the neighbors. Not the police. No one."

"When will the war end?" Fannie asked.

"Soon."

"Gizella?"

"Yes?"

"When it ends . . ."

"Yes?"

"How will I find everyone?"

Winter arrived, and brought 1944 with it.

As the war raged on, supplies became scarce. There was less to eat. Even bread was expensive. Gizella took on additional sewing and washing. She stitched most of the night, washed clothes in the river during the morning, and made deliveries in the afternoon. Some evenings, when Fannie snuck into the house, she found Gizella sleeping head-down on the sewing table. She looked older than that first day when they met in the woods.

"Let me help," Fannie offered. "I used to mend clothes with my mother."

"All right," Gizella said.

After supper, the two of them spent hours sewing together, Gizella teaching Fannie the finer points of attaching buttons or hemming a dress. This went on for many weeks. One night, Gizella put a garment down and reached over to place her hand atop Fannie's.

"May I tell you something?"

"Yes?"

"I believe God sent you to me. Before Sandor left to fight, we were hoping to make a baby. He said he wanted a daughter. I asked him, 'Why not a son?' He said a son could become a soldier and a soldier could go off and die. He said he wouldn't want me to worry about losing a child."

She bit her lip. "Instead, I lost a husband."

Fannie squeezed her hand.

"What I'm saying," Gizella whispered, "is that when this war is over, if you want to stay with me, you can."

Fannie felt a warmth rising inside her, something she hadn't felt in a long time. At thirteen, she lacked the vocabulary to explain it. But I can tell you what it's called.

Belonging.

∞

The next day, after Gizella left, Fannie decided to do more to help her. There was a great deal of sewing still left unfinished, and she felt worthless hiding in the hay, passing the hours with the same few books Gizella had given her. She was careful to sneak from the coop to the house, crawling along the ground to avoid neighbors spotting her. Once inside, she set to work. She felt refreshed and purposeful, seeing sunshine spill through a window for a change. It was her first sense of normalcy since all the madness began in Salonika.

By midday, having drunk three glasses of water, she needed to use the latrine. She was careful when she slipped outside. But when she returned to the house minutes later, she walked into the sewing room and came face-to-face with a gray-haired woman in a green overcoat and matching hat, holding a bundle of clothing.

The woman's face registered surprise. Her thick eyebrows raised.

"Who are you?" she asked.

Fannie was so startled at seeing this woman—or anyone, for that matter—that she couldn't form a response.

"I asked your name," the woman said.

Fannie swallowed. She couldn't think straight.

"Gizella . . ." she whispered.

"You are not Gizella. I know Gizella. Gizella is supposed to have fixed the buttons on these shirts."

"I meant . . . I help Gizella." Then she added, "*Csókolom*," the Hungarian greeting for an older woman.

The woman tilted her head back, as if sniffing the air around Fannie.

"What is that accent? You are Bulgarian?"

"No."

"Your hair. Are you Greek? Where do you come from?"

"I don't know . . ."

"You don't know where you come from?"

"I am from here. From here!"

"You're lying. Where is Gizella? Does she know you are in her house? I want to see Gizella!"

Fannie's heart was pounding so fast, she thought she would drop right there on the floor. All she could think of was to run. So she did. Out the back door and into the woods as the woman's screaming words "*Where are you going, girl?*" faded behind her.

Fannie hid in the trees until the sun went down. She kept waiting to hear a siren, or the heavy boots of soldiers. But nothing came. Finally, she saw a light turn on in Gizella's kitchen. This was usually the sign that it was safe for Fannie to come from the coop. She crawled on her knees until she reached the house, then tapped lightly on the door. Gizella opened it.

"What's wrong?" Gizella asked. "Why are you on the ground?"

Fannie glanced left and right. Everything seemed normal.

"Fannie? What happened?"

In that moment, Fannie could have confessed the truth. She could have told Gizella about the encounter with the gray-haired woman. Perhaps things would have been different.

But a lie comes in many disguises; sometimes, it looks like safety. Fannie did not want Gizella to get scared, or decide it was too dangerous for Fannie to stay. So she did not mention the incident at all.

"Everything is fine," Fannie said, getting up. "I'm sorry to have frightened you."

"I saw the sewing you did. Thank you."

"You are welcome."

"But, Fannie, please don't try that again. It is dangerous. Someone could have seen you."

Fannie nodded. "Yes. You are right."

Gizella paused for a moment, then went to her bedroom and came back with her pouch of rosary beads. She was wearing a pair of white gloves, the ones she wore to church.

"Do you see these beads?"

"Yes."

"Do you know what they are?"

"You pray with them."

"Yes. But these are not normal rosary beads. These are peas. Jequirity peas."

"They're pretty."

Gizella lowered her voice. "They are poison. If you eat even just one, it can kill you."

Fannie stared at the little red objects. They seemed so innocent. Gizella put them back in the pouch. "My husband gave these to me before he left. He paid a lot of money to someone who imports them. I have two sets. Mine and his."

She exhaled. "I want you to have one."

"Why?"

"Because I know the enemy. I know what they can do."

Gizella looked straight at Fannie. "If we are ever caught, if there is ever no hope and they are going to do certain things to you? Sometimes . . ."

"What?" Fannie said.

"Sometimes it is better to leave this world by your own hand than theirs."

She pushed the pouch into Fannie's palm, then rose and left the room.

For the next five months, as summer came then faded away, they continued their routine, sewing, washing, eating, sleeping. Fannie stayed in the coop, and even got used to the ammonia-like scent of chicken droppings. She all but forgot about the screaming gray-haired woman.

But just because you forget about a lie does not mean it forgets about you.

∞

I have mentioned this is a story of great truths and deceptions. You will find the big ones and the small ones interconnect.

When Hungary's leader, Miklós Horthy, made his alliance with the Wolf, he lied about his ongoing conversations with the Wolf's enemies. And when the Wolf found out, he lied, too, inviting Horthy to a phony meeting to lure him out of his country while the Nazis invaded it.

When Horthy learned of how he'd been duped, he was furious. Before meeting with the Wolf, he hid a pistol in his clothing, planning to execute the Nazi leader in cold blood. But he put the gun back just before he left his room, later claiming it was not up to him to take a life. Perhaps, if he had gone through with it, the war might have ended sooner, and what happened next to Nico, Fannie, Sebastian, and Udo might never have come to pass.

But that is fantasy. And I do not traffic in fantasy.

Here is the reality: Horthy was promptly replaced, a puppet government was installed, and the Nazi forces, sensing the war was slipping away, swept through Hungary with the fierceness of a bleeding animal. The Wolf put his top people in charge of expelling all Hungarian Jews to the death camps. In this task, they had eager help from the Arrow Cross, a hateful Hungarian political movement that, in mirroring the warped view of the Wolf, believed Hungarians also had a racial purity that needed protecting.

The Arrow Cross was as vicious as any Nazi outfit, and its soldiers swept through the countryside, rounding up all those they viewed as undesirable. They raided schools, synagogues, bakeries, lumberyards, shops, apartments, houses.

And one October morning, before the sun came up, they swarmed through a hillside village and followed a tip from a gray-haired woman in a green coat who told them, "The lady in that house is hiding a Jew." They kicked in the front door and discovered a seamstress and a teenager eating oatcakes.

"Who is this girl?" one of them yelled.

"This is my daughter!" Gizella answered. "Leave us alone!"

A soldier whacked her with a club and told her it was a good thing she loved Jews so much, because now she would get to die with them. Fannie screamed as the Arrow Cross took her away, dragging her past the gray-haired woman, who nodded approvingly, her arms folded across her chest. Fannie could only stare in disbelief.

The little lie had caught up to her.

In war, there is no limit to repeated horrors.

Fourteen months after being shoved inside a cattle car, Fannie Nahmias was shoved inside another one, this time heading to Budapest, where bombs were falling and buildings were in ruins. Later she was herded into her second ghetto, and forced to sleep in a lightless room with nine other people whose names she never learned.

Then, in November of 1944, Fannie and dozens of other Jews were marched at gunpoint through the streets of the city. It was dark, nearly midnight. Snow blew through the air. The prisoners were dragged up a long bridge, then led down steps to the banks of the Danube River. There, shivering in the cold, they were forced to remove their shoes. Their bodies were tied together with rope, three or four in a group. Fannie caught the eye of a young Arrow Cross soldier, staring at her pretty face. "It won't hurt," he mumbled, and looked away.

The prisoners were turned toward the dark water, which was moving rapidly. Fannie tried to see how long this lineup went. It was at least seventy or eighty people, many of them children, the snow landing on their heads and naked feet. For a few minutes, the soldiers huddled and pointed here and there. Finally, at the far end of the line, an Arrow Cross guard stepped forward, lifted his gun, and fired at one Jewish man's head, watching him and the bodies tied to him fall into the freezing river, the swift current whisking them away.

He moved to the next group and fired again.

Fannie squeezed her eyes shut. Her heart was pounding like a fist on a door. She thought of Gizella and wondered if she were still alive. She thought of her father, knowing he was dead, and her neighbors from Salonika, who were probably dead as well. She thought of the bearded man on the train, who whispered to her, "Be a good person. Tell the world what happened here." She realized she would never do that now. She was trembling uncontrollably, her knees, her hands, her jaw. Amid the sobbing of her fellow prisoners, she told herself this would all be over in a minute, she could die and be with her loved ones in heaven. There was nothing to miss about this world anymore.

She heard sudden yelling and commotion. As a frigid wind blew across her face, for some reason, she thought of Nico. She saw him so clearly in her mind that she actually thought she heard him calling her name.

"Fannie?"

She stopped breathing.

"Fannie? Is that you?"

She opened her eyes to see a taller version of the only boy she'd ever kissed, draped in a Nazi officer's coat. At the sight of him, she promptly fainted, pulling the two people tied to her wrists down to the ground and nearly falling into the blood-stained river.

Nico, from Lie to Lie

Now I must tell you about Nico's journey. For me, this is painful, like a mother speaking about her son's time in prison.

The boy who never lied shed his honest skin on those Salonika railroad tracks in 1943. By the time he appeared on the banks of the Danube, now nearly fourteen years old, he was barely recognizable—to me, or to those like Fannie who knew him in his earthly form.

Adolescence did not so much arrive for Nico as pounce upon him. He sprouted six inches in height. His lovely features grew sharper. His voice deepened to a soft baritone, and he put on twenty-two pounds. This does not count the weight of his deceptions, which is beyond calculation.

But those deceptions kept him alive. Nico became, as Udo had labeled him, "a good little liar," undoing a lifetime of honesty almost overnight. This is not without precedent. Did Adam not lose paradise with a single bite of an apple? Was Lucifer not a good angel before his eternal expulsion? We are all one fateful act from a redirected destiny, and the price we pay can be immeasurable.

Nico paid such a price.

He lost me.

He could no longer speak Truth. He shunned it like the devil's breath. Saying true things only reminded him that his honesty may have condemned his family to death. Who among us could stare at such a blazing sun of accountability and not go blind?

So lying became Nico's new language. He used countless falsehoods to move from place to place. He was helped in these endeavors by certain people he met along the way.

But first, he was helped by a passport.

That passport had belonged to a broad-shouldered German soldier named Hans Degler, who had been rounding up Jews in Salonika, got terribly drunk one night in a Greek taverna, and fell off a rooftop where he had taken a woman for pleasure. His body was found the next morning, sprawled and lifeless in an alley next to a deserted automobile.

Udo had kept the young man's passport, planning to turn it in upon his arrival in Germany. That was before the day of betrayals, and Nico's fortuitous discovery of the leather bag hidden in the crawl space, which, in addition to money and badges, also held the now-deceased Hans Degler's identification. It may strike you as odd, all the benefits a single bag from a former tormentor might bestow. But those who do you the most harm, if you survive them, can inadvertently lead you to good.

Nico disembarked a northbound train in the small Greek city of Edessa, not far from the Yugoslavian border, in search of someone with a camera. His goal was to switch a photo of himself onto Hans Degler's passport, which would declare him as eighteen years old. Nico knew that was a stretch, but what choice did he have? Nazi soldiers could insist on seeing "papers" anytime. With a German passport, they might leave him alone.

As he walked through the town with the badge pinned to his shirt, Nico drew stares, but no one challenged him. The people of Edessa, like those of Salonika, had already felt the wrath of the Nazi forces. They didn't want more trouble.

Nico spent hours looking for a photographer, but could not find one. Late in the day, tired and sweaty, he passed a barbershop and noticed pictures of customers displayed in the window. He entered to the tingling of a bell. A tall, pock-faced man emerged, wearing a short-sleeved tunic and sporting the thickest mustache Nico had ever seen.

"How can I help?" the man said, eyeing Nico's badge. Nico reminded himself he was playing the part of a German. He tried to look stern.

"*Ich brauche ein Foto,*" he said.

The man stared at him, confused.

"Photo? You need a photo?"

"*Ja,*" Nico said, pointing to the pictures in the window, "*ein Foto.*"

"All right. First, the haircut. Yes?"

The man motioned toward the barber chair. Nico had no desire for a haircut, but he didn't want to arouse suspicion. He sat down, and twenty minutes later, his blond hair was clipped short and he looked older. The mustached barber went into the back, emerged with an old camera, and snapped several shots.

"Come back in two days," the man said, holding up two fingers. Nico popped from the chair and started to go. The man cleared his throat and rubbed his palm, looking for payment. Nico opened his bag and pulled out a few Greek coins. He noticed the man staring and quickly zipped the bag shut.

"*Ein kleines Foto*," Nico said.

"Eh?" the man said.

Nico repeated, until the man seemed to understand. A small photo. Passport size. That's what he wanted.

"*Ich werde zurückkommen*," Nico said. I will come back.

For the next two nights, Nico slept in the train station. He ate some bread and sausage that he'd stuffed in the bag, and drank water from the sink in the bathroom. He found a nearby bookstore and purchased a German language phrase book, which he studied for hours on end, practicing the words by holding imaginary conversations with himself.

On the third day, when he returned to the barbershop, the mustached man was waiting, and motioned Nico into the back room.

"I have your photo here," he said.

Nico walked through the door and was immediately tackled by two teenaged boys, who held him down while the barber ripped open his bag. He rummaged through the food, clothing, and money, but when he saw the badges, he recoiled.

"Who are you working for? Why do you have Nazi badges?"

Nico writhed against the grip of the two boys.

"I work for Herr Udo Graf, the *Hauptsturmführer*! And he will have you killed!"

Only then did he realize he had yelled this in Greek.

The barber looked at the teenaged boys, and nodded for them to let Nico up.

"You're from Salonika," the man said. "I hear it in your accent. You may look like a German, and you may speak their language, but you're one of us. A Greek. Why are you pretending?"

Nico scowled. "Give me back my bag."

"You can have the bag, but I'm keeping everything in it. Unless you tell me what you're doing."

"I need a photo. For a passport."

"Where are you traveling?"

Nico hesitated. "To the camps."

"The camps? The *German* camps?"

The barber looked at the teenagers and started laughing.

"Nobody goes to those camps willingly. They take you there like a captured animal. And you never come back."

Nico tightened his jaw.

"Tell me, boy," the man said. "Who's in the camps that you need to see so badly?"

"None of your business."

"You're a Jew?" the barber asked.

"No."

"We could pull down your pants and see quickly enough."

Nico clenched his fists. The teenaged boys eyed one another. The barber waved them off.

"Never mind. Maybe a Jew, maybe not a Jew, but a boy who

speaks German and needs a passport to go *into* the camps. That is something interesting."

He stepped away and rifled through the bag. Beneath the clothes and the sausage, he discovered more papers folded at the bottom. He took one out, then chuckled to himself. He turned back to the teenaged boys.

"Bring him to your grandfather," he said.

Who were these people?

The barber's name was Zafi Mantis, and the teenaged boys were his sons, Christos and Kostas. They were Romani, often referred to in those days as "Gypsies." They, too, were hiding from the Nazis, the barbershop being a front for their real intentions.

The three of them led Nico to the outskirts of town, a deserted block with just two buildings standing. Nico noticed a cluster of tents behind one building, and some women bathing children in a large metal tub. He was led up a set of stairs. On the second floor, Mantis knocked on a door four times, waited, knocked three more times, then knocked once more.

The door opened, and a short, bearded man wearing a smock let them inside.

"Who is this?" he asked.

"Our gold mine," Mantis said.

Nico looked around. There were paint cans and canvases and various works of art on easels. At the back end, a large tarp hung from floor to ceiling, and some stools sat in front of it, as if for models.

"Look at this," Mantis said, opening Nico's bag and pulling out papers. "Identification documents. *German* documents!"

A flash of fear shot across the bearded man's face.

"Relax," Mantis said. "They're not his. He's a Jew on the run. Or not a Jew on the run. Look."

The bearded man held the papers up to a light bulb. He turned back to Nico. His blue smock was covered in paint stains.

"Where did you get these?"

"I'm not telling you anything unless you give me back my bag," Nico said. "And the photo I paid you for." He was trying to sound brave, but his voice warbled.

"He speaks German," Mantis said.

"Really?" The bearded man raised an eyebrow. "Can you read it, too?"

Nico sniffed and nodded. The man reached into his pocket and produced a folded paper.

"Quickly. What does this say?"

Nico read. It was an official list of names, under a paragraph of instructions. Nico had seen papers like this on Udo Graf's desk.

"It says these people are to be arrested on the twenty-eighth of August and taken to the train station. That their bags cannot weigh more than six kilos. And that women and children are to be separated from the men before they board."

Mantis frowned. "The twenty-eighth? That's the day after tomorrow."

Nico handed back the paper.

"Are you all Jews?" he asked.

The bearded man shook his head.

"Worse," he mumbled.

What could be worse?

Allow me to interject. The Romani lived in nomadic communities all over Europe, with a rich history, strict faith, a love of music and dance, and a deep sense of family. But the Wolf considered them as poisonous as the Jews. He labeled them *Zigeuner*, and called them "enemies of the state." Wherever Nazi forces discovered Romani, they transported them to death camps, or murdered them on sight. The Wolf's soldiers were particularly cruel to the "Gypsy swine" they so detested, raping their women, hanging their men, playing games for sport by making them choose between being shot in the head or having to run into electrified fences.

Before the war was over, more than half of the Romani living in Europe would be wiped out. Some say three out of every four were put to death. Descendants would refer to this period as Porajmos, which means "devouring," or Pharrajimos, which means "cutting up," or Samudaripen, which means "mass killing." You cannot blame them for having multiple terms. Could a single word really describe such horror?

But back to the attic.

Nico remembered how his own family had been herded onto the trains. He thought about the large man who had lifted him by the armpits. *They're taking us to die.*

"You need to leave this city right now," Nico warned.

The men nodded at each other. Mantis zipped the leather bag and handed it over.

"Good luck trying to reach the camps."

He turned to his sons. "Take him back to the shop."

"Wait," the bearded man interrupted. "The boy needs a photo."

Mantis scoffed. "Why should we help him?"

"Because he helped us."

The bearded man turned to Nico. "That paper you translated was stolen by a maid who works for a Nazi officer. We couldn't read it. Now, thanks to you, we know we must go."

Nico nodded. He felt badly for them. They were just trying to stay alive, same as him.

"This is my son, Mantis," the bearded man said, pointing. "And these are my grandchildren, Christos and Kostas. You can call me Papo, as they do. It means 'grandfather.'"

"Papo," Nico repeated.

"And what do we call you?"

Nico swallowed.

"Erich Alman."

"All right, Erich Alman, where is the passport you need help with?"

Nico hesitated. Part of him felt he had already shared too much with these people. But something in the bearded man's eyes made him think of his own grandfather. It filled him with a longing, and a remembrance of trust. He removed his shoe, took Hans Degler's passport from inside it, and handed it over. Papo saw the brown cover with the black eagle and the swastika above the words *Deutches Reich*. A huge smile spread across his face.

"A German passport? You have given us a second gift, Erich Alman."

"You can't keep it!" Nico yelled.

"Oh, I don't want to keep it."

He yanked back the tarp to reveal a drafting table, bottles of ink, jars of chemicals, and a sewing machine.

"I want to copy it," he said.

Despite his paint-stained smock, Papo was not an artist.

He was a forger.

His family had been providing false documents to the community for over a year. Identification cards. Marriage certificates. Always changing the spelling of names to avoid detection as Romani. This small workshop, hidden behind the guise of a painter's studio, was impressive. Nico saw stacks of paper, rubber stamps, cups of colored water, various dyes, even a pile of different-colored passports.

"I've never had a German one before," Papo said.

"Can you put my picture in it?" Nico asked.

Papo examined the pages. "I'll have to erase this blue stamp and create another. But I can use lactic acid. It works well."

Nico didn't know what the man was talking about. But he was fascinated. Here, in this abandoned building, was a place of reinvention, where old identities could be destroyed and new ones created. For a chameleon like Nico, it was perfect.

"Teach me to do what you do," Nico said.

"Teach you?" Papo said.

"Yes."

"No."

"I'll pay you."

"Listen up, boy," Mantis said. "We are packing and heading out in a few hours. We'll be gone by tomorrow night."

Nico set his jaw. "Then I'll go with you."

Udo Gets a New Job

Forgive me. I realize, in my detailed accounts of Nico, Fannie, and Sebastian, I have ignored the progression of their tormentor, our fourth character, Udo Graf.

Udo arrived in the camp known as Auschwitz on the same day as Nico's family. He stepped from his train car to witness the mayhem of passengers and guards. It repelled him. The awful stench, the stacking of dead bodies, all these skeletal figures running through the mud in their striped pajamas. *What was he doing here?*

The answer came within the hour. While arriving prisoners were being pushed, clubbed, shaved, disinfected, or led into gas chambers, Udo was escorted to a villa at the far corner of the camp, a stately brick structure with well-tended gardens surrounding it. The workers there—a groundskeeper, several maids—kept their eyes low when Udo walked past. Once inside, he looked out the windows. He noticed high walls and large trees that blocked much of the view of the camp, particularly the large chimney of the crematorium. The place felt like a country house, pleasant, almost pastoral.

Udo was led to a study with a mahogany desk. A canter

of vodka sat atop it. As he waited, he heard a constant engine noise coming from outside. He would later learn that during the gassing of prisoners, a guard would rev the engines of a motorcycle to drown out the muffled screams of those taking their last breaths.

Suddenly, a high-ranking member of the SS entered the room, his shoes clacking on the polished wooden floor. He filled two glasses with vodka, handed one to Udo, and informed him that he had been summoned to assist him with the operations of this camp, effective immediately. This man was the new *Kommandant*. When a confused Udo asked what happened to the previous *Kommandant*, the new man lowered his voice.

"There was an unfortunate relationship with a female prisoner. An intimate one. A child resulted. He has been sent back to Germany pending a complete investigation."

The *Kommandant* paused. "I trust we will have no such problem with you, Herr Schutzhaftlagerführer?"

The word meant "camp director." So *that* was his new job. That was why Udo had been summoned. It wasn't a betrayal. It was a promotion.

"No such problem, *Kommandant*," Udo said.

"Good. Now. In this place, we have one overriding rule. Keep what is worth keeping, get rid of the rest."

"Can you be more specific?"

The man lowered his glass. "How's this? When the filthy Jews arrive, sort through them like the trash that they are. Old women, mothers with babies, feeble old men, anyone showing the slightest bit of resistance? Kill them immediately.

"Anyone else, strong men, useful women, you put to work. You did see the sign at the gate, didn't you? *'Arbeit macht frei'*? 'Work sets you free'?"

The *Kommandant* grinned. "Of course, we don't really mean 'free.'"

Udo tried to grin back. His stomach rumbled. He took a sip of vodka and wondered how many people he was expected to exterminate.

∞

Prior to his arrival at Auschwitz, Udo had mostly been on the logistical side of murder. Encircle the enemy, bring it to its knees, then ship it off to be dealt with elsewhere. This was different. *Kill them immediately?* It gave Udo pause. A better conscience would have balked. Walked away. Asked for another assignment.

But you serve the Lord or you serve man, and if you choose man, there may be no limit to the orders you will have to follow, or your cruelty.

So Udo became an exterminator, and discovered he was quite efficient at it. Under his direction, arriving trains were unloaded in a hurry, the prisoners led to gas chambers often within hours. Although every one of them was someone's terrified mother or father, or someone's crying child, they were shuffled with equal dispassion to their deaths, like rice being swept off a table. Udo kept copious details in his notebook diary, the numbers, the tallies, his feelings of pride when a day's exterminations went smoothly.

He also wasted no time bloodying his own hands. Before

Auschwitz, he hadn't done much killing himself. He'd shot one old Jewish rabbi who'd been pleading to keep soldiers from burning down a Salonika synagogue. And he'd shot two men who'd broken out of the Baron Hirsch ghetto, after an SS soldier had trouble with his rifle. It was embarrassing, Udo felt, the way the soldier fumbled with it, while the two Jews were on their knees. Udo couldn't take their whining, so he put a quick end to the matter with his luger.

But those were select occurrences, and Udo had stared at the bodies after his bullets silenced them, feeling a tinge of regret, even anger, that the confrontations had escalated to such a point.

Here at the camp, figuring the guards would be motivated by his actions, Udo insisted on shooting at least one Jew a day, and two on Saturdays. After they were dead, he asked for the numbers that were tattooed in blue ink on their wrists. He wrote those numbers in a list in his notebook.

In all his time at Auschwitz, Udo never learned the name of a single prisoner.

Except one.

Sebastian Krispis.

The brother of his little liar.

Udo remembered him from the train platform. He recalled how, when Nico's family was yelling and crying and rushing to him, only the older brother held back.

Then, on the train car, when Udo threw that baby out of the window, all the passengers had looked away except this one, again, the brother, who stared Udo down. Udo could have shot him for that. He'd thought about it.

Instead, once inside Auschwitz, Udo instructed the guards to assign the boy only the most gruesome tasks.

"If you hate that one so much, why not just kill him?" an officer once asked.

"Killing the flesh is easy," Udo said. "Killing the spirit is a challenge."

Sebastian Grows Weaker, Gets Stronger

Killing the boy's spirit, it turns out, would not be as simple as Udo imagined. Stripped of his mother and his siblings, his petty jealousies replaced by starvation and exhaustion, Sebastian matured quickly. He grew stronger. Bolder. His shifting jobs gave him a wider view of the camp and how to survive it. He snatched potato peels from garbage bins. He scooped dog food from bowls. He made connections with other Greek prisoners, who shared information about which block had the fewest inspections, or which guards could be distracted. They invented nicknames to identify them.

"Look out for Big Ears today, he's on the warpath."

"I saw Vampire sleeping outside the latrine."

"The Ferret shot two prisoners yesterday, steer clear."

Sebastian even connected with some Polish civilians who were brought in as day workers to labor alongside the Jewish prisoners. The two groups were not allowed to speak. But one morning Sebastian found himself shoveling gravel next to a thick-necked laborer who wore an eye patch.

"You're a damn skeleton," the man whispered to him. "What are they doing to you in here?"

Sebastian swallowed. He hadn't thought about how he looked to other people. None of the prisoners commented on one another's appearance. Everyone was equally diminished—shaved to the nubs, bruised, scarred, open-sored, grease-stained, bone thin. But the Pole's question: *What are they doing to you in here?* How could this man, who obviously lived nearby, be so clueless about what was happening in his neighborhood?

Part of Sebastian wanted to start from the beginning, the cattle cars, the separations, the disinfecting, the beatings, the morning punishments, the evening plop of tasteless soup, the coughing, vomiting, typhus, scarlet fever, the bodies found dead in their bunks.

On the other hand, if it got back to the guards, he would be hanged in front of the whole camp, and his father and grandfather with him. It was a deadly multiplier the Nazis employed; for every prisoner caught stealing food, five would be tortured. For every attempted runaway, ten would be killed. How could Sebastian reveal the Truth, when the Nazis were choking me inside his throat?

"Can you get me some food?" he finally mumbled.

The man with the eye patch shook his head and kept shoveling, as if to say, *Why did I bother?* But the next day, when the guards were elsewhere, he slipped Sebastian a single potato and a tin of sardines, which Sebastian hid in his underwear until he got back to his block. He shared it with his father and grandfather.

"Tonight, I am grateful for our brilliant Sebastian," Lazarre said, smacking his lips. "I don't think a potato ever tasted this good."

Lev smiled and rubbed his son's head. He noticed the curved scar above his collarbone, a souvenir from a dog bite after Schutzhaftlagerführer Graf had ordered the hounds on a group of prisoners.

"How is it healing?" Lev asked.

Sebastian glanced down. "Still hurts."

"When you put on a collared shirt, you won't even notice it."

Sebastian smirked. "When am I putting on a collared shirt?"

"One day," Lev said.

Lazarre leaned in. "Never be ashamed of a scar. In the end, scars tell the story of our lives, everything that hurt us, and everything that healed us."

Sebastian touched the wound lightly.

"I'm proud of you, Seb," Lev whispered. He blinked back a tear. "I never realized how strong you were. I'm sorry. I guess I didn't pay enough attention."

"It's all right, Papa," Sebastian replied.

"I love you, son."

Sebastian shivered. He thought about those words, and the many times he'd wished his father would say them to him. Now, however, words were no longer critical. Food was. Water was. Avoiding the guards' gaze was. It is a sad fact I have noticed with humans. By the time you share what a loved one longs to hear, they often no longer need it.

∞

One night, in the late summer of 1944, the prisoners were startled by the distant sound of explosions. The next day, the work they had been doing was replaced by the hurried construction of air raid shelters.

"We're being bombed," one of them whispered.

"They're coming to free us!" whispered another.

"But what if they *hit* us?"

"It's the end of the war! Don't you see?"

Sadly, it was not the end. The Allied forces were indeed bombing, but not the death camp itself, rather the factories surrounding it. Day after day, the sound of airplanes rumbled the sky. The Germans ran to their shelters, which were off-limits to prisoners, who could only lie in a muddy waste field, one atop the other.

During these raids, Lazarre caught a virus, likely from the hours spent beneath his fellow prisoners. He grew weaker by the day and struggled to get through his labors. Every step seemed a challenge. He was hunched over, bent like a pipe cleaner, the vertebrae of his spine visible through his skin.

As his coughing grew more violent, Lev and Sebastian feared Lazarre would not pass the next "selection," a weeding-out process the Nazis used to discard the weak and make room for new bodies. The camp had been flooded with Hungarian Jews lately, and the block quarters were jammed. Some prisoners would have to go.

"Give him your portion," Lev told Sebastian when the nightly soup was ladled out. Sebastian did. Lev did the same. They hoped to nourish the old man to better health. But when the day of the selection arrived he was little improved.

That afternoon the prisoners were stripped naked and squeezed into a large room. One by one, they were told to run across the yard and hand a card with their number on it to the inspecting officer. That officer, based on a cursory look that lasted two seconds, would determine who would be executed and who would not.

"Move your grandfather to the back," Lev whispered. He and Sebastian maneuvered Lazarre behind a cluster of other prisoners. Once the quota was met, they hoped, the inspector might not care so much.

"Remember, Nano," Sebastian said, "keep your head up, chest out, move as fast as you can, look strong."

Lazarre nodded, but could barely stand. Only a few naked men remained ahead of him. Suddenly, he began coughing hard, loud, violent expulsions. He bent over in pain.

Lev bit his lip. Tears filled his eyes. He glanced at Sebastian, who saw something in his father's face that he had never seen before. Then, with one furtive move, Lev grabbed his father's card from his hand, shoved his own number into Lazarre's palm, and pushed out into the yard, running naked past the inspector, his chest forward, his eyes on heaven, saving his father, condemning himself.

Budapest

Fannie spread jam on a roll and bit into it quickly. Even here, in the basement of an apartment building in Budapest, she ate in a hurry, as if the food might be taken at any moment.

There were twenty-two other children around her, some as young as five, others as old as sixteen. They ate in silence, careful not to clang spoons or forks. They had all been rescued from the banks of the Danube River and had been hiding in this basement for nearly three weeks now.

From what Fannie could gather, she'd been saved by a rather fantastical series of events. A famous Hungarian actress had arrived at the riverbank just as the Arrow Cross had begun their executions. This actress brought with her gold and furs, and she moved among the guards, offering bribes to let the prisoners go free. Fannie never saw the woman—she'd passed out before that—but the older boys said she was very attractive, sultry even, with heavy eye makeup and bright red lipstick. At times, they said, she seemed to be flirting with the soldiers.

Her efforts, however, were only partly successful. The Arrow Cross let her take the children, but not the adults. The youngsters were loaded into automobiles that were driven, in the middle of the night, to this empty apartment building, which apparently was not where the actress lived but on the other side of the city. They were hurried downstairs and given blankets for sleeping.

In the basement, they were fed twice a day by a cook, who Fannie assumed worked for the actress. They had books to read and even a board game to share. Each day, when the cook came to deliver meals, Fannie asked the same thing. *Have you seen a boy named Nico? Was he there that night on the river-bank?*

The answer was always the same. Nobody knew that name. By the time December came, and the cook brought down sugar cookies with green sprinkles as a treat, Fannie wondered if she'd imagined the whole thing.

I can tell you she did not.

So what was Nico doing on the Danube River?

It all began with forgery, a talent he perfected during his time with the Romani refugees. Hiding in the high woods near the border of Greece and Yugoslavia, Papo taught Nico about inks and dyes, how to create stamps from woodblocks, how to perforate paper, and how to remove markings with lactic acid taken from dry cleaning shops. Nico's talent for drawing served him well, he was a natural, and by the winter of 1943, he had already produced dozens of identity cards and packs of food ration certificates, all of which helped keep Romani refugees alive. He also now possessed three passports for himself,

Hungarian, Polish, and, most importantly, the German one bearing the name Hans Degler.

At night, Nico would sit with the Romani families by their campfires, kept small to avoid Nazi detection. He would share from a pot of rabbit stew with onions and listen to songs played on wooden guitars. He heard the elders' plaintive singing and was reminded of Sabbath evenings in Salonika, how his grandfather would loudly chant the Hebrew blessings, and how Nico and Sebastian would stifle a laugh when his voice warbled on the high notes. Nico ached for such memories. He was desperate to see them again.

One morning, Mantis awoke to see Nico fully dressed and zipping up his leather bag.

"What are you doing, boy?"

"I have to go."

"To find your family?"

"My family is in Germany, safe and sound."

Mantis raised an eyebrow. "Is that so?"

"Yes. It is. Anyhow, I have to go."

"Wait a minute."

Mantis retreated to his tent. Moments later, he returned with Papo, who was carrying two loaves of bread, a can of jam, and a satchel filled with pens, ink, stamps, and three stolen Hungarian passports. He smiled warmly and handed the satchel to Nico.

"I knew this day was coming."

"I'm sorry, Papo."

"Be careful. Trust no one."

Nico choked up. Part of him wanted to stay here, with the

nightly fires and the pleasant songs and the fellow Romani who had taken him in without questions. It felt like family. But his real family needed him. Having learned the art of forgery, his plan was to create enough doctored paperwork to set them free.

"Thank you for everything," he told Papo.

"We should be thanking you. You saved our lives."

Mantis exhaled deeply. "You know, if you go to those camps, they'll kill you in a second."

Nico didn't reply.

"I'll tell you this, Erich Alman, or whatever your name is, you have some guts."

The wind blew leaves across the frozen mud. Papo walked Nico to the edge of their encampment.

"Always remember this," he said. "*Si khohaimo may pachivalo sar o chachimo.*"

"What does it mean?" Nico asked.

"'Some lies are easier to believe than the truth.'"

∞◇∞

Employing that philosophy, Nico walked, rode trains, hitched rides with wagons and automobiles, and made his way toward Poland by traveling through Yugoslavia and into Hungary, adopting whatever identities suited him. In Belgrade, he posed as a student and ate for a week in a school lunchroom. In Osijek, he found work as a printer's apprentice, staying long enough to steal paper and supplies for more forgeries. He always had a story ready, should some authority figure stop him. He was a Hungarian musician, visiting his grandparents.

He was a Polish athlete on holidays with his uncle. *Some lies are easier to believe than the truth.* Nico's truth, that he was a Jewish boy from Greece who had been tutored by a Nazi *Haupsturmtführer*, had deceived his own people on a train platform, was taught the art of forgery by Romani, and now was traveling to a death camp from which he had been spared, was far less believable than his cover stories.

One night, in the Hungarian city of Kapsovár, Nico was walking a busy street when a group of Nazis pulled up in transports and ran inside a department store. The owners, three Jewish brothers, were marched out at gunpoint and lined up by the store's front windows. A young German soldier, bony and tightly muscled, removed his coat and hat and placed them on a bench. As the brothers were restrained, the soldier beat each of them senseless.

A crowd gathered to watch, some of them cheering with each new blow. *"Hit him again!" "It's about time!"* The German was energized, and when the brothers lost consciousness, he demanded they be propped up for more strikes. When he finally finished, his knuckles were raw and his shirtsleeves were stained in blood. He took congratulatory slaps from his fellow troops and exhaled in satisfaction.

But when he went to retrieve his coat and hat, they were gone.

Nico was already blocks away.

∞

As the weeks passed, Nico studied Hungarian from people he met in his various identities. He found a job washing dishes in a café in Szeged. The cook took a shine to him and would teach him phrases as they played cards after work. Having already learned parts of eight different languages, Nico had a system. Learn certain key verbs (do, want, see, make, go, come, eat, sleep), certain key nouns (food, water, room, friend, family, country), memorize all the pronouns, then begin to fill in the rest.

One night, Nico put on the German soldier's coat and hat and walked to the city center. Although he admittedly looked young for the Nazi uniform, nobody questioned him. Quite the opposite. They feigned smiles and stepped out of his way.

Near the center of town, Nico spotted a swarm of people in front of a cinema. He approached to see what was happening. There, in the middle of the crowd, stood a beautiful, wavy-haired woman who, from what he overheard, was an actress in the new film playing there. She had come to Szeged to promote it. She wore a sparkly gown and white gloves, and people crammed around her for autographs.

"Katalin!" they yelled. "Over here, Katalin!"

Nico had never seen a movie in his life. While the crowd fussed in front of the theater, he snuck around the back and found an unlocked door. He slipped inside and took a seat in the rear. When the other seats filled and the room went dark, he felt a moment of trepidation. Then the screen lit up.

The film was about a Hungarian count who, through a magic time machine, travels back two centuries to win the hand of a woman, played by the actress outside the theater. Nico was captivated, not only by the film itself, the images, the action, the larger-than-life characters, but also by the story, and the idea of traveling backward. The whole experience was magical. For a few moments, he didn't think about the war, the trains, or his lies. He just watched the screen, his mouth agape. He didn't want it to end.

But it did end. Abruptly. A loud commotion shattered the peace, reminding Nico of the moment his home was swarmed by troops as he hid in a crawl space. The lights burst on, and Nico heard men screaming in German. SS troops. They ordered the patrons outside.

"*Schneller!*" they yelled. Faster!

Nico waited until the theater was mostly empty, then marched out slowly with his hands behind his back, as if he had helped to clear it. When he saw the other Nazis, he edged away, his heart pounding. It was one thing to present phony papers, or walk the streets alone in this outfit. It was another to play the part of a Nazi in front of other real ones. Fortunately for Nico, the war at this point was depleting German personnel, and members of the Nazi youth were being deployed more and more. It wasn't that unusual for a teenager to be pressed into service.

The soldiers at this theater—there were only five of them—were more concerned with the owner and the actress, whom they accused of pushing propaganda. They hollered about the film being "forbidden" and a "violation" of protocol. They forced the actress into the backseat of a transport, presumably to arrest her.

Nico knew he should slip away while he could. But this woman, whom he had just watched moments earlier on a giant screen, froze him in place. She seemed otherworldly. So glamorous. Even in the transport, she showed no signs of fear. She folded her hands in her lap and looked straight ahead.

The Nazis began to argue with some of the patrons, who were demanding their money back from the theater owner. A fight broke out, and the soldiers pushed in to break it up. One ran past Nico and, seeing his uniform, pointed to the transport and yelled in German, "Watch the woman!"

Nico nodded and hurried to the vehicle. The actress kept staring straight ahead, appearing more angry than frightened.

"Do you have a way out of here?" Nico whispered in Hungarian.

She turned, and Nico felt goose bumps. She was beautiful in a way that could knock you back with a flash of her eyes. The woman studied him for a moment, then pinched two fingers under her lipstick-painted mouth.

"My driver is over there," she said.

Across the plaza sat a black vehicle with a man inside it. Without thinking, Nico pulled the transport door open.

"Go."

The actress looked both ways, as if this were a trick. Then, as the fight by the theater grew more raucous, she slipped out quickly and ran to the waiting vehicle.

Nico closed the transport door, lowered his head, and walked around the corner. As soon as he was alone, he took off the Nazi coat and hat and walked briskly to the café where he worked, so he could retrieve his bag. He was breathing fast and kept blinking his eyes, as if not believing what he had just done. What if the Nazis found him? How much trouble was he in? Why did he take a risk like that—for a stranger?

Once he got his bag, he ran toward the train station. He ducked down an alley and raced through it. As he emerged on the other side, he heard a screeching of tires and jumped back just before he was hit by an oncoming car.

Its rear door swung open.

"Get in," the actress said.

∞

Her name was Katalin Karády, and she was once the biggest movie star in Hungary. Raised the poor daughter of a shoe-maker, she became a singer and film icon and rose to great fame. She had an unusual voice that attracted legions of fans, and her sultry look and fashion style were copied by thousands of Hungarian women, who dressed, did their hair, and fixed their makeup just like her.

Katalin's personal life was often in the news, which gave her even greater celebrity. But when the war came, she was fiercely anti-German, and since everything she did or said quickly became public, it cost her dearly. As Hungary slipped deeper into Nazi control, her songs were banned and eventually her movies, too.

The night she snuck Nico into her car, they drove to Buda-pest and she let him stay in her apartment, which was more luxurious than anything Nico had ever seen. A chandelier hung in the middle of a large sitting room, and lace curtains draped every window.

"So," she said, pouring herself a glass of wine. "You haven't told me your name."

"Hans Degler," Nico said.

"You're German?"

"*Ja.*"

She grinned. "Young man, I am an actress. Don't you think I can tell when someone is pretending?"

Nico presented his German passport, which made her smile.

"Even better," she said. "An actor with papers."

She shrugged. "It doesn't matter. I haven't used my real name in years. My manager created 'Karády.' He thought it sounded more Hungarian." She sipped her wine. "These days, everyone is whoever they need to be."

Nico studied the woman. The color of her cheeks. The way her eyelids were painted.

"Aren't you afraid they will come for you again?" he asked.

"Oh, I know they'll come for me. If you stand for something during a war, you are going to pay a price."

She looked Nico straight in the eye.

"What do you stand for . . . Hans Degler?"

Nico hesitated. He had never been asked that question. *What did he stand for?* He could only think of his grandfather, the most principled person he knew. He thought of the story he had told Nico and Sebastian at the White Tower, about the prisoner and his offer to paint his way to freedom.

"A man, to be forgiven, will do anything," Nico said.

Katalin chuckled. "The face of a schoolboy, the clothes of a Nazi, and the words of a philosopher.

"You should be in the movies."

Nico found Katalin fascinating. She found him amusing.

That night, they stayed up until dawn, with Nico asking endless questions about films. Where did the clothes come from? Who wrote the stories? How did they make it seem like she traveled back in time? Katalin was charmed by his naivete, and it helped take her mind off her worry that what happened in Szeged would soon follow her here.

It didn't take long. Two days later, German transports roared to her apartment building, and she was arrested and carted off to jail. It wasn't the first time. It wouldn't be the last. The Hungarian authorities accused her of spying, and in a prison cell, she was beaten and tortured. This went on for several months.

Finally, through the help of a government official, Katalin was released. But her apartment, during her incarceration, had been stripped by the Nazis. She returned to empty rooms. Even the curtains were gone.

She collapsed in the corner and pulled her knees to her chest. Her legs and arms were gashed. Her once beautiful face was blotched with purple bruises.

As she wiped away tears, she heard a noise outside the living room window. She sucked in her breath. She saw one hand, then two, appear in the frame, followed by a shock of blond hair and Nico's smiling face. He pushed up the glass pane and tumbled through it.

"You again?" she said.

"Are you all right?"

"Do I look all right?"

"No."

"The bastards." She motioned to the empty room. "They robbed me blind. They took everything."

Nico smiled.

"Not everything," he said.

The Words of a Blessing

There is a prayer that Jewish people recite when they learn of a death. While the words are in Hebrew, the translation is roughly this:

Blessed are you, Lord our God, the Judge of Truth.

Of all the things you could say when someone dies, why mention me? Why reference truth at all? Why not ask for forgiveness? For mercy? For a soft landing in a glorious heaven?

Perhaps it's because the lies you die with are the first thing the Lord peels away—the lies you have told, and the lies that have been told about you.

Or perhaps I am more important than you think.

After Lev switched number cards with his father in the selection line, it was just a matter of time before the Germans came for him. At night, in their bunks, Lazarre pleaded with his son to admit what he had done, to tell the SS men he was only trying to save his elderly father. But Lev shook his head.

"Then they will just kill both of us."

He was right, of course. So Lev remained silent, his father wept, and Sebastian waited, feeling so powerless his hands and feet went numb. On the third morning, a chilly, rainy day, the SS guards read the numbers of those "selected" and pulled the subjects from the roll call lines. Lev was one of them. He heaved a huge breath and Sebastian saw his father's hands trembling. Just before they took him away, he leaned into his son.

"I love you, Sebby," Lev whispered. "Never give up. You survive for me, OK? Watch over Nano. And find your brother one day. However long it takes. Tell him he is forgiven."

"No, Papa," Sebastian pleaded. "Please, please don't leave . . ."

A guard smacked Sebastian's face as Lev was yanked away. Sebastian felt hot tears streaming down his cheeks. He wanted to howl. He wanted to kill these soldiers, grab his father, and run. But where could he go? Where could any of them go?

Suddenly he heard these words:

"Blessed are you, Lord our God, the Judge of Truth."

His grandfather, hunched over, was mumbling the blessing in Hebrew. Sebastian burned with an anger that singed his soul. He swore at that moment he would never pray again. There was no God here. There was no God anywhere.

"Get back to work!" the Nazi officer yelled.

A horn sounded. The prisoners hurried to their tasks. Thick clouds swallowed the morning sky.

Twenty minutes later, Lev Krispis was gone from this earth, a single bullet to the head having separated his soul from his body, which was tossed into a muddy trench, dug the day before by a dozen haggard prisoners, including Sebastian.

A son should never have to dig his father's grave. I'd like to think this was part of the truth that the Lord judged when Lev arrived at heaven's door.

But then, I am down here with you. So how would I know?

Four Days of Snow

Only the dead see the end of war. But individual wars do reach their conclusions, and the Second World War would end with the Nazis defeated. That defeat, however, did not arrive at the same time everywhere. Instead, the curtain dropped for months, with some celebrating liberation while others suffered final, brutal consequences.

Allow me to present a single day, Saturday, January 27, 1945, experienced from four different perspectives, to illustrate how the war ended differently for Fannie, Sebastian, Udo, and Nico.

All four involved snow.

Fannie was walking in a long line of prisoners.

She didn't know what day it was. She didn't know what month it was. Only that it was terribly cold, and that she and the others had to sleep on the frozen ground every night, without as much as a sheet to keep them warm.

The Nazis, in their final desperate acts, were marching captured Jews back to the motherland, to keep them from telling liberators of the atrocities they had suffered, and to use what was left of their labor before murdering them.

It is hard to conceive that, even as the concentration camps were burned and abandoned, those who had survived them were not done with their torture. Instead, they were rounded up, ghostly and emaciated, and forced to walk hundreds of miles without food or water. Those who fell, stopped to rest, or even squatted to defecate were quickly shot, their bodies left unburied by the side of the road.

You might ask why the Wolf, in the waning days of his attempted world domination, would care so much about killing helpless Jews when there were military battles to be waged. But questioning a madman is like interrogating a spider. They both go on spinning their webs until someone squashes them out of existence.

Fannie and the other children hidden by Katalin Karády were discovered one night after a neighbor informed the Arrow Cross about unusually large food deliveries coming to the building. Soldiers burst into the basement and started screaming orders and waving rifles. The youngest children were taken away. Teenagers like Fannie were herded to a detention barracks at Teleki Square, where they waited with crowds of starving adults, clueless about their fate.

Then, one morning, they were forced out into the winter cold, joining a thousand other Jews in a thick line that filled the street. That line was flanked by Nazi guards, who shouted a single direction.

"Marsch!"

They were walking to the Austrian border.

The journey would later be labeled a "death march" for all the shootings and fatal collapses of its victims. Fannie found the only way to survive was to step into the muddy shoeprints of those in front of her and stare straight ahead, never stop, never look back, not when an old woman next to her dropped into the snow, not when a skinny man gasping for breath stopped to urinate and was pushed to the ground by an SS soldier. Fannie squeezed her eyes closed, knowing a bullet was coming. Bang! She shuddered and marched on.

The war's constant grip had sapped the adrenaline from the poor girl's bloodstream. Her body was rake-thin, her cheeks hollow. There was so little left of her emotionally that she found herself fingering the small pouch of red rosary beads given to her by Gizella, as a voice inside her whispered, *"Enough. We are a wisp. Swallow a bead. Get it over with."*

She might have surrendered to that voice, if not for a memory that played endlessly in her head: the crowded train car from Salonika, and those final words from a bearded stranger:

"Be a good person. Tell the world what happened here."

The only way to do that was to survive. It was her last shred of purpose. So she lifted one foot, then the other, and she kept herself awake by slapping snow against her face, and hydrated by shoving it into her mouth when the guards weren't looking.

On her fifth day of marching, she found herself beside a young boy, maybe seven years old, who was struggling to stay upright with a pack on his back.

"Take your pack off," Fannie whispered. "Leave it."

"I can't," the boy said. "I have cheese in there. I will need to eat when we arrive."

Fannie wondered how he had managed to get cheese, or to have a pack at all, since most of the others were denied even the smallest satchel. But it wasn't helping. He kept stumbling, and crying, and he fell in the snow several times. Fannie yanked him up before the guards noticed.

"Give me the pack, I'll hold it."

"No. It's mine."

He fell again and Fannie lifted him. She kept his arm in her grip for the next three hours, until it looked like he would pass out.

"Let me help," Fannie said. "I promise I will give it back."

The boy no longer protested. Fannie slung the pack on her shoulder. It was heavy, and made her steps more labored. She wondered if there was really cheese inside.

"Where do you live?" she asked the boy.

"No place."

"What about your family?"

"I don't have any."

He corrected himself. "Anymore."

He began crying again, and Fannie told him to stop, it would tire him out. Her shoulders ached. Her feet were throbbing. When nighttime fell, the marchers stopped and she told the boy to sleep and maybe the next day they would be liberated.

"Then where will I go?" he whispered.

"You can live with me."

"Where?"

"We'll find someplace."

They fell asleep next to each other. Fannie awoke at dawn to the shouting of Nazi commands. The prisoners around her slowly rose, but the little boy did not. Fannie jostled him.

"Wake up, boy."

He didn't move.

"Wake up. Come on."

"Leave him!"

An SS guard was hovering over her, his gun drawn.

"No, please, don't shoot! He's just sleeping."

"Marsch!"

She stumbled ahead, carrying the pack, pushed along by the crowd behind her. She glanced back at the boy's small body. She tried to remember the words from the kaddish, but could only recall the first two lines, which she whispered under her breath. A man standing next to her overheard this and whispered along with her.

Five hours later, her eyelids heavy, she threw the pack off her shoulders and left it in the mud. She never even opened it.

∞

Now, I've warned that this is a story which might, in its twists and turns, make you question the coincidence of certain events. I can only confirm what happened next:

On that day, Saturday, January 27, 1945, the sky was dark, and word came that the death march line was drawing close to Hegyeshalom, a town by the Austrian border. Fannie shivered when she heard that word. *Austria?* No! Once they entered the Wolf's birthplace, no one would ever help her, even if she escaped. She had to do something. But what?

At the precise moment of Fannie's deliberation, snow began to fall. And as the wind whipped it into a squall, a large group of Hungarian refugees suddenly appeared, trudging up the road perpendicular to the Nazi march. The SS guards blew whistles and hollered, trying to let the refugees pass. But the refugees swarmed them, hands out in desperation.

"Give us food . . . Give us water! Please! Some water!"

In the chaos of the crowd, Fannie saw her chance. The guards were preoccupied. She took a deep breath, then slipped from the line with her head down. She quick-stepped into the refugee group and, once there, began shouting the words they were shouting in Hungarian.

The annoyed Germans kept waving the refugees on. "Out of the way! We have nothing for you! Move!"

Fannie nudged up to a man in a yellow raincoat and grabbed his shoulders. With her last ounce of strategy, she pushed up a fetching smile, and the man smiled back. He yanked off his raincoat, draped it about her, and kept his arm around her neck. They walked that way through the intersection, beneath the impatient gaze of SS guards. Fannie's heart was pounding so hard, she swore the soldiers could hear it.

Head down. Take a step. Take a step.

Moments later, the SS fired guns in the air and continued marching their prisoners north to the border. The refugees, heading west, disappeared into the blinding white. Fannie felt her knees buckle. The man holding the raincoat grabbed her chin and turned it his way, repeating a single Hungarian word.

"*Lelegzik.*"

Breathe.

And that, for Fannie, was the end of the war.

Udo removed his boots.

He tossed them into the fireplace, which was already burning his uniform, hat, and overcoat. For the first time in years, he was dressed without the slightest symbol of authority. Just a flannel shirt, black pants, work shoes, and a wool coat he had taken from a local farmer who delivered food to the camp.

It was January 27, 1945. In the previous days, explosions could be heard around Auschwitz. The Russian Army was at their doorstep, and orders had come to evacuate the surviving prisoners back to Germany, but only those strong enough to make the walk. The others—the weak, sick, or elderly—were to be left behind. There wasn't even time to kill them.

Udo watched the flames swallow his uniform. Had he been the type of man to face me, he would have known it was over. The Wolf was finished. The Reich had been crushed. But faithfully convinced that his was a superior race, Udo focused only on the next steps of this war, which meant destroying all evidence of his evil.

He had already torn down the gas chambers and crematoriums and murdered all the Jews assigned there, so they could never testify about it. Warehouses full of stolen goods were burned. Records were destroyed. Piece by piece, Udo was covering his tracks.

But all this took time, and he did not know how much time he had left. His *Kommandant* had already fled. The coward. Udo stayed to finish the job. Now, with the prisoners evacuated and his guards either marching with them or battling the Russians, it was time to preserve himself. Get back to the Wolf. Live to fight another day.

His plan for escape was simple. He had already paid a Polish laborer for his papers and thus had a new identity, Josef Walcaz. He would walk out of the camp in these civilian clothes, blend into the nearby town, and take a prearranged car to the German border. Once there, his contacts would welcome him back home.

What Udo did not know was at that very moment, the Russian Army, dressed in white coats that nearly blended with the snow, was rapidly approaching the Auschwitz gates. Their horse soldiers and jeeps would soon burst through. Udo might have avoided them had he left twenty minutes sooner. But he used those twenty minutes finding bullets for his luger and contemplating whether to take it with him. If the enemy found this gun on him, it could be damning. On the other hand, could he dare flee without protection?

Holding his pistol, his mind raced back and forth. For some reason, he remembered the night in Salonika when he fired a shot and heard a thump in the crawl space and discovered the hiding Greek boy named Nico, who helped Udo mastermind his successful deportation of nearly fifty thousand Jews.

What a time that was. Such power. Such control. Udo felt a wave of pride in what he'd accomplished for *Deutschland über alles,* and he took it as a sign that he should keep his gun with him. He loaded the bullets, tucked the luger in his belt, then pulled on the farmer's coat and yanked a cap over his head. With his officer's uniform still burning in the fireplace, he headed out the door.

∞

To visualize what happened next, try to think of a triangle's three vertexes.

The first vertex was the Russian troops, heading up the hill to liberate the camp.

The second vertex was Udo Graf, in his civilian disguise, walking toward them.

The third vertex was a barbed wire fence, behind which stood a line of feeble Auschwitz survivors, leaning on crutches or draped in threadbare blankets, still wearing the filthy striped uniforms that hung off their skinny bones. As the Russians approached, these prisoners, too weak to speak, merely stared in curious confusion, the way a deer across the river stares at an approaching human.

Udo spotted the troops and took a deep breath. He looked at his feet. Running was now out of the question. He could only continue walking, hands in his pockets, as if none of this was his business. *You are a farmer. You're passing by. You made a delivery.* People often practice their lies when facing a confrontation. Udo kept repeating his. *A farmer. Cabbage and potatoes. Keep walking.*

The first horse soldiers trotted past him. Udo fought a grin. A jeep passed by as well.

They are too stupid to notice you. Keep to your plan.

Another jeep. A third. The ruse was working.

And then, a voice.

"Stop him! Somebody stop him!"

It was hoarse and strained and came from behind the barbed wire. It sounded like the yowl of a wounded animal.

"Stop him! He's a killer! *Stop him!*"

Udo glanced sideways and saw a single male prisoner pushing through the others, jumping, waving, pointing through the fence and screaming. Udo knew immediately who it was.

The older brother.

Sebastian Krispis.

Why isn't he dead?

∞

Now, I should tell you how Sebastian, at sixteen, came to be shouting among the sick and elderly that day.

When word spread that the SS was planning to march the survivors out of Auschwitz, Sebastian made a decision. He wasn't going anywhere. His grandfather, Lazarre, was still alive, weak and unable to walk, but alive. He had contracted lice, and the lice had infected him with typhus. The effects of that disease had covered his eyes in a filmy pus that left him nearly blind. He'd been taken to the infirmary, where Sebastian traded items he'd stolen from camp storehouses to keep the guards from executing the old man.

"I won't leave you, Nano," Sebastian had said the last time they'd spoken. "No matter what. I'll stay."

"Don't be foolish . . ." Lazarre had croaked. "I'll be dead soon . . . If you get a chance to run, run."

"But—"

"Don't think about me, Sebastian!"

"But, Nano—"

Lazarre reached for his grandson's hand and squeezed it gently, which stopped the boy from finishing his sentence. Had he done so, Sebastian would have added these words:

"You're all I have left."

∞

In the end, it was something Udo Graf did that changed Sebastian's fate. Auschwitz, by January of 1945, was no longer the efficient killing center it had once been. Order at the camp had broken down. The guards, worried about capture, were leaving their posts. So much of the place was in chaos or shambles that keeping track of where prisoners went was a challenge.

When the orders came for evacuation, Sebastian slipped away just after morning roll call, found a shovel and a piece of pipe, and began piling snow atop a wooden crate near the last remaining crematorium. Since the building was no longer being used, he figured guards would not be looking there. And since he appeared busy, nobody in the current confusion bothered to stop him. His plan was to hide inside the buried crate until they marched everyone out.

Once the crate was covered in snow, he banged the pipe

through the center until he felt it break through the wood. Then he crawled inside, pulling the shovel in with him.

He had no idea how that would save his life.

Minutes later, on the other side of the crematorium, several SS guards, under Udo's orders, loaded packs of dynamite into holes that were bored in the walls, then detonated them to destroy the building. The explosion sent rocks and debris flying everywhere, including all around a snow-covered crate that nobody would bother with now.

That afternoon, tens of thousands of prisoners were marched out of Auschwitz, heading for the German border.

Sebastian remained inside the crate, breathing through the pipe, for two days.

When he emerged, using what little strength he had left to push the top open with his shovel, he blinked back the sunlight. The camp was deserted. He heard the wind whipping through the yard. He tried to stand, then tumbled into the snow, his legs too weak to support even his meager skeleton. He stayed down for a long time, sucking in the air, wondering what to do next.

When he finally rose, he stumbled toward the rear entrance of the camp. There he saw a cluster of prisoners standing by the barbed wire fence. No guards. No dogs. No sirens. No alarms. They were huddled together, as if waiting for a bus.

He dragged himself into the group, and stared at what they were staring at: the Russian Army was approaching. A rush of relief flushed through Sebastian's body, followed by a shuddering concern.

Nano. Where is Nano?

He started limping toward the infirmary when a figure caught his eye. A man in a coat and cap was walking out of the camp. Even dressed that way, Sebastian recognized the man's gait. His frame. His down-turned face.

The *Schutzhaftlagerführer*.

He was walking out as if going home after a day's work, and no one was stopping him. No. No! This could not be! Sebastian's throat was raw and parched, he had not spoken in days.

But he began to scream.

∞

"Stop him! Stop that man! He kills! He's in charge!"

The boy's words were damning—but they were in Ladino, a language the Russians did not comprehend. Udo kept walking, feeling the sweat bead under his cap. *Ignore him. They don't speak his language. You are a farmer. You have no reason to look back.*

"Stop him!" Sebastian screeched. "Somebody stop him!"

A fifth jeep passed by. *Not much farther now*, Udo thought. He would turn at the intersection and disappear into town.

And then, from the other side of that barbed wire, came a single screamed word, a word that in any language meant the same thing.

"NAZI!"

Udo shivered. *Keep walking. Don't react.*

"NAZI! NAZI! NAZI!"

Suddenly, a second voice shouted Udo's way.

"You! Stop!"

Udo clenched his jaw.

"Yo! Hey! You! Stop!"

A Russian soldier was yelling from a transport.

Damn that Jew boy. I should have killed him on the train.

Had Udo merely halted and addressed the soldier, presented his Polish papers, shrugged at the screaming teenager, he might have slipped away. But Sebastian's incessant yelling bored its way into Udo's brain. *NAZI! NAZI!* This filthy *Jude*, yelling at him with such disdain. How dare he? Yes, Udo was a Nazi, and intensely proud of it. This Jewish scum was screaming the word like a curse!

Udo would not have it. In a split second that changed everything, he spun toward the barbed wire fence, pulled out his luger, and fired at Sebastian, who twisted grotesquely with the bullet's impact and went down like a dropped marionette.

That was the last thing Udo saw before taking a bullet of his own, just above his knee, dropping him to the ground as two Russians pounced on his back, pushing him into the frozen earth.

Back at the fence, the other survivors scattered, leaving alone the body of a teenager who'd been shot at the very moment of his liberation, his blood now turning the white snow red.

And that is how the war ended for Udo and Sebastian.

Half a mile away, Nico heard two gunshots.

The soldiers beside him ducked their heads. Their jeep continued in a line of Russian transports, following railroad tracks until they reached an entrance. Nico saw iron letters arched over the gate. Three words in German:

ARBEIT MACHT FREI

Auschwitz.

Nico shivered. Seventeen months after chasing the train that stole his family, seventeen months of changing identities, switching papers, speaking different languages, doing anything and everything to get to this place, finally, he had reached it. He was still just a teen, but there was little youthful about Nico Krispis anymore, not in his appearance, and not in his soul. War had shown him cruelty, brutality, and indifference. But above all, it had shown him survival through lying. Nothing—least of all the Truth—could get in the way.

Nico's newest name, according to his "official" papers, was Filip Gorka, a Polish Red Cross worker. Before that, he had been a Czech carpentry apprentice named Jaroslav Svoboda. Before that, Kristof Puskas, a Hungarian art student.

How he managed to get onto this Soviet transport, on the very day that Auschwitz was liberated, is an unlikely story rife with deceptions.

Here, briefly, is the path Nico took.

∞

You remember, in Hungary, Nico told the actress Katalin Karády that "not everything" had been taken by the Nazis. A day before they raided her apartment, Nico had broken in and hidden her jewelry and furs in two garbage cans in a nearby alley. Weeks later, those items enabled Katalin to barter for the lives of Jewish children about to be executed on the Danube River, including Fannie, whom Nico recognized and convinced Katalin to include in the trade.

Did Nico ever speak to Fannie?

He never got the chance. The rescued children were hidden in the basement of a building a few miles from Katalin's apartment. Meanwhile, word of her daring rescue spread fast. She was arrested again, this time by the Arrow Cross. Nico escaped by hiding on the roof until the soldiers left, then grabbed his bag and forgery tools and ran to the train station.

From there he traveled through Slovakia, renting a room for two weeks from a carpenter, who agreed, for a price, to take Nico via wagon to the Polish border, where he met a Polish Red Cross worker in a café. The man told him the Red Cross was mobilizing to join the Allies in liberating Nazi camps.

"There's one just outside of Oświęcim," he said.

"Is it called Auschwitz?" Nico asked.

"I think so."

Nico took a deep breath. By the end of the night, he had traded a pack of forged food ration cards for the man's Red Cross arm badge. From there he traveled north through the Tatra Mountains and found sanctuary in a Polish church in the ski resort town of Zakopane, where the priest brought him to the nearest Red Cross team, which was short-staffed and largely women.

One of those women, a young nurse named Petra, took a

liking to the good-looking new arrival, and when he told her he was hoping to help Jewish war prisoners, she took him to a house on a dimly lit street and put a finger to her lips as they moved down a stairway. At the bottom, she found a flashlight leaning against the door. She picked it up, entered the room, and turned it on.

There, staring back at them, was a room full of wide-eyed children.

"They are all Jews," the nurse whispered.

Nico took the flashlight and moved it around the young faces, catching their dull expressions and tired, blinking eyes. He never said he was hoping to see his baby sisters, Elisabet and Anna. Would he even recognize them now?

The flashlight caught some writing on the wall, and as he got closer Nico saw that it was everywhere. In various languages, children who'd been sheltered there had scribbled messages above their names: "I am alive" or "I survived" or "Tell my parents I went to . . ." with various directions for their loved ones to find them.

Nico felt a choking in his chest. He turned to the nurse.

"How do I get to Auschwitz?"

His chance came three days later, after the Nazis who'd been controlling Zakopane abruptly departed. The next day, Nico saw why. Russian soldiers rode through the town in tan leather coats with sheepskin collars. The Polish families cheered them from their porches. When those soldiers stopped to replenish food and supplies, Nico saw his opening.

Dressed in his Red Cross uniform, he helped load medical equipment onto their jeeps, all the while telling anyone who could understand him that he spoke German and could be useful if they took Nazi prisoners.

One Russian captain agreed. It didn't hurt that Nico offered him a bottle of expensive vodka, which he'd stolen from a guesthouse.

"You can ride with the medics," the captain said, looking over the bottle. "We leave at sunrise."

So it was that, on Saturday, January 27, 1945, that battalion, targeting Oświęcim, stumbled upon a series of camps a mile away, and Nico's transport pulled up just in time to witness Soviet soldiers ramming open the Auschwitz gate locks with their rifles. This was the opposite end of the camp from where Sebastian had just taken a bullet from Udo Graf. But Nico could not know this. Instead, he watched dazed survivors in striped uniforms push out of the gate, embracing their liberators or stomping the frozen ground, unsure of what to do with their sudden freedom.

Nico, having come so far, could no longer restrain himself. He leaped from the transport and ran through the entrance, checking every gaunt face in search of his family. *Not him. Not her. Not him. Where are they?* The Russians advanced in military posture, guns high, anticipating resistance. But they quickly lowered their weapons in shock.

What they saw, what Nico saw, none of them could believe. Amidst the smoldering remains of the camp, starving prisoners sat motionless in the snow, staring, as if someone had just awakened them from their graves. Hundreds of corpses pocked the frozen ground, unburied, flesh rotting. Behind the destroyed crematorium was a mountain of ash that had once been human beings. The stench of death was everywhere.

Nico felt his legs trembling. He couldn't find his breath. Until this point, like many soldiers around him, he had believed places like Auschwitz were labor camps. Hard labor, certainly. But not this. Not a killing ground. He had honestly expected to find his family alive, waiting for liberation. But the Wolf's deceits had fooled even the little liar. It was left to Truth to open his eyes.

I am the harshest of virtues.

"Hello? Does anyone here speak Greek?"

Nico was wedging through what was left of an infirmary, crowded with shivering bodies too sick to go outside. There was no medicine. No pills. No serums. The departing Nazis had stripped the place of even a single aspirin. The patients, bone thin and moaning, occupied every decrepit bunk, every space on the filthy floor.

"Does anyone here speak Greek?" Nico repeated.

From the corner, he heard a grunting noise. He looked over to see an old man raising his hand. He hurried to his side. Only when he was inches away did he recognize the familiar jowls, nose, and mouth.

"Nano?" Nico whispered.

"Who is that? Who is here?"

Nico's throat went dry. Could this really be his vibrant, cheerful, barrel-chested grandfather? His body was a fraction of its old size. His neck could fit in Nico's hand. His hair was shaved white stubble, and his eyes were covered in a grayish goo.

"Can you help me?" the old man croaked. "I can't see anymore. But I have a grandson . . ."

"Yes, it's m—"

"His name is Sebastian. He's all I have left."

Nico swallowed. *All I have left? What does that mean?* In his coat pocket, Nico held newly forged identification papers for his father, his mother, both his grandparents, his siblings, his uncle and aunt. He'd created them so they could escape this place and go home. All the lies Nico had told were to serve that single mission: a return to Salonika. A return to their house. A return to the sun-soaked Sabbath mornings when they walked to synagogue and the starry nights strolling the promenade to the White Tower. *All I have left? Why did he only ask about Sebastian?*

"Sir," Nico said, in a practiced adult tone, "where is the rest of your family?"

Lazarre sniffed in deeply. He looked away.

"Dead."

Nico repeated the word without even realizing it.

"Dead?" he whispered.

"They killed them all. These devils. They killed them all."

The old man began to weep without tears, his face melting

in pain, as if he wanted to say more, but no words came. In the corner, a woman howled when a nurse touched her. Across the room, Russian soldiers lifted crying patients onto stretchers.

I would like to tell you that Nico dropped his charade at that very moment and embraced his beloved grandfather. That the two of them were reunited after all that suffering. But nothing cements a lie more than guilt. So in that infirmary, believing he had ushered his loved ones to their deaths—*they killed them all*—Nico Krispis finally lost me forever, like an astronaut losing the cord out in space.

"You must go to a hospital, sir," he said, rising.

"I don't think I will make it."

"You will. Believe that you will."

The old man tried to blink away the pus.

"What is your name?" he whispered.

Nico cleared his throat.

"My name is Filip Gorka. I am a doctor with the Red Cross. Stay here. I will find someone to help you."

He turned, wiped the tears from his eyes, and walked away.

And that is how the war ended for Nico.

Part III

1946

Truth is universal. You often hear that expression.

Nonsense.

Were I truly universal, there would be no disagreement over right and wrong, who deserves what, or what happiness means.

But there are certain truths that are experienced universally, and one of them is loss. The hollow in your heart as you stand by a grave. The lump in your throat as you stare at your destroyed home. Loss. Yes. Loss is universal. Everyone in their lifetime will know it.

Salonika, by 1946, was a monument to loss. A city of ghosts. Less than two thousand Jews remained, the "lucky" ones, who had hidden like hunted animals in the nearby mountains, and the less fortunate who dragged home from the camps, dead yet somehow alive, searching for something but uncertain what for, having lost everyone they loved and everything they knew.

Sebastian Krispis, now fully grown but bone thin, stood in front of No. 3 Kleisouras Street on a chilly February morning and banged on the door. He wore a coat provided by the Red

Cross, pants and shirt from a relief agency, and boots he was given by an empathetic Polish shoe merchant. His shoulder still ached from the bullet he had taken a year ago.

A middle-aged man with heavy stubble answered in an undershirt. Sebastian stood up straight.

"Hello, sir," he said in Ladino. "My name is Sebastian Krispis, son of Lev and Tanna Krispis. This is my house."

"*Ti?*" the man replied.

"This is my house," Sebastian repeated, switching to Greek.

"What are you talking about?" the man said. "It's mine. I bought it."

"From who?"

"A German."

"That German never owned it. He took it."

"Well, however he got it, he sold it to me. I paid the money. So it's mine."

He tilted his head, studying Sebastian's clothes. "How old are you anyway? You look like a teenager. Go back to your family."

Sebastian felt his jaw tighten. *Go back to your family?* He'd had headaches for almost a year, ever since waking up in a Kraków hospital with that bullet beneath his shoulder. The doctors could not remove it, they said, because it was too close to a major artery. A cyst had formed above the wound, a permanent reminder of Udo Graf's terror.

Go back to your family? Sebastian spent weeks in that hospital bed, then months in a displaced persons camp, where survivors passed around newspapers, desperately searching for lost relatives. He asked repeatedly for any news of his grandfather, but when a Greek survivor arrived and claimed that Lazarre had died in the infirmary, Sebastian was denied permission to leave and search for the body. Even here, the Jews were treated like inmates. At times, they were actually forced to share quarters with captured Nazis.

Go back to your family? As months passed, some well-meaning Jewish groups tried to create a cultural life for the refugees, inviting schoolteachers and staging sporting events. Sebastian was asked if he wanted to take part in a musical. *A musical?* All around were the Wolf's withered victims, so haunted by trauma they could barely drag themselves through the day. Some, having survived the worst of German starvation, died from taking in too much food too soon. They called it "refeeding syndrome," a new form of Jewish extermination.

Go back to your family? Once his strength increased, Sebastian moved from camp to camp, scanning the weary faces for the only two people left from his life: Fannie and Nico. He asked to see lists, but the names were endless and the information incomplete. After months of fruitless searching, he gave up and sought help getting back to Greece. He was eventually sent, via train, through Poland, Czechoslovakia, Hungary, and Yugoslavia. He stared out the windows at destroyed towns, bombed buildings, farmers walking through razed fields, children playing in the ruins of churches.

Go back to your family? When he arrived in Athens, he was sent to a gymnasium and given biscuits, cigarettes, and ouzo. His fingerprints were taken. Eventually, a truck drove him to

Salonika. When he got there, it was nighttime and he had no place to go. He slept, shivering, on a bench near the harbor, and was awakened by the sound of fishing boats bringing in their morning catches. As he rubbed his eyes, he wondered if life in his hometown had gone on like this every morning while he, his father, and his grandfather were being herded like animals into the Auschwitz yard. How could fishing boats keep rolling in so innocently? How could the world eat when all those prisoners were starving? How could things look so terrifyingly normal here, when there was nothing left of normal for Sebastian?

Go back to your family?

"Everyone in my family is dead," Sebastian said.

The man looked him up and down. "You're a Jew."

"Yes."

The man rubbed his chin. "They took you away? On those trains?"

Sebastian nodded.

"I heard things. Awful things. Were they true?"

"Please, sir," Sebastian said. "I tell you again. This is my house."

The man looked sideways, as if thinking. Then he turned back.

"Listen. It's too bad, whatever happened to you. Maybe the government can help. But this is my house now." He scratched his chest over his undershirt. "You really need to go."

Sebastian teared up.

"Where?" he rasped.

The man shrugged. Sebastian wiped his eyes. Then he lunged

forward, threw his hands around the man's neck, and did not let go.

The next day, Fannie was on Egnatia Street.

She was staring at what used to be her father's apothecary. It was a shoe store now. The Jewish bakery was a laundry. The Jewish tailor's shop was a solicitor's office. Although she recognized certain landmarks, everything within them had changed, and everyone moving about them seemed different. She saw no Jewish men with graying beards, or Jewish women wearing shawls. She heard no Ladino being spoken.

Fannie had also endured an arduous journey home. Hiding in the hills in northern Hungary, it took her months before she felt safe enough to admit her true identity. Eventually, like Sebastian, she was sent to a displaced persons camp, this one in Austria, the very country she had run away from on that snowy day. She slept in a bunk and ate meager rations of food. She waited days to see a doctor. She was constantly fending off unwanted advances of male camp workers, who seemed to act as if she should be grateful they were helping her and tried to put their arms around her waist or kiss her neck.

After months of paperwork, she was finally given train passage to Athens, where she passed her sixteenth birthday sleeping on a cot in a warehouse. In February 1946, more than a year after escaping the death march out of Budapest, she traveled back to Salonika with a young woman named Rebecca who had survived the camps by being a seamstress for Nazi uniforms. Rebecca wore a wool skirt made from a camp blanket, and had a scar below her left ear. Her gaze rarely shifted from straight ahead.

When the two of them arrived in Salonika, they were housed in one of the two remaining synagogues in the city, alongside several dozen Jews who had hidden in the mountains. It was a Friday. That evening, for the first time in years, Fannie witnessed a Sabbath service. The sanctuary was dimly lit, and some of the survivors prayed softly. Fannie remained silent. Later the group shared bowls of soup and small portions of chicken.

That night, after most of the others had gone to sleep on the floor, a group of men who'd been part of the Greek resistance huddled around the two new arrivals.

"What's that on your wrist?" one of them asked Rebecca.

"My number."

"What for?"

"Every prisoner was tattooed with a number."

"Why aren't there more of you?"

"Most died when they got there."

"Died?"

"Killed."

"Killed how?"

"Gas," Rebecca said.

"What happened to the bodies?"

"The Germans burned them."

A pause.

"That's true?"

"Of course it's true."

The men looked at each other. They shook their heads in disbelief. But one of them, a broad-shouldered, mustached man, leaned forward and pointed a finger.

"Then how are *you* here?"

Rebecca blinked. "What do you mean?"

"They didn't burn *you*. Why not?"

"I . . . survived."

"How?"

"I had a job—"

"What kind of job? Who did you collaborate with? Who are you collaborating with now?"

Fannie could not believe what she was hearing. But the truth of the death camps was incomprehensible to most. A lie of collaboration was easier to accept.

"What about you?" the man asked, turning to Fannie.

Another man tried to stop him. "She's just a teenager—"

"Where's the number on *your* wrist?"

"I wasn't in a camp," Fannie said.

"Why not? Who did *you* collaborate with?"

"Nobody. I—"

"Who did you condemn so you could survive?"

"Stop it!"

"WHO—"

"Leave her alone!" Rebecca screamed. "Isn't it enough that we lived? Do you want us to be ashamed of that, too?"

The man looked angrily at the others. He cleared his throat and spat into a handkerchief.

"Just stay away from me," he said.

⋞∞⋟

Fannie did not sleep that night, wary of the men snoring loudly on their cots. The next morning, when the sun came up, she left the synagogue and walked down to the sea.

The harbor was littered with hulls of ships destroyed during the war. Many of the cafés were closed. Salonika was not only missing its Jewish community, it was missing the joy of its mornings, the bustling of its markets, the mingling of its many cultures. In the aftermath of war, the city was starving, broken, and its people were fighting among themselves.

Fannie walked along the old promenade, following the cable car tracks. She headed east toward the White Tower, but when she saw it in the distance, she felt a catch in her throat. The Germans had painted it in camouflage colors to avoid targeting by bombers. Instead of white, it was a tangled mess of fading greens and tans. For some reason, this tore at Fannie's heart.

As she approached the structure, she remembered the time she and the Krispis boys got to climb to the top, courtesy of their grandfather. The sky that day had seemed indescribably vast and the mountains across the water had fresh snow on their peaks. The world felt so alluring, so full of promise.

Now, Fannie wanted nothing to do with the world. She just wanted to sit still. A shop owner emptied a mop bucket onto the cobblestone and set out with a broom, which made a harsh, scraping sound. Where would she go now? What would she do? She had been hiding for so long, freedom felt like its own prison.

Despite promising herself that she would never cry if she

made it back home, Fannie teared up. And at that very moment, when she felt the most alone in her life, she heard footsteps behind her, and a man's voice say the following words:

"Marry me, Fannie."

She spun to see Sebastian, his face mature and whiskered, his forehead scraped by wounds and dried blood, as if he'd been in a fight.

"Oh my God," Fannie said. "Sebastian? Is it really you?"

She threw herself into his embrace, overcome with the sight of anyone from her past who was still alive. She felt his strong, narrow shoulders and the brush of his short hair against her temples.

"I've been looking for you everywhere," Sebastian whispered.

Those words, and the way they made Fannie feel, that someone still considered her existence worthy of a search, wrapped her in a sensation that had been dormant since that brush of a kiss with Nico. She and Sebastian sat in the shadow of the White Tower and tumbled into conversation, questions, head shakes, more questions, tears. Sebastian blurted out what he'd been hoping to say for three years. "I'm sorry for pushing you to the train window." Fannie said she understood, and after hearing what happened in the camps, it was probably for the best. They stayed away from awful details that neither wanted to revisit. At times, they just held hands. When the midday sun had turned the gulf a sapphire blue, Sebastian said, "Let's walk."

They walked all over the city, stunned by the changes. They

went north along the shoreline, pointing at mansions along the *Leoforos ton Exochon* that had once belonged to wealthy Jewish families, but had been stolen by the Germans and repurposed by the Greeks. They went west until they reached the old Baron Hirsch quarter, where they had been imprisoned before their deportation, and saw how the entire neighborhood had been torn to the ground.

By the time the evening darkness fell and streetlamps lit the intersections, the two of them had come to the same conclusion: Salonika was no longer theirs. The word *home* had been blown up letter by letter.

A city of ghosts is no place for a young couple. So when, in the moonlight over the gulf, Sebastian took Fannie's hands and repeated the request "Marry me," Fannie nodded and said, "I will."

At the same time, in an Italian monastery . . .

A man stepped inside the confession booth. He spoke to the shadowy face.

"Do you have the papers?"

"Yes."

"It's been a long wait."

"These things take time."

"They permit me to book passage?"

"Yes."

A deep breath. "Finally."

"Do you have enough money?"

"It's come in slowly. But enough now, I believe."

"Thanks be to God."

"God did not send the money, Father."

"God is responsible for all things."

"If you say so."

"Only through God can you earn absolution."

"As you like."

"May I ask where you will go now?"

Udo Graf leaned back against the wall. Where would he go? He had been so many places in the past year. First, he escaped Poland—only because the Russians, after his capture, were foolish enough to put him in a hospital instead of a prison cell. An orderly got word to his connections in Kraków, and two men came in the middle of the night to sneak Udo out. His leg was severely injured by the Russian gunshot and he had to be carried to a transport, which embarrassed him greatly.

The vehicle drove until morning. When it arrived in Austria, Udo hid with one of many wealthy families still sympathetic to the Nazi cause. He slept in a guesthouse on the rear of their property and joined them on occasion for dinner, although he steered clear of any discussion of his actions at Auschwitz, referring to himself as a midlevel officer just following his orders. At night, he smoked in his room and listened to German music on a Victrola.

Once he was well enough to walk, Udo was guided across the mountains into Italy, to the first of several monasteries to offer him shelter. These well-established escape routes were referred to by the Germans as *rattenlinien*, or "ratlines," meant for fleeing. In this venture, they had ample help from Catholic priests in Italy and Spain. You might ask why men of the cloth, supposedly true to God, would be willing to help those responsible for the deaths of so many innocent people. But clergymen can distort me as easily as anyone else.

"The war was unjust."

"His crimes were exaggerated."

"Better free to repent than to rot in a prison cell."

Udo hid in a back room of a cathedral in Merano, Italy, near the Sarentino Alps, and spent many mornings staring at their snowcapped peaks, wondering how the Wolf's brilliant plan had come undone. Months later, he moved to Rome, where papers were organized for a new name and a new passport. Eventually, armed with this fresh identity, Udo came to a church near the port city of Genoa, where he waited for enough money and proper travel documents to assure his passage abroad. He privately found it humiliating, having to rely on Catholics to save him, when he had no belief in their faith and little respect for their pompous rituals. But they had plenty of wine. He took advantage of that.

Where will you go? South America was the obvious destination. Several governments on that continent had made clear their willingness to look the other way should Nazi officers need a safe haven.

"Argentina," he told the priest. "I will go to Argentina."

"May God watch over you."

"As you like."

But Udo was lying. He knew too many SS officers who had already been shepherded to South America. Ever the strategist, he reasoned that if one of them were discovered, it would be easy to connect the dots to the others.

No. Udo was determined to fight another day, to finish what the Wolf had started, and to do that, he needed to study the enemy from within. He'd told the priest "Argentina," but that would just be temporary. In his head he'd already decided on a better hiding place.

He would go to America.

Part IV

———

What Came Next

If you think of our story as a child's snow globe, then this is the moment when we shake it hard and the various pieces churn in the water, dancing with gravity on their way to a new resting place.

Decades passed. Locations changed. Work was found. Children were born. But even oceans apart, Nico, Sebastian, Fannie, and Udo were still affecting one another, their lives braided together by their truths and their lies.

Shake the globe, and twenty-two years after we last saw them, this is how each of them landed.

Nico became rich.
Sebastian became obsessed.
Fannie became a mother.
Udo became a spy.

Allow me to elaborate:

First, to Nico's story.

My precious child who had always told the truth slipped away from me for good after Auschwitz. Seeing how the Wolf had murdered his people and turned their corpses to ashes—and realizing he had inadvertently played a part—sent the once honest boy into a world where I do not exist.

Psychologists call it "pathological lying." It refers to lies that do not serve a purpose, or even help the person telling them. They are simply choices made out of a disorder, a mental illness, or, in Nico's case, because the trauma of truth was so blinding it burned his eyes to me forever.

Nico, who had deceived to do the nearly impossible—sneak his way into Auschwitz—now began lying about the simplest of things. What books he liked. What he'd eaten for breakfast. Where he purchased his clothes. He couldn't help it. Every straight line became crooked.

∞

I mentioned that Nico became rich. Lying helped that happen.

By 1946, he had made his way back into Hungary, with hopes of reuniting with Katalin Karády. He still carried all his forgery tools, but the money from Udo's bag was mostly gone. He needed funds.

On a train heading toward Budapest, Nico fell asleep and was nudged awake by a conductor asking for his ticket and papers. Groggy, Nico reached into his bag and began to remove the brown German passport, before realizing his mistake and grabbing the Hungarian one instead. The conductor didn't notice. But the passenger sitting next to him did. He looked to be about thirty years old, with a scar on his left hand. He stared at Nico until the conductor moved on. Then he leaned over and spoke in German.

"Can you get me one of those?"

"One of what?" Nico said.

"A Hungarian passport."

"I don't understand."

"Sure you do. I saw that German one. You don't fool me. A man with two passports these days can get three."

"I don't know what you're talking about."

"Come on. How else would you speak German? You get me a Hungarian passport, I'll make it worth your while." He held out his hand. "I'm Gunther. From Hamburg."

Nico thought for a moment.

"Lars," he said.

"From?"

"Stuttgart."

"You have an accent."

"My family moved to Hungary when I was young."

"What are you now, sixteen, seventeen?"

"Eighteen."

"Listen to me, Lars. I need that passport."

"Why not go home to Germany?"

He looked away. "I can't. I have something to do, and once I do it, I need to start fresh."

"Well, I can't help you," Nico said. "I'm sorry."

Gunther snorted and looked out the window, as if contemplating his next move.

"Listen," he whispered, "I can make us both rich."

Nico studied the man's clothes. A turtleneck sweater, gray

slacks, dirty coat, fur hat. He didn't look like a man who could make anybody rich.

"How?"

"Not long ago, there was a train, more than twenty cars long. It was full of gold, jewelry, cash—all things we took from the Jews. It was heading to Germany to fund the Reich."

"So?"

"It made stops."

Nico waited.

"It made *stops*," Gunther repeated. "And at one of those stops, some crates . . . were taken off."

He leaned back in his seat.

"I was a guard on that train. There were lots of us. And a few of us know where those crates are hidden."

"Where?"

The man grinned. "Of course you ask me that. But I'm not telling you. I'll just say there's a church here in Hungary with a basement that has enough for a lifetime."

He measured Nico with his eyes. "You get me a new passport, I'll take you there."

∞

Three months later, on a damp, moonless night, a large truck sat in muddy grass that surrounded an abandoned Romanesque church in the small town of Zsámbék. The church, built centuries ago, was destroyed by the Turks in the seventeenth century and was never repaired. It had been a tourist attraction until the war. After that, there were few visitors.

From what Nico was told, Gunther and a fellow guard, who

were supposed to be doing a nighttime inventory on that Nazi train, had secretly unloaded several crates of gold, cash, and jewelry into a transport, then had driven it here in the middle of the night. Gunther said they'd paid off a night watchman to let them unload it into a basement chamber. They'd put a padlock on the door.

"What happened to your partner?" Nico asked.

"He's dead," Gunther said. "The Russians got him."

"What about the night watchman? Didn't he know what you were doing?"

"Not a clue."

"How do you know he stayed quiet?"

"He did. We took good care of him."

The stone floor beneath the church was wet and smelled of mold. Nico and Gunther found a heavy door with a padlock, and Gunther used an axe to break it. They pulled the door aside and lit the room with flashlights. Sure enough, there were four crates sitting inside.

"What did I tell you?" Gunther said, a huge grin on his face.

The two men carried out the crates, one at a time, straining to get them up the old staircase. Gunther could barely contain himself.

"There is more in here than you can spend in a lifetime, Lars!" Based on how heavy they were, Nico figured he was right.

It took over an hour to load them into the truck. Nico was sweating through his clothes. He kept searching the area for anyone who might be watching, but there were no lights from nearby structures and no noise besides the nighttime crickets.

When the final crate had been wedged inside the truck, Gunther leaned back and exhaled a whooping sound into the darkness.

"This is what I've waited for! The whole stinking war! Finally. Something for me!"

"Let's get out of here," Nico whispered.

"Wait, wait, I have to show you what kind of loot we have."

"Not now."

"Don't be a *lusche*," he said. "Don't you want to see how rich I'm making you?"

He held his flashlight down by his waist, so the beam illuminated his face.

"Look at me, Lars. Look at me! This is the face of a rich, new Hungari—"

The bullet hit before Nico heard the sound. Gunther's head snapped back and his collar bloodied red. A second bullet went through his chest and dropped him like a sack of flour, his flashlight tumbling to the mud.

Nico froze. He heard footsteps approaching. Suddenly, he was staring down a rifle held by a redheaded boy, who kept the barrel pointed straight ahead as he studied Gunther's body, now dead and bent against the truck's rear tire.

Nico raised his hands in surrender, but when the boy saw his face, he lowered the gun. He looked to be about ten years old.

"Why?" Nico gasped.

"He killed my father," the boy said, flatly. "I've been waiting every night for him to come back. Him and the other soldier."

He paused. "Not you."

"No, not me," Nico said quickly. "It wasn't me, I swear."

The boy squeezed his lips together. He seemed to be fighting tears.

"Your father," Nico said. "He was the night watchman?"

"Yes."

"I'm sorry. I didn't know."

"Where's the other man?"

"Dead."

"Good."

He kicked Gunther's body. It fell into the mud.

"I'm going home to tell my mother."

He turned to walk away.

"Wait." Nico pointed to the truck. "Don't you want the crates?"

"What's in them?"

"Gold, I think. Money. Jewelry."

"It's not mine," the boy said.

He cocked his head.

"Is it yours?"

"No," Nico said, "it isn't."

"Well. Maybe you can give it back to whoever they took it from."

The boy threw the rifle strap over his shoulder, stepped across the flashlight beam, and disappeared into the darkness.

∞

Many things transpired after that night, too numerous to detail here. I will share that Nico used some of those riches to educate himself, realizing his last true day of school was when he was eleven and the Germans invaded his home. Posing first as a Hungarian teenager in Budapest, then as a French university student in Paris, and later, after perfecting his English, as a member of the 1954 class of the London School of Economics, Nico, using the name Tomas Gergel, became well educated, particularly in the ways of business. He was single-minded about learning to make money, seeing how it enabled him to navigate the war years. He showed maturity in his classes and was admired by his professors. Thanks to the crates in the church, he maintained a private bank account that would astonish his fellow students, but he lived alongside them in the dormitories, and often spoke of having barely enough to eat. His good looks caught the eyes of many young women, and he was never alone if he did not want to be. He told his dates that his Hungarian family had been wiped out during the war, so there was never a question of a mother or father or a home to return to on holidays. His romantic relationships were intense but brief. He was not one for getting close.

He graduated with honors, and when he received his diploma, he took it to a hotel room near an airfield in Southampton. He felt the need to start anew, as pathological liars often do. Using his forgery tools, he removed the name "Tomas Gergel" from the parchment.

He thought back to his childhood, his grandfather, the trip to the White Tower and the story of the Jewish prisoner who offered to paint the entire structure for his freedom. Nico took his pen, and in perfect penmanship, wrote the name of that inmate, "Nathan Guidili," on his diploma.

The next morning, he boarded his first airplane, the initial leg of a trip that would take him west, then farther west, until he found himself in the blinding sunshine of a state called California and a city called Hollywood, where playing false roles was not only common, but commerce.

Katalin Karády had once told Nico, "You should be in the movies."

Soon, thanks to his money, he was.

Now to Sebastian and Fannie, who shared a name.

They were married in a Jewish welfare office three weeks after reuniting in Salonika. Fannie wore a white linen dress that an aid worker loaned her. It was too large and she had to avoid tripping over the fabric. Sebastian wore a dark coat and tie given to him by a rabbi.

It was a brief ceremony, with two dockworkers brought in to sign as witnesses. The couple had no family or friends to invite, only ghosts, whom they pictured in their minds as their vows echoed in the otherwise empty room. Once the rings were exchanged, they kissed awkwardly, and Fannie was ashamed that for a fleeting second, she remembered kissing her new husband's brother.

At that moment, at such a young age, it would be safe to say that Sebastian was fulfilling an adolescent dream, while Fannie was clinging to the only piece of her old life that was left. It was not a thoughtful marriage. Nonetheless, they became husband and wife, eighteen and sixteen years old, and if not equals in passion, they were united by one idea: neither wanted to stay a moment longer in Salonika.

As soon as they received some assistance, they boarded a boat heading south (Fannie refused to get on a train), and after several stops, they disembarked on the mountainous island of Crete. The sky was streaks of white against a brilliant blue, and the heat felt good on their necks.

"Where should we live?" Sebastian asked as they walked through the port city of Heraklion.

"Not here," Fannie said. "Someplace quiet. Away from people."

"All right."

"Maybe you could build us a house?"

Sebastian smiled. "Me?"

Fannie nodded, and when he realized she wasn't joking, he stopped himself from saying he had no idea how to build a house, and simply answered, "If that's what you want, I'll do it."

It took him more than a year, making many mistakes borne from bad advice. But eventually, on a patch of land by an olive grove near the east end of the island, Sebastian constructed a three-room house made of bricks and cement, with a wooden roof covered in clay tiles. On their first night in this tidy domicile, Fannie lit the Sabbath candles and said a blessing she hadn't recited since her father was alive.

"Why now?" Sebastian said.

"Because," she said, "now we have a home."

That night, they made love in a gentle, passionate manner that had been missing from their earlier efforts. And soon they welcomed their first child, a little girl whom they named Tia, after Sebastian's departed mother, Tanna. Fannie showered the child with all the love she had locked away during the war. As she held the baby and kissed her wispy locks of hair, she felt a breath fill her lungs that was tingly and new, and she shifted her heart into a warm and wondrous place called contentment.

Sebastian tried to let go of the war.
But it would not let go of him.

The contentment Fannie found eluded him. Like many who suffered in the camps, his nights were haunted by the dead. Their faces. Their bony frames. The times he dropped them in the mud or snow. Small horrors would return during his sleep and wake him bathed in sweat, his hands shaking. He would gasp for air and tears would rush down his cheeks. It happened so often, he kept a wooden spoon by his bedside to bite down on, so Fannie wouldn't hear him sobbing.

Sebastian, like his brother, Nico, had never finished his schooling. But without the money to do so, his work options were limited. He knew the tobacco business from his father, and in time he found a job with a company that imported cigarettes to Crete. That brought in enough money for food and clothing, and Fannie, happy with her daughter, did not ask for more.

One night, for Tia's fourth birthday, they took a rowboat

out from a nearby fishing village and looked back at the harbor. Oil-lit streetlamps framed it in a ring of light.

"I think Tia needs a sister," Fannie said.

"Or maybe a brother?" Sebastian said.

Fannie touched her husband's hand. "Do you ever wonder about your own brother?"

Sebastian scowled.

"No."

"What if he's alive?"

"He probably is. He always found ways to get what he wanted."

"You're still angry at him?"

"He was working with the Nazis, Fannie. He was telling their lies."

"How do you know?"

"I saw him! You saw him!"

"I saw him for a second."

"And he told you everything would be OK. There would be jobs. Families united. Right?"

She looked down. "Yes."

"Like I said."

"But why would he lie? What was in it for him?"

"They let him live."

"Maybe they lied to him, too. Did you ever think of that?"

Sebastian clenched his teeth. His anger toward his brother took physical forms.

"What were you doing with him that day?"

"What are you talking about?"

"You know. In the house."

"This again?"

They had rehashed that morning so many times. Fannie had explained over and over about hiding in the crawl space, about being too scared to come out, about holding Nico's hand, about leaving an hour later. She hated this conversation because, step by step, it always led to her father's death in front of the apothecary.

"Never mind," Sebastian said. "It doesn't matter."

But it did matter. Jealousy rarely forgets. The part of Sebastian that sensed Fannie had once preferred Nico was a devil born in his adolescence. And even though Fannie had taken his hand in marriage and had given him a daughter, that devil, at times like these, still whispered in his ear.

∞

One day Sebastian read a magazine story about a man in Vienna who had created an agency dedicated to finding former Nazis. Apparently, many of them were hiding with new identities. This man had funding, an office, even a small staff. Some called him "the Nazi Hunter." He'd already had several ex-SS officers arrested.

For days, as he unloaded crates of cigarettes at work, Sebastian thought about this man. One night, after Fannie and Tia were asleep, he began to write a long letter detailing what he remembered about his time in Auschwitz: the tasks he had been given, the names of the officers who ran the crematorium and the gas chambers, the number of people he remembered certain SS guards killing, and the many atrocities committed by the *Schutzhaftlagerführer* Udo Graf. His list took up nine pages.

When he finished, he sent it off to the man in Vienna. He had only the man's name and his organization, no street address or numbers, so he doubted it would ever find its way there.

But four months after posting that letter, Sebastian received one in return—from the Nazi Hunter himself. He thanked Sebastian for the information he'd shared and expressed admiration for its keen level of detail. He said if at some point Sebastian could travel to Vienna, he would like to meet him personally to verify the details, and take a formal statement of accusation. It might be helpful in pursuing the escaped criminals, particularly Udo Graf, whom, according to the information the agency had gathered, had fled a Polish hospital and disappeared.

Sebastian read that letter at least a dozen times. At first, he was furious, almost physically ill, realizing that Graf was still alive. But with each reading, Sebastian also felt a strength returning to him, like the warming of fingers that had gone numb with cold. He could do something now. He could take action. For so long, his time in the camps had been a rope that held him bound and tied. This man in Vienna was the knife to cut him free.

Sebastian did not tell Fannie of his correspondence.

He hid the letter from the Nazi Hunter. In this way, he deceived his wife. It is nothing new; the lies spouses tell one another are most often omissions. You skip this detail. You don't share that fantasy. You leave out certain stories altogether.

You justify these acts by deeming me, the Truth, too agitating. *Why stir things up? Why make waves?* Sebastian, for example, had never mentioned to Fannie his previous marriage to the girl named Rivka. That poor child had died from typhus in Auschwitz, and Sebastian had barely spoken to her. In his mind, the entire relationship—the hurried wedding, the mumbled vows, his grandmother's ring—was a mistake of someone else's doing, and he didn't want to be reminded of it. He also didn't want to upset Fannie.

So he deceived her out of kindness, or at least that's what he told himself. Fannie, in her own way, did the same thing. Knowing Sebastian's envy of his brother, not once in their marriage had she mentioned that she had seen Nico again, on the banks of the Danube River, or that she believed he had saved her life.

∞

When Sebastian finally showed his wife the letter, she was taken aback.

"Why would you contact that man?" she asked.

"What he's doing is important."

"So let him do it. We have a life here in Greece."

"But you read what he said. My information can help."

"Help what?"

"Help him find those bastards."

"And do what?"

"Hang them. Hang them until they rot!"

Fannie turned away. "More killing," she mumbled.

"It's not killing. It's justice. Justice for my parents, my

grandparents, my sisters. Justice for your father, Fannie! Don't you want that?"

Fannie wiped away a tear. "Do I get him back?"

"What?"

"If you find these Nazis, do I get my father back?"

Sebastian scowled. "That's not the point."

"It is to me," she whispered.

"I want to go to Vienna."

Fannie blinked hard. "And leave Tia and me?"

"Of course not. I would never leave you." He reached for her hand. "I want us all to go. We can move there. I can work for this man. I know it."

Fannie shook her head, slowly at first, then faster, violently, as if seeing something terrible coming for her.

"Austria? No, Sebastian, no! I ran away from Austria once! No, please, no!"

"It's different these days."

"It's not! It's where they all live! It's where they came from!"

"Fannie. I need to do this."

"Why?" She was sobbing now. "Why can't you leave this behind?"

"Because I can't!" he screamed. "Because I see it every night! Because people have to pay for what they did!"

Fannie squeezed her eyes shut. She heard her daughter crying from the other room. Her shoulders slumped. When she spoke again, her voice was shaking.

"Is this about your brother?"

"What?"

"Is this about Nico? You want revenge?"

"Stop talking foolish. I want to help this man find Nazis and give them what they deserve, that's all! And I'm going to do it!"

He glared at her, his jaw set tight. But he had to look away because, and I should know, she was right. Yes, a big part of him wanted Udo Graf captured, convicted, and executed a thousand times over.

But part of him also wanted this man in Vienna to track down someone else, a certain young Nazi helper by the name of Nico Krispis.

And bring him to justice.

Udo Visits an Amusement Park

The enemy of my enemy is my friend. That expression goes back centuries. But in the aftermath of the Second World War, it played out with such astonishing speed, few people even realized what was happening.

High-ranking Nazis had long been targets of the American military. But as the Reich began to crumble, America set its sights on a new enemy. Even before the Wolf swallowed a cyanide capsule and put a bullet in his head—and his nation surrendered eight days later—U.S. intelligence agents had made a quiet shift in strategy. Germany was done. The Soviet Union was the next major threat. And nobody knew, hated, or fought harder against the Russians than the Nazis.

So when the war ended, and the ratlines allowed thousands of SS members to escape, many of them were secretly invited to come work for the United States government, which would provide new names, new jobs, new homes, and new protection, so long as they helped take down their old Russian nemesis.

Such recruitment was never shared with the American public, nor would it be for many decades. This should not surprise you. When it comes to lies, governments can outlast anyone.

Udo Graf, who'd taken a slow ship across the Atlantic Ocean, had been living in a Buenos Aires apartment for a year. He had a false name and a job at a butcher shop. He'd learned enough Spanish to get by. *This is all temporary*, he told himself, part of a long, deliberate plan to return to power. He kept his voice low and his ears open.

By early 1947, Udo knew of at least three other relocated Germans living within five miles of him; all had been officers in the SS. They met secretly on weekends. They shared rumors of fellow Nazis who were recruited to the United States. Udo let it be known that he would welcome such an opportunity.

One Saturday, while he was cooking a veal cutlet, Udo heard a knock on his apartment door. A voice, steady, low, and in perfect German, recited the following words from the hallway:

"Herr Graf. Please let me in. It is safe. I bring an offer. I think you will want to hear it."

Udo removed the frying pan from the flame. He slid toward the door. He kept a pistol in the pocket of a coat on a nearby hook. He put his hand on that pistol now.

"Where is this offer from?" he said.

"Don't you want to know what it is first?"

"Where is it from?" Udo repeated.

"Washington, D.C.," the man said. "It's in—"

Udo opened the door. He grabbed his coat.

"I know where it is," he told the stranger. "Let's go."

∞

Six months later, Udo Graf was working in a laboratory in suburban Maryland, under the new name of George Mecklen, whose paperwork indicated he was a Belgian immigrant. The Americans who recruited him had learned of Udo's science background and assumed he'd utilized it in the SS. They'd been eager to learn what he knew about the Russian military. Udo, so skilled at destroying me whenever he got the chance, lied boldly about having such knowledge, even boasting that he spent most of the war working on espionage and weaponry. The more he said the word *Communists* the more the Americans were inclined to believe anything he told them.

"And what about these reports that you were at Auschwitz?" an American agent had asked him during an interview in a wood-paneled office. The agent, stocky and crew-cutted, spoke fluent German. Udo answered his questions cautiously.

"Auschwitz? I traveled there, yes."

"You didn't work there?"

"Certainly not."

"What was the purpose of your visits?"

Udo paused.

"What did you say your name was, officer?"

"I'm not an officer. Just an agent."

"Apologies. Your German is excellent. I assumed, with such skill, you were a superior."

The agent pushed back in his chair and smiled with false modesty. Udo took note. *A man who enjoys compliments can be molded*, he told himself.

"Ben Carter," the agent said. "That's my name. I learned German from my mother. She was raised in Dusseldorf."

"Well, Agent Carter, you must understand that Auschwitz was more than a camp. It had many factories vital to our war efforts. I visited those factories to share plans in case of air attack."

He added, "By the Russians."

The man's eyes widened.

"And what do you know of the atrocities that took place in Auschwitz?"

"Atrocities?"

"The gas chambers? The executions? The many Jews they say were murdered there?"

Udo tried to look horrified. "I only learned of such accusations after the war. I was focused on our defense. Of course, I was shocked to read about what may have gone on."

He saw Carter holding his pen, studying Udo's eyes.

"As a German, naturally, I wanted my country to prevail," Udo continued. "But as a human being, I cannot condone such brutality against Jewish prisoners. Or anyone."

When the agent began writing, Udo kept going, his words and thoughts racing in opposite directions.

"Some terrible things may have been done."

We were kings. And we will be again.

"If so, such inhumanity is not right."

Unless your victims are subhuman.

"I regret what others may have done in the name of our nation."

I regret nothing.

Once Agent Carter finished his notes, he closed the folder. And when he leaned over and said, "Let's talk about Russian missiles," Udo knew he had been absolved of his sins. The priest was wrong. He didn't need God at all.

∞

In short time, Udo Graf, aka George Mecklen, became an unofficial spy for the U.S. government. He had his own town house, his own phone, a car in the garage, and a barbecue in the backyard. As the years passed, and the cold war intensified, he worked on missile development at the lab. But he was deemed most valuable outside it, gathering information on Communists. His old country, Germany, had been divided in two, with one side loyal to the West, the other to the Soviets. The agency wanted Udo to gather intelligence from his former contacts. They arranged for him to listen to German wiretaps and read intercepted messages. Suspicion ran so high that Udo was able to make up much of the information he shared, and no one could prove it wrong. He sometimes created shadowy enemies entirely from his imagination.

Through the 1950s, this was enough to justify his salary. Udo's English improved greatly. He blended into American life. He mowed his front lawn. He attended Christmas parties. On one company outing, he visited an amusement park and rode a roller coaster with his fellow workers.

He met a woman named Pamela who answered telephones at the lab. She was short and pretty with wavy blond hair and a penchant for decorating and smoking filtered cigarettes. The first night she made hamburgers for Udo, he decided she would be an excellent American cover. Udo had given up on his dream of finding a perfect German wife to raise a family. He needed a partner in his ruse. Pamela had typical American habits—she watched soap operas, chewed gum, and seemed enamored with Udo's status at work, especially his compensation. When he proposed, she first asked if she could have her own car. When Udo said yes, she said yes as well.

They married in a church. They played tennis with friends. They made love regularly. But for Udo, the woman was companionship, nothing more. He judged Americans as an undisciplined people. They ate too much dessert. They watched too much television. When their nation went to war in Vietnam, they protested. They even burned their own flag!

Such disloyalty was repulsive to Udo. But it made him think that this so-called mighty nation could be defeated by the right enemy.

That gave him hope.

What gave him concern was a story in the newspaper.

A man in Vienna, a Jewish survivor of the camps, had formed an entire organization devoted to exposing former Nazis. This crazy *Jude* was releasing lists of names to foreign governments. On some occasions, the men were actually brought to trial!

Udo wondered how many people knew he was in America. He doubted anyone would come across an ocean to find him. But in 1960, one of the Wolf's top architects, a man named Adolf Eichmann, was captured in Argentina, drugged, brought to Israel, convicted, and hanged. Udo realized he was not safe. None of them were. He needed to stop this Jew in Vienna.

For that, he would need more than a false identity.

He would need power.

∞

The opportunity came soon enough.

Agent Ben Carter, who worked with Udo for years, had left the agency in 1956 and gone into politics, winning a state election in Maryland, then another, then another, eventually running for a Senate seat in 1964.

Udo and Carter had stayed in touch. Udo figured it would be good to have an elected official in his corner, and the two men enjoyed drinking brandy together at a particular bar, away from their wives. Over the years, Carter had confessed a certain admiration for the Nazi Party, their organization, their dedication to pure ideals, pure bloodlines.

"Don't get me wrong," he'd told Udo late one night, "you can't just go around gassing people. But a country has the right to deal with undesirables, doesn't it?"

Udo humored Carter. He complimented him often. He knew someday he could use this man.

His chance arose during Carter's Senate campaign. He and Udo met at the bar one night. Carter was distraught and drinking heavily. After some prodding, he admitted to Udo that his campaign was in jeopardy, that "everything is about to come apart," all because of a woman whom, as Carter put it, "I should never have gotten involved with." For years, she had been smuggling diamonds into the country and selling them at a great profit. Carter had used his government position to acquire phony paperwork for her efforts, in exchange for half of the money. But now that he was running for national office, he told her they had to stop, it was too risky. That made her angry. She was threatening to expose him.

"Once my opponents get ahold of this," Carter groaned, "I'll be finished."

He put his head in his hands. Udo swigged his drink and slammed the glass down hard. He was embarrassed by Carter's weakness. A woman?

"Give me her name," Udo said.

"What?"

"Her name and where she lives."

"This isn't some spy thing."

"No," Udo said. "It's easier."

A week later, having followed the woman several times and knowing she went for walks at night over a bridge near her home, Udo stopped his car on that bridge, took out a jack, and pretended to be working on a tire.

When the woman appeared, by herself, Udo, on his knees, nodded up at her.

"Sorry to be in your way," he said.

"Trouble?" she said.

"A flat."

He glanced both ways, assuring there was no one in sight.

"Would you do me a favor? Would you hold this for one second?"

"Sure."

He stood up to hand her a wrench, and as she took it, he pulled a revolver from his jacket and shot her once in the forehead, a silencer masking all but a soft plinking sound of the bullet. Moments later, he tossed her body over the bridge and heard it splash in the rushing river below. He put the wrench and jack in the trunk, drove off, and left the car at a prearranged junkyard, where it was crushed before noon the next day.

Carter won his election by a large margin. And the man named George Mecklen gained a permanent position on his staff. Pleased at how easily killing came back to him, Udo Graf poured himself a drink. He was one step closer to real power now, the kind of power that could get rid of that Jew in Vienna, and see the Nazi dream restored.

The Envied Eccentric

I must confess a confusion in this world. Why, if people so loudly value the Truth, are they so fascinated by liars?

Your literature has been about it for centuries. Molière's *Tartuffe* is a fraudster from the start. So is the title character in *The Great Gatsby*.

Your modern films celebrate liars and cheats. *All About Eve. The Godfather.* Perhaps this is why Nico was attracted to movies. Nothing is real. Everything is pretend.

One afternoon, during his time with Katalin Karády, Nico had asked why she'd chosen to be an actress.

"Because I can disappear," she said. "I can hide inside someone else. I can cry their tears, scream their curses, love their loves, but when the day is over, none of it touches me.

"I get the experience without the pain."

Experience without the pain. The idea was alluring to Nico. When he arrived in California, he immediately asked how he could enter the movie business. The fastest route, he was told, was to find work as an extra. It was an easy way to get onto a set and observe the process.

Many films in those days were being made about the war. On one such project, Nico was hired for a day's work as a background soldier in a battle scene. He was fully costumed when an actor tripped over a piece of sheet metal, gashed his leg, and was taken away for medical care.

"You!" someone yelled at Nico. "The blond guy! Can you do a line?"

Nico had never said a word during a production, but he promptly responded, "Yes, of course." He was told to run to a fallen body, roll it over, look up, and yell, "He's gone!" Then wait for the director to holler "Cut!"

They practiced this once, and Nico lifted the body of the other actor, whose eyes were closed. When the director shouted, "Let's set it up!" the actor opened his eyes and said, "Hey, where'd the other guy go?"

"He got hurt," Nico said.

"Oh. That's a shame. Nice fella."

"Yeah."

"I'm Charlie Nicholl."

"I'm . . . Richie."

"Richie what?"

"Richie James."

It was a name he'd invented on the spot.

"So. You done a lot of films, Richie?"

"Oh yes."

"Which ones?"

"Lots. Hey. We should prepare for this scene, right?"

"What's to prepare? I lie here. You find me. At least you get a line."

"Yeah." He squeezed at his pants leg. "These uniforms are stiff."

"No worse than the real thing."

"I guess."

"Richie?"

"Yes?"

The man squinted.

"You serve?"

"Serve?"

"The war."

"Oh. Yeah. Yes. I was in the war."

"Me, too. South Pacific. Guadalcanal. This beats the hell out of that, huh?"

"It does."

"Where were you?"

"Europe."

"Where?"

"Lots of places."

"Oh, yeah?"

"Yeah."

"Richie?"

"Yes?"

The man sniffed. "You kill anybody?"

Nico blinked. For a moment, he thought about the train platform. The people swarming him, day after day, as he moved through the crowd, telling them lies.

"Only Nazis," he said.

"Nazis?"

Nico turned his head. "Yes. Nazis. I killed lots of them."

"Wow, Richie." He shouted to some other actors, sitting in the dirt. "Hey, fellas! We got a bona fide war hero here! Killed lots of Nazis!"

The other men shrugged. A couple of them clapped.

"Are we set?" the director bellowed.

They did the scene. Nico yelled, "He's gone!" and the director, satisfied, moved to another setup. A man approached Nico and told him where to go at the end of the day to get money for saying a line.

"Thank you," Nico mumbled. But as soon as the others had departed, he walked straight to the parking lot, boarded a bus, and never again returned to a movie set.

Instead, Nico found success in films by financing them.

He met a young director named Robert Morris at a swimming club. Robert had an idea for a movie about King Solomon. When he lamented lacking the money to make it, Nico said, "I can help with that."

Together they went to a studio, which, encouraged by a partner who would share the risk, invested in the project. The movie became extremely popular and earned Nico's money back many times over. Soon he had his own office at the studio, where he listened to people's ideas for films and decided which ones to pursue. The more successes he had, the richer the studio became. His skill at judging popular ideas greatly impressed his industry colleagues, but it was no surprise to me. A good liar knows what people want to hear; why wouldn't he know what they want to watch?

Nico's influence increased exponentially. People whispered about his success rate. They clamored to meet with him. He was using the name Nathan Guidili, which was on the diploma that hung in his office. He told people to call him Nate.

The 1950s passed, with films becoming more popular, more complicated, and more expensive. Nico grew even more valuable to the studio. He was well compensated and was permitted to keep his own schedule, which often saw him disappear for days at a time.

From the outside, it appeared to be an enviable existence. A high-paying job. A glamorous business. A private office in a movie factory where one's wildest dreams turned to celluloid reality.

But the lies you tell by daylight leave you lonesome in the dark. Nico's sleep was haunted. He rarely had a night where a war memory did not wake him, gasping. He would see Nazis shooting bodies into the Danube River. He would see the gates of Auschwitz. He would see corpses stacked in the mud. But mostly he would see the thousands of fellow Jews he had lied to on the train platform, their sallow faces, their trusting eyes, the obedient way they entered the boxcars to their doom, after Nico had told them everything would be fine.

Sometimes the ghosts of his parents would come to him in dreams, always asking a single question: "Why?" On such occasions, Nico would get so agitated he would have to leave his house, walking hours around his neighborhood until his breathing eased and his nerves calmed.

As a result, he rarely came to work in the morning. He

became more and more dependent on sleeping pills, and would sometimes not arrive until the midafternoon. He always had an explanation. Car trouble. A doctor's appointment. Because his talent was so valuable, the studio indulged his excuses.

Eventually, Nico only took meetings at night. He kept his office lights low, concerned that visitors might see the anxiety on his face, or the effects of the pills he was taking. He became known around the studio as eccentric, but in the film business, the more eccentric a successful man acted, the more his colleagues hailed the eccentricity. Soon others at the studio began taking their meetings at night, too.

In the summer of 1960, the studio was producing a very expensive motion picture, a western, one that Nico had approved. To help create publicity, the studio owner, Robert Young, gave an interview to a major newspaper. He shared what he knew about the eccentric Nate Guidili, which, it turned out, was the reporter's real interest. The reporter began to dig into where Mr. Guidili came from. He made calls to the London School of Economics and discovered there was never a student there by that name. He shared this information with the studio owner, who, the following night, confronted Nico as he was leaving work.

"Nate, I gotta ask you," he said. "You have the diploma on your wall. But did you ever really attend that school?"

Nico felt his skin tingle. It was the first time in America he'd been confronted with his lies. His mind raced. *How did they find out? What else do they know?* He thought about his classes in England, and how well he had done under the name Tomas Gergel. *Did he ever really attend? Of course he did.*

"No, I didn't," he said. "I'm sorry. I thought it would impress people."

The owner shrugged and exhaled deeply. "Well. Makes no difference to me. I guess I shouldn't have talked to that reporter. We'll take care of it."

"What do you mean?"

He slapped Nico's arm. "Don't worry about it. You keep picking winners. But no more lies, OK?"

Nico watched him leave. He waited, day after day, for the story to appear. But it never did. The western came out and was a huge success. Nico was given a bonus. Three months later, he quit the studio and started his own company, where his office had a back door directly to his parking space and no one saw him come or go.

The Heart, and What It Yearns

Let me speak here of love. You might ask, what does Truth know about that subject? But which word do humans choose to describe love's purest form?

"True."

So hear me out.

You have debated for centuries about what true love means. Some say it is when another's happiness means more to you than your own. Others say it is when you cannot imagine the world without your partner.

For me, true love is easy. It's the kind where you do not lie to yourself.

Fannie, if she were being honest, had never truly loved Sebastian. She'd run to him as shelter. She'd embraced him as relief. When they found each other by the White Tower in Salonika, they were both alive, but not sure why. A wedding gave meaning to their survival.

But tragedy arranged that marriage, and death attended the ceremony. Their love was less for each other than for all the ghosts around them. As the years passed, those ghosts whispered differently to Fannie than to Sebastian. Hers was just her father, who said, "Live your life." His was three generations murdered in the camps, screaming in his head, "Avenge us!"

So, despite his wife's objections, Sebastian eventually moved the family to Vienna, where he could work with the Nazi Hunter.

And Fannie never forgave him.

She hated being in Austria. She hated the memories. She hated the cold. She refused to learn German or visit the mountains or learn to ski. She focused only on raising Tia, hovering over her after school, reminding her of her Jewish roots. Tia grew into a shy, intelligent teenager, who read a great deal and, like her mother, was largely unaware of her beauty. She often asked when they could return to Greece, where it was warmer and she could swim in the sea.

Sebastian found a night job as a security guard, which left him hours during the day to help the Nazi Hunter review lists, make phone calls, write letters, and chase information. There was a small group of equally dedicated workers at the agency, most of them survivors of the camps. They smoked and drank coffee. They kept photos of escaped Nazis on a wall and celebrated every arrest or deportation. Sebastian skipped many meals with his wife and daughter to work with these people, and when he came home, he wanted to speak of the progress they were making, which Fannie forbade.

"Not in front of Tia," she said.

"Our daughter should know what happened to her family, Fannie. She should know why she has no grandparents or cousins!"

"Why? So it can haunt her, too? Why can't you let it go?

Why do you want to keep talking about Nazis, Nazis? Why must you always go to the past?"

"I'm doing this for everyone I lost."

"What about the ones you still *have*?"

This argument repeated itself, in various forms, at least once a month. He felt it was a reason to live. She felt it was ruining them. Each would tell you they didn't want to fight about it, but, in time, the fight was all they had in common.

As Sebastian advanced at the agency, he began to take trips to foreign cities, in hopes of pressuring governments to pursue ex-SS officers living there. Always in his mind were Udo Graf, which he told Fannie about, and Nico, which he did not. Although their sins were hardly equal, he considered each of them war criminals. He hoped to punish them both.

The more Sebastian went away on these trips, the further he moved from Fannie's heart, until one day, when his train was delayed and he missed his daughter's high school graduation ceremony, he edged outside it altogether.

As Tia cried in the school auditorium, Fannie squeezed her hand. She told her it was unavoidable, don't fret, don't be mad. She took her daughter for ice cream and later kissed her good night. When Sebastian finally arrived, after midnight, Fannie didn't yell. She didn't fuss. She barely spoke. The truth of love is that when it fades away, you don't really care less. You don't care at all.

A few years later, once Tia had departed to attend a university in Israel, Fannie opened a suitcase, packed her clothes, and told Sebastian she was taking a trip of her own. It was a Saturday, the Sabbath, a day on which observant Jews would not travel. Fannie didn't care. She watched her husband stand in the doorway, arms crossed, brow furrowed, as she buttoned her coat and lifted her bag.

"When will you be back?" he said.

"I'll call and let you know," she said.

But she already knew; she wasn't coming back. And deep down, because true love cannot lie, so did he.

Fannie's first stop was Hungary.

For nearly twenty-five years, she had wondered what became of Gizella, who had shown her such kindness during the war. The day the Arrow Cross captured Fannie was the last day she had seen the poor woman. The soldiers said she would die for her treason. But Fannie needed to know for sure. She thought about the poison rosary beads. She prayed that Gizella never had to use them.

She traveled from Vienna to Budapest. From there she took three trains to reach the hillside village where Gizella had lived. Fannie spent nearly a full day walking before recognizing the old road. So much had changed. The architecture. The streetlights. Gizella's house had been replaced with a larger, more modern one, and Fannie might have passed the property altogether, were it not for the chicken coop on the slope behind it, which was still there.

She walked up the pathway carrying her suitcase. She felt her pulse quicken. She remembered the day the gray-haired woman discovered her, and the morning the guards dragged Fannie away.

She knocked on the door. A stocky, middle-aged nurse answered.

"Hello," Fannie said, straining to remember her Hungarian. "I am looking for . . . I used to know . . . There was a woman who lived here once. Her name was Gizella?"

The nurse nodded.

"Do you know if . . . Well . . . Is she still alive?"

"Of course," the nurse replied.

Fannie exhaled so hard, she bent forward. "Oh, thank God. Thank God. Do you know where I can find her?"

The nurse seemed confused. She pulled back the door, and Fannie glimpsed a woman in a wheelchair, sitting near the fireplace. Her right eye was covered with a patch, and that side of her face drooped. But upon seeing Fannie, she let loose a high-pitched squeal, and Fannie ran to her and threw herself at her feet and began sobbing so hard in her lap that all she could get out was, "I'm sorry, I'm sorry, I'm sorry."

The Arrow Cross had dragged Gizella to an interrogation room and had beaten her when she denied the girl she was hiding was Jewish. For three weeks they withheld food, water, even medical attention, trying to get her to talk. Only when an elderly priest from Gizella's church arrived at the door and paid an undisclosed sum of money was she set free.

The beatings left her blind in one eye and unable to walk without a cane. As the years passed, her hips deteriorated, and she now needed a wheelchair to get around. Fannie apologized so many times that Gizella forbade her to use the words

"I'm sorry," insisting that the war had so many victims, just being alive was something to celebrate.

That first night, Fannie helped the nurse prepare a meal. When Fannie carried over a bowl of soup, Gizella smiled and said, "Remember when I did this for you?"

"I could never forget it."

"Look at you now. Such a face. Such hair. And your figure! Fannie, you are beautiful."

Fannie blushed. She hadn't felt beautiful in a long time.

"I never stopped thinking about you, Gizella."

"And you were in my prayers every day."

"So much happened," Fannie said. "Terrible things . . ."

"Do you want to tell me?"

"I don't know where to start. I almost died at the Danube. And then, on a march, we had to walk in the snow for days. There was this little boy . . ."

She started to choke up. She felt ashamed even mentioning her struggles when Gizella, in a wheelchair, had endured so much herself.

"Whatever you suffered," Gizella said, "there is a reason you are still here."

"What's the reason?"

"God will show you when it's time."

Fannie bit her lip.

"Why were you so kind to me?"

"I told you, dear, many years ago. You were sent to fill the hole in my heart. And now, you have done it again."

Fannie smiled as tears spilled down her cheeks.

"Eat," she whispered.

Gizella slurped a spoonful of soup.

"It's good."

"The soup?"

Gizella took Fannie's hand.

"This," she said.

∞

Now, in the interest of moving our story along, I will not detail all the joy that Fannie and Gizella shared in the two weeks they spent together, although their reunion was the most satisfying time either had spent in years. I will mention one conversation that came up quite innocently, but irrevocably changes the course of our tale.

Fannie was making dumplings in the kitchen, remembering the process she and Gizella had done years ago. She used yeast flour and curd cheese and rolled them together.

"When did you build this new house?" Fannie asked.

"Oh, a long time ago," Gizella said.

"It's very comfortable."

"Thank you."

"Why did you keep the chicken coop?"

Gizella smiled. "In case you came back looking for me."

"Well, it worked," Fannie said, laughing. "Honestly, if not for the coop, I would have gone right past it."

She carried a dumpling to the table and sat down. She lowered her voice.

"If it's all right to ask . . . how did you pay for such a nice home? I mean, after what . . ."

"They did to me?"

Fannie frowned. "Yes."

"Darling. I thought you knew."

"Knew what?"

"The boy."

"What boy?"

"The boy with the red hair."

"What boy? Who is he?"

"He never says his name. But he started coming a few years after the war. He brought a bag of money. He said it was for me and not to ask why.

"The next year he came again. The next year, again. He's a grown man now, but every year, there he is, on the same day, August 10. He gives me the bag, then he leaves."

"Wait," Fannie said. "I don't understand. Who is sending you this money?"

Gizella's eyes widened.

"I thought it was coming from you."

The date Gizella mentioned was significant.

Perhaps you remember it. Fannie did. She was still thinking about it a few weeks later as she exited a railway station in Budapest.

August 10.

The day her train left Salonika.

Fannie would never forget that morning. The platform. The confusion. Nico. Her being shoved inside the cattle car, the light disappearing, the air evaporating, the car rumbling horribly in its departure. It was the turning point of her life.

But how was it connected to Gizella?

Why was money being delivered to her in Hungary—on that day of all days? Was it just coincidence? Was the government reimbursing her? No. That made no sense. Why would a redheaded boy deliver the bags?

Fannie tried to recall if she'd told anyone about Gizella. Only Sebastian. Could he have something to do with this?

From a phone center at the train station, Fannie had an operator call the apartment in Vienna. She waited a long time. No answer. She hesitated, then gave the operator Sebastian's number at the agency. Someone answered and said he was there.

"Hello?"

His voice sounded thin and distant.

"Sebastian, it's me."

"Where are you?"

"Budapest."

"Why?"

"Do you know anything about Gizella?"

"Who?"

"Gizella."

"Who's that?"

"The woman who found me after the train."

A pause.

"Is that who you're seeing?"

"I found her, yes. She's alive. I was so relieved. But, Sebastian, she is getting money sent to her. Every year. A lot."

"From where?"

"I don't know. I was going to ask you if you had anything to do with it?"

"Me?"

From the sarcastic tone in his laugh, Fannie immediately knew he didn't.

"Never mind," she said. "It was a stupid thought."

"Sorry."

"Goodbye then."

"Wait."

"What?"

"Fannie?"

"Yes?"

"Are you coming home soon?"

She touched her chest.

"I'm going to keep traveling for a while."

A long silence.

"I thought you were calling to tell me you found my brother."

"Why would you think that?"

"I don't know. Never mind."

"Goodbye, Sebastian."

"Will you call again?"

"Yes. I'll call."

"When?"

She rubbed her forehead. "I'll call."

She hung up.

∞

That afternoon, Fannie found herself walking the banks of the Danube. The summer breeze was strong and blew the dark curls off her shoulders. She had worried this visit might be too painful a memory, but in broad daylight, more than two decades later, there was nothing familiar about it. Just a mighty river slicing through the city, running across the continent and out to the Black Sea.

Fannie stared at Budapest's massive parliament building, its Gothic facade and huge central dome. She took in the churches that sat along the banks. She wondered what all the people in these buildings had been doing two decades ago, when Jews were being shot at night and dumped into the river.

She had blocked so much of that event. It was just her way. While Sebastian fretted over every flashback, Fannie built a wall inside her brain to shield her from the dark memories. That afternoon, she might have stayed on the safe side of that wall, had she not taken a seat on a bench by the Danube as the sun was centered in the sky.

Moments later, an old man arrived, carrying a prayer book. He walked to the edge of the embankment and began to sway back and forth. Fannie recognized his prayers. They were in Hebrew.

When he finished, he wiped his face with a handkerchief and walked past her.

"Who are you mourning?" Fannie asked.

He stopped, surprised.

"You know the kaddish?"

She nodded.

"My daughter," he said.

"When did she die?"

"Twenty-three years ago. They killed her here." He looked out at the rushing river. "Not even a grave. Just water."

"I'm very sorry."

He studied her face.

"You are not from Hungary. Your accent."

"Greece. But I've been here before. On this river. At night. With my hands tied."

She looked off. "I was luckier than your daughter."

The old man stared. Tears moistened his eyes. He sat down and gently touched Fannie's shoulder. He saw that she was crying, too.

"*Baruch hashem*," he whispered. "I've never met anyone who lived through it. Tell me. Who saved you?"

"I don't know," Fannie blurted out. "All these years, I still don't know. I'd heard it was an actress, but I never saw her. It was dark. They took us to a basement. We lived there for weeks."

The old man leaned back. He looked stunned.

"Katalin Karády," he mumbled.

"Who?"

"The actress. I'd only heard rumors."

"You knew her?"

"Every Hungarian knew her. She was very popular. Then she stood up against the government, and they destroyed her. Beat her. They pounded on her pretty face. They broke her jaw, I heard.

"There were stories, rumors, that she sold jewelry to the Arrow Cross in exchange for saving Jewish children. But you're telling me it's true? You were really one of them?"

"Yes!" Fannie said. "Where is she now? Please! I need to find her!"

The old man shook his head. "They drove her out of Hungary a long time ago. They ruined her reputation. She couldn't work.

"I read somewhere that she is living in New York City. She has a shop there, I think. A hat shop, or something."

Fannie's head dropped. *New York City?* She began to cry.

"What is it?" the old man asked.

"Nothing. I just . . . I wanted to find her. I wanted to thank her. And I needed to ask her about somebody, a boy I knew, a boy I saw that night. I think he was working with her."

She looked up at the old man's face. "I think he was the one who saved me."

The wind blew hard. The old man wiped his eyes with his handkerchief.

"Do you know what the Talmud says about saving a life?"

Fannie nodded. "If you save one, it's as if you saved the whole world."

"That's right." He crossed his hands. "How old are you?"

"Thirty-eight."

"My daughter's age." He gave a sad smile. "Had she lived."

"I'm sorry. This must be very hard to hear."

"Oh, no, my dear. You've given me more joy than you can imagine. You survived. You beat them. One life saved. As if the whole world was saved with you."

He placed his hand on hers. "Do you have children?"

"A daughter."

"The best revenge," he said, grinning.

He looked at the river, then glanced up at the sun. He put away his handkerchief and rose to his feet.

"Would you come to my office with me?" he asked. "It's not far from here."

"Why?" Fannie said.

"I want to help you find what you're looking for."

∞

Fannie went to the old man's office, on the second level of a carpet factory. He introduced her to several of his workers and showed her a photo of his daughter when she was a child. Before Fannie left, the man went to a closet, opened a safe, and filled an envelope with enough money for a plane ticket to New York City. I mentioned this story has fortuitous twists. Certainly, this is one of them.

When Fannie initially refused his kindness, the old man smiled and insisted, saying he had saved the money for a reason, and that this made him feel as if he were helping his own child, who died with her dreams unrealized.

Fannie hugged the old man as she left. He recited a blessing over her head. Then he added, in a final whisper that made her shiver: "Tell the world what happened here."

She left the building dazed. Three weeks later, she was walking down a street in New York City, holding a piece of paper and searching for an address.

Part V

She Laughs, She Lies

In the Bible there is a story about Abraham and Sarah. When they were both in their nineties, they were visited by three strangers, who were actually angels of the Lord. Sarah was inside, preparing food. Meanwhile, outside, one of the angels gave Abraham some stunning news.

"I will return to you next year around this time," the angel said, "and your wife will have a son."

Sarah, inside the tent, overheard this and laughed. She said to herself, "After I am worn out and my husband is so old—now I will have this pleasure?"

Of course, talking to yourself in the presence of the Almighty is never really talking to yourself. The angel immediately asked Abraham, "Why did Sarah just laugh? Why did she say, 'Will I really have a child?' Can't God do anything God chooses to do?"

Abraham called for his wife, who, when confronted, grew fearful and lied.

"I did not laugh," Sarah said.

"You did laugh," the angel replied.

Now. You may take from this anecdote that God does not put up with deceptions, even small ones.

On the other hand, when the angel repeated to Abraham what Sarah had said, you'll notice he left out the part about Abraham being too old to father a child. He skipped right over it, rather than insult the husband and cause a rift between the couple.

So you might conclude that angels lie, too.

I see the story differently. To keep harmony, there are things you might not say, even if you know them to be accurate. It is, technically, an act of deceit. It is also an act of love. The two are more connected than you think.

As we will soon see.

Postcards from the Past

Fannie entered the shop on East Twenty-Third Street. Hats covered every space—on hooks, on shelves, on mannequin heads. There were no other customers. Soft classical music was playing from a small speaker.

"Good afternoon," a voice said, in accented English.

Fannie saw a middle-aged woman emerge from a back room. It was her. The actress. It had to be. She looked to be well into her fifties but still maintained a stark beauty. Her face was heavily made up, her eye shadow a deep blue, her lipstick the color of grapes. Her dark hair was puffed high in the style of the day.

"*Jó napot*," Fannie said in Hungarian.

The woman's eyes shot straight at Fannie's, so piercing it made her shiver.

"Who are you?"

"Please. I need to ask you something."

"Do you want a hat?"

"No."

"Then I can't be of service."

The woman turned toward the back room.

"Wait!" Fannie blurted out. "On the banks of the Danube in 1944, there was a group of Jewish people about to be killed. They say you were there. And there was a boy, dressed like a German officer. Please. Do you know who he is?"

The woman slowly turned.

"Who are you with?"

"Nobody."

"Who are you *with*?"

Fannie shook her head. She felt dizzy. She grabbed a shelf to steady herself.

"Nobody. I'm with nobody. I don't have . . . anybody left."

The woman watched in silence. She crossed her arms as Fannie began to cry.

"What was this boy called?"

"Nico. His name was Nico."

"I've never heard that name."

"He was from Greece."

The woman shook her head.

"I'm sorry. I don't know him."

"May I sit down? I don't feel well."

The actress motioned to a chair by a mirror. Fannie sat as the woman moved behind her. Their reflections filled the glass.

"How old were you in 1944?" the actress asked.

"Fourteen."

"What were you doing on the Danube?"

"I was tied to other people, about to be murdered by the

Arrow Cross. Somebody saved me. Someone risked their own safety. And because of that, I'm alive."

She wiped her eyes. "More than alive. Because of that, I was able to grow up. I was able to marry. I was able to have a child of my own and give her the things I never had."

The woman said nothing. But Fannie saw her lower lip begin to tremble.

"It was you, wasn't it? You were the one who saved me."

Fannie grabbed her hand.

"It was *you*."

"It wasn't me," the woman replied, taking her hand back. "It was my money. There is a price for everything. A price you pay for someone's life to be spared. And a price you pay for sparing it."

She touched her jaw.

"I heard they were terrible to you," Fannie said.

"Less terrible than they were to others."

"There was more than just me that night. There were at least twenty of us."

"Twenty-three," the woman said, softly.

She moved behind the counter and, from underneath it, opened a small safe. She rustled through the contents and pulled out an envelope. Inside was a piece of paper. She unfolded it and placed it in front of Fannie.

It was old and faded yellow at the corners. But the handwriting was clear. A list of names with birth dates. Twenty-three of them.

"Are you here?" the woman asked.

Fannie scanned the lines. When she reached number nineteen, she gasped, and placed her fingers beneath the words.

Fannie Nahmias, 2/12/1930

"It's you?"

Fannie nodded.

"Then I am very sorry I treated you so coldly." She put her hand on Fannie's shoulder. "I am glad you are alive."

"What about the others?" Fannie said. "What happened to them?"

"The younger ones survived. The older ones were put in a ghetto. After that, I don't know what happened."

"I do," Fannie said.

The woman sat down.

"Tell me."

"They marched us to Austria. For days and days, we had to keep going. It was so cold. There was no food. No water. We slept on the ground. You couldn't stop walking or they would shoot you. So many died. Women. Children. They didn't care. They left them in the mud."

The woman sighed. She pointed to the paper.

"Fourteen of these names are still alive. Fifteen now, with you. A woman in Budapest keeps track of them. Some are still in Hungary. Some in Israel, some here in America. They have husbands, wives, children. They suffered awfully. But I am relieved to know they are well taken care of."

Fannie looked up. "What do you mean?"

"Every year, they get money. Nobody knows from where. It's been going on since the war ended."

The actress noticed the look on Fannie's face.

"You get this money, too?"

"No. But I know someone who does. Every year, on the same day—"

"August tenth," the woman said.

"August tenth," Fannie repeated.

The actress pursed her lips, then took the paper and folded it back inside the envelope. She looked at Fannie for a long moment.

"Wait here," she said.

She went into the back and was gone for a bit. When she reemerged, she was holding a pack of postcards, held together by a rubber band.

She sat down, undid the band, then laid the postcards on the table in front of Fannie. There were at least two dozen. Each announced the premiere of a new movie.

"I've been getting these for years," the actress said. "No message. No signature. Just the postcards. The boy you are looking for? Did he have blond hair? A nice smile?"

Fannie nodded quickly. "Yes. Yes, he did!"

"If it's him, then he was the cleverest boy I've ever met. Spoke many languages. Could charm anyone. He hid some of my jewelry and furs from the Nazis. If not for that, I'd have had nothing left to trade with the Arrow Cross. But he wasn't called . . . what name did you say again?"

"Nico?"

"No. His name was Erich Alman. At least when I knew him. I told him once he should go into the movies."

She pointed at the postcards. "I think he did."

She stacked the cards together and put the rubber band around them. She handed the stack to Fannie.

"Find the man who made these films," she said, "and you'll find the boy you're looking for."

Vienna, 1978

At this point in our story, you'll notice three of our four characters have landed in America. The fourth would arrive as well, to witness something he thought he would never see again. To explain, I must move our timeline ahead to 1978, ten years after Fannie had discovered Katalin Karády.

Sebastian Krispis had grown into one of the Nazi Hunter's top staffers. He was working full-time for the agency, which had lost some of its personnel over the years. It was still being funded by a few large contributors, but interest in war criminals was fading. Money was hard to find.

Living by himself in a three-room apartment, Sebastian had thrown himself into the cause. He came in early. He stayed until dark. There were moments, late at night, eating a cheese and mustard sandwich in his office, when he realized the cause was all he had.

He kept a photo of Fannie and Tia near his bed. It tore at his heart that his family was not with him. Still, he sometimes went weeks without speaking to them. He didn't know what to say. He grew frustrated trying to explain himself, or why justice against these Nazi monsters was, to him, the highest calling he could think of, and the only one he thought worthwhile. He couldn't understand why they didn't feel the same way. Deep down, he was depressed by his obsession with the horrors he'd endured, yet furious with those who had not paid a price for inflicting them.

In the end, he blamed himself for misaligning his life. He shouldn't have. His mind was not his own. War still takes hostages, long after it is over.

∞◇∞

What brought Sebastian to America was the stunning news that a new party of Nazis planned to march in a small suburban town in Illinois called Skokie. The town had an unusually large number of Jewish Holocaust survivors, who had come to make a life in America. There were nearly seven thousand in Skokie alone.

Which is why the Nazis had targeted it. During their march, they planned to wear the brown-shirted uniforms, wave the flags, display the swastikas on their armbands, and raise their straight right palms in Nazi salutes.

When Sebastian read about this, he was repulsed. In America? This couldn't be true! But evil travels like dandelion seeds, blowing over borders and taking root in angry minds.

When the Wolf stirred his followers in the 1930s, it worked not because Germans were inclined to hate Jews, but because all humans are inclined to hate others if they believe they are the cause of their unhappiness. The trick is to convince them.

It isn't hard. Just find a group that feels aggrieved and point at another group as the source of their woes. The original Nazis did that with the Jews. And while the new Nazis that were springing up did not carry the Wolf's fervent allegiance to Germany, they sang his same song of racial purity, and the need to purge the impure before they ruined life for the deserving. Hate is an ancient melody. Blame is even older.

Sebastian convinced the Nazi Hunter that this event in Illinois might be an opportunity to weed out former SS officers. Perhaps some would attend? Watch from afar? Photos could be taken. Information could be gathered.

The Hunter agreed. And soon Sebastian was on his way to the United States, planning publicly to observe the rise of a hate group, and privately to seek clues about Udo Graf and Nico Krispis.

Only when he boarded the plane did he admit to himself he was hoping to see Fannie, too.

Udo had taken notice of the march.

Living outside Washington, D.C., he was well aware of the green shoots of rising Nazism. It made him proud. And hopeful.

It had been more than three decades since he'd followed that ratline from Italy to Argentina then America. His cover remained secure. Thanks to various unseemly tasks he handled for the senator, Udo had risen to the post of "special adviser." He had his own office, and drew a large salary. Meanwhile, unofficially, he continued to work with the American spy agency, which, in its fervid war against communism, had elevated his status. He listened to tapped phones. He translated stolen documents. They even sent him to Europe once, to pursue his supposed intelligence connections.

Udo had hoped to visit his homeland on that trip but was told it was too dangerous. Someone might remember him. It vexed him to be that close, yet unable to set foot in his beloved Deutschland, even if it had been cleft in two, the East and the West, and his childhood city of Berlin was divided by a massive wall. Still, it pleased him to learn of a growing resistance by certain Germans to keep apologizing for the war. Some even objected to the Holocaust memorials being built in their cities.

"Enough," they said. "Time to move on."

This is how it begins, Udo told himself. *Time passes. People forget. Then we rise again.*

∽∘∽

Udo was now in his early sixties, but he kept himself fit with a regimen of morning exercise that he never missed: two hours, every day, rising before sunrise, pushing himself through sit-ups, pull-ups, weights, and running. He refused to eat junk food—even though his American wife, Pamela, stocked the cabinets with it. He took care of his teeth. He stayed out of the sun. He dyed his hair brown to fight the gray. Thus, when he looked in the mirror, he saw not an aging man but the nostalgic form of a soldier, ready to resume his duties when called. In his mind, he remained a warrior, hiding in the bush.

The Illinois march was too risky for Udo to attend. A

small town. Lots of Jews. No doubt some of them had been at Auschwitz. There was always a chance one might remember him. He had heard of a fellow Nazi hiding in Baltimore who had been shopping in a supermarket when a survivor spotted him and began yelling in Yiddish, *"Der Katsef! Der Katsef!"* ("The Butcher! The Butcher!"). She made such a scene that police arrested the man, and eventually, thanks to paperwork from that old Jew in Vienna, his past was exposed. He was extradited to Germany and found guilty by a court.

Udo wanted none of that. He wrote in his notebook the mistakes other SS officers had made and how to avoid them. But when the small-town march in Skokie was canceled in favor of a rally in Chicago, he reconsidered. A big city like that? He could hide in the crowd. Blend in with the onlookers. See how ripe this country might be for a Nazi resurgence. He so missed belonging to something he believed in. The temptation was hard to resist.

He arranged the trip to Chicago on the premise that he was visiting Pamela's family. A small lie, in the scheme of things, and, in Udo's mind, well justified. On the plane ride there, he imagined witnessing an impressive military scene, young, strong Nazi men, hundreds if not thousands of them, marching in step, neat and disciplined, demonstrating the power of a superior race, sending a message to the world.

∞

What he saw on the day was quite different. When he arrived at the park that Sunday morning, it was already rimmed with anti-Nazi groups shouting slogans, and young Black militants carrying signs. Hundreds of police officers milled about, wielding clubs, wearing helmets. Long-haired teenagers bunched in circles, smoking, looking for amusement. By Udo's estimate, there were at least several thousand people, and none of them were Nazis.

Finally, two vans pulled into the park, one black, one white, and a group of men, maybe two dozen, spilled out. They dressed in Nazi uniforms but were hardly what Udo would call fit, disciplined, or even organized. They struggled to climb atop their vans as people screamed, "Nazis, go home!" Much of what the men tried to say was drowned out. Onlookers hurled things. Police began shoving protesters back. Some were arrested and put in handcuffs. Udo saw people laughing, others smoking, drifting in and out of the chaos.

The whole scene disgusted him. This was no call to action. It was a circus. A handful of men disgracing his nation's uniform, yelling more about Blacks moving into white neighborhoods than about the Wolf's principles of a master race. *Look at these slobs*, Udo thought. The leader screamed, "I believe there was no Holocaust!" As he did, a protester yelled, "Go to hell, Martin!"

A man next to Udo leaned over and pointed. "Did you know his father is Jewish?"

"What?" Udo said.

"The little guy, on the van, the leader. His father's Jewish. What's he even doing up there?"

Udo was incensed. This was the final indignity. The son of a Jew? Wearing the uniform? He moved toward the vans, wedging through the police, who were tangling with scream-ing Black youths. He drew closer, and made eye contact with the short imposter. He even formed the sounds in his mouth to holler: "Get down! You are a disgrace!"

He never got the chance. His fury was interrupted by two words he had not heard in decades, words so unexpected he could not help but turn to see their source.

"UDO GRAF!"

There, across the park, was a tall, skinny man, his expres-sion almost maniacal. Udo recognized the face, older now, no longer a teen. The Brother. Sebastian. *But I shot him! How is he alive?*

"UDO GRAF!"

Udo dug his hands in his pockets and moved swiftly in the opposite direction. *Why did I come here? It was reckless.* He heard his name being called again and again, but tried to ig-nore it in the cacophony of protesters and the short man atop the van screaming, "If you want a holocaust, we will give you one!" Udo's head was throbbing. *Think. Think.* He passed a police officer and leaned into him.

"Officer, there's a crazy man yelling 'Udo Graf' back there. He has a gun. I saw it."

The police officer grabbed a partner and raced off as Udo kept his feet moving, hurrying but not running, head down, talking to himself, *Don't look up, don't look up*, just as he had talked to himself thirty-three years earlier when he walked past those Russian soldiers. His temper had gotten the better of him that time, and the pugnacious Jew had done him in. He would not succumb twice.

He kept moving, exiting the park, crossing a busy street. He saw an approaching bus, which he flagged and jumped aboard, handing the driver a dollar bill and moving swiftly to the back, away from a window. Only when he sat down did he realize his shirt, socks, and undershorts were soaked with sweat.

∞

Sebastian bent to catch his breath. His throat was raw from screaming. He looked up and down the streets, but he could not spot the old man. Still. It was him. He knew it. His suspicions had been correct. The thought of Nazis rising had been irresistible to the former *Schutzhaftlagerführer*. He'd been drawn out of the weeds.

Sebastian's mind was racing. More than thirty years of haunting dreams, midnight screams, visions of vengeance, all the while never knowing if the man was even alive to face his punishment. *But he was! I saw him!* The same jutting jaw. The same steely eyes that used to stare at Sebastian across the Auschwitz yard. His hair was even the same color.

He had chased Udo through the park, but the police grabbed Sebastian and protesters blocked his view. Part of him sagged with the thought that a once-in-a-lifetime opportunity had slipped through his fingers.

But the other part felt his actual fingers. They were gripped like talons around an object that gave him comfort, a shred of hope that justice, finally, had a chance.

It was a camera.

And Sebastian had taken at least twenty photos.

His first call was to the Hunter.

He could barely contain his enthusiasm. "I found him!" was how Sebastian began, followed by a detailed description of all that had taken place. The Hunter was pleased but measured in his response, reminding Sebastian that seeing the devil and capturing him are two different things.

Nonetheless, the photographs, combined with Sebastian's eyewitness testimony—considering he personally spent nearly two years under Udo Graf's torture—should be enough to engage the U.S. authorities, the Hunter said. But he cautioned Sebastian to remember that for the Americans to help locate a former Nazi, they might be forced to admit they had harbored him.

"Proceed cautiously," he warned. "Learn who you can trust."

Sebastian hung up and ran his hands through his hair, scratching his head, rubbing his temples. The proof he had been waiting for had finally come to pass, and now his instructions were "proceed cautiously"?

He drank a miniature bottle of vodka from the hotel refrigerator. Then he called the front desk and asked them to put through a call to California. He read them the digits he had scribbled in an address book. It was the last phone number he'd had for his now ex-wife.

Hollywood, 1980

"Start the movie, please."

The film was fed through the projector upside down as an intense light passed through lenses and spilled images onto a screen. Somehow, during the process, the picture turned right side up. Twenty-four frames were projected each second, and each one flashed three times, yet the scenes played smoothly on the screen, as if the actors were right in front of you. Every part of watching a motion picture is some kind of deception. But this occurred to me, not so much the weary man in the screening room.

"The lights," Nico said.

"Yes, sir, sorry," said the projectionist.

The room darkened. The film ran. It was the third time in three weeks that Nico had watched it by himself. The movie, which had not yet been released, was about a German clown during World War II who, through his drunken behavior, ends up in an internment camp. There he performs for Jewish children who are imprisoned. Upon seeing how he makes them laugh, the Nazis use the clown to convince those children to board the trains to the death camps. Against his will, he does this again and again. Finally, in the end, feeling guilty for his deceptions, the clown himself goes to Auschwitz and takes the hand of a child, as they enter the gas chambers together.

The film, which Nico had financed, was a work of fiction, but every time it reached its conclusion, he felt his body tremble.

"Again, sir?" the projectionist asked when it finished.

"No. That's enough."

"It's heartbreaking, isn't it?"

Nico rose and looked toward the booth's bright light.

"What did you say?"

"I'm sorry, sir," the projectionist mumbled. "Excuse me." The light went off, quickly followed by the clumsy noise of a film canister dropping.

Nico shook his head and sat back down. This projectionist was new and obviously did not know the rules: no speaking during the screening process, unless spoken to.

Nico had developed a nickname in Hollywood, "The Financier," pronounced the French way *"fee-nan-cee-yay."* He was now one of the most powerful people in his business. Despite the glamour of actors and directors, it was money that moved Hollywood, and The Financier had more of it than most. But unlike many in his field, he shunned attention and wanted only to view the films privately upon their completion, not to attend their premieres or visit their working sets. Most of his movies made handsome profits, which he reinvested in new projects and made more.

Even in his forties, Nico's deep-set blue eyes, wavy blond

hair, and tall, lanky frame drew glances in a business where good looks matter. But people did not see him often. He arrived at odd hours. He stayed late. He did not have an assistant and conducted most of his business by phone. He never gave interviews. He found his job relatively simple. Pick stories that people wanted to hear. Make sure the budgets were responsible. Proceed.

In between, he would disappear for many days at a time, and calls to him would often go unanswered. When he did respond, he fabricated stories: an ankle injury, a sudden trip to New York, a car problem. People waited months for an appointment. If he canceled, they waited months more.

He stared now at the white screen, thinking about the final scene of the film he'd just watched, the clown walking into the gas chamber. He rubbed his temples, then tapped his hand three times on the armrest.

"I changed my mind," he announced to the projectionist. "Play it again."

Now, I hear your question: Did Fannie ever find Nico?

The answer is right in front of you. But it took twelve years to reveal itself. Here are the important steps along the way:

1968

After meeting Katalin Karády, Fannie returned to Europe. Her ticket restrictions, passport paperwork, and lack of further money made traveling beyond New York impossible.

She kept the movie postcards with her.

1969

Fannie revisited Gizella in her Hungarian village, and stayed with her through the summer, circling the date of August 10 on the calendar.

On that day, a redheaded man with ruddy skin and a thick torso arrived with a bag of money. Fannie confronted him.

"Who are you? Who sent you? Where is this money coming from?"

He shook his head at every question. When Fannie persisted, he got into his small car and drove away.

1970

Fannie traveled to Israel, where her daughter was living, and the two of them spent months together, often by the sea, which Tia loved. They spoke about Tia's plans upon graduation, and a young man she had met who was about to enter the army. Sometimes they spoke of Sebastian. One night, while walking along a beach, Tia asked, "Are you ever going back to him?" and Fannie said she didn't know, and Tia asked, "What happened between you two?" and Fannie sighed and said, "First we were friends, then we were refugees, then we were parents, and now we feel like strangers."

1971

Fannie returned to Hungary and stayed with Gizella, helping her with the housework and pushing her wheelchair on walks through the village. When the redheaded man arrived on the morning of August 10, Fannie was ready. She again asked where the money was coming from. When he refused to answer, she ran to his car and got in the front seat. "I am not leaving until you tell me," she yelled.

The man stared at her for a moment, then walked away, leaving the car behind.

1972

Fannie returned to Israel, where her daughter and her new husband welcomed their first child, a baby boy. The couple named him Shimon, after Fannie's father, which left Fannie happy and sad at the same time.

1973

At her daughter's urging, Fannie visited a memorial for the Jewish victims of the "Holocaust," a now-common term for what had happened under the Nazis. It came from the Greek word *holocauston*, which means a burned sacrifice. Fannie said the phrase was inappropriate. When Tia asked what word she would use, Fannie said there was no word, and there should never be one.

The memorial, called Yad Vashem, was built into a hillside in western Jerusalem. There, Fannie saw detailed photos from the camps. She saw images of the sick, the starving, the emaciated, the dead. Alongside some of the photos were printed testimonies from survivors, detailing what they had endured.

She read one account of a mother who had lost her seven-year-old son. His name was Yossi. He had been ripped from her arms by Nazi soldiers. For some reason, it made Fannie recall the death march out of Budapest, the boy with the back-pack who died in the snow. What if that was Yossi? What if Fannie knew the child's fate but his poor mother did not?

She began to cry, slowly at first, then uncontrollably. "What's wrong, Mama?" Tia asked. "What is it?" But Fannie could only shake her head. The bearded man on the train had said, "Tell the world what happened here." But she could not yet speak that Truth. She did not want to talk about what really happened, not with anyone, not even her own daughter.

1974

Fannie returned to Hungary. Gizella, now in her late sixties, was in failing health. She forgot many things. At night during the winter, she would sit by the fire, holding Fannie's hands, and sometimes she would turn to the other room and speak to her long-lost husband, telling him to "bring in more wood from outside, our daughter will be cold."

1975

One morning, lying in her bed, Gizella asked that Fannie remove her eye patch.

"Why?"

"Because I am going to see Jesus."

"Please don't leave me. Not yet."

Gizella reached for her hand. "I never left you all the time we were apart. How could I leave you now?"

The autumn sunlight shifted through the window.

"Oh, Gizella," Fannie said, her words cracking, "I keep

thinking you'd have been better off if I never came into your life."

The old woman could barely shake her head.

"Without you, I would have died a long time ago."

She squeezed Fannie's fingers.

"Please? My eye?"

Fannie slowly removed her patch. Although the wound was difficult to look at, she did not turn away. Gizella rolled her head back, as if gazing at something above them.

"He is waiting for you," she whispered.

"Who?" Fannie said.

Gizella took her final breath and died with a smile.

1976

In August, when the redheaded man showed up, Fannie was sitting on the porch. As he approached with the bag, she lifted a blanket in her lap to reveal a pistol pointed straight at him.

"I need to know who is sending this money. Now."

The redheaded man dropped the bag and raised his arms. He took a step back.

"I don't know," he said. "Honestly. I get paid like everyone else, once a year. He warned me if I ever say anything, the money stops."

"Who warned you?"

"The Gypsy."

"Is this his money?"

"I don't think so. Not the way he dresses."

"Then who?"

"If I had to guess, I'd say it's the money my father died for."

"Your father?"

"He was shot by Nazis after they hid crates in his church. I never knew what was inside those crates. But a year later, two men came back for them. One was the man who killed my father."

"Where is he now?"

"I shot him dead."

"And the other one?"

"I never saw him again."

"He took the crates?"

"Yes."

"Why would he give away what was in them?"

"I don't know."

"Can you describe him?"

The man shook his head. "It was a long time ago. He looked like a Nazi. Young. Not much older than me."

Fannie thought about the night she saw Nico on the Danube. *He looked like a Nazi. Young. Not much older than me.*

"I could have killed him as well," the man said. "But I didn't. Maybe that's why I'm getting money, too."

1977

Fannie boarded a plane with Katalin Karády's postcards tucked in her purse. She was heading to America, hoping to get answers.

Upon arriving in Los Angeles, Fannie rented a room in a single-story motel with a palm tree in the parking lot. On her first day, she showed the postcards to a man behind the front desk and asked if he knew who made those movies. When he didn't know, she asked the woman sweeping the hallway. When she didn't know, Fannie crossed the street and asked the owner of a diner. Although he knew nothing about films, when he heard her accent he said, *"Eísai Ellinída?"* (Are you Greek?) and she said, *"Naí"* (Yes), and by the time they were done speaking, Fannie had a job making coffee and eggs and pancakes. She used that job to improve her English. And she used her English to learn how the movie business operated.

1978

When she finally discovered who was responsible for making those films—a mysterious, rarely seen man, they said, whose last name was Guidili—she went to the studio where he supposedly worked. She wore her nicest dress, entered the building, and asked the receptionist in the lobby if there were any jobs available.

She did this every week for eight months, always being told no.

1979

One spring day, on Fannie's weekly visit, the studio receptionist, who by this point had come to like her, smiled when Fannie asked if any jobs had opened up.

"You're in luck," she said. A training position had just come free. Low pay at first. But a foot in the door. Was Fannie interested?

She started the next day. She had hoped to encounter the man she believed to be Nico in a hallway or in the lobby, but she soon learned that no one had access to him. He came and left through a private entrance. He never met with employees. Fannie wondered if all this effort had been a huge waste of time.

1980

After a year of apprenticeship, Fannie was told by Rodrigo, the man who'd been training her, that he was retiring. Health reasons. He congratulated her on being an astute student and told her she was ready to move up.

"What do you mean?"

"You're replacing me."

Fannie had to catch her breath. She knew what this meant.

"Just remember," Rodrigo warned. "Always be on time. Do exactly what he asks. And never speak to him unless he speaks to you."

She nodded. And in November, she officially took over.

As The Financier's private projectionist.

Four Confrontations

The more you confront the truth, the more upset you are likely to become. But if you believe that old expression that truth can set you free, then am I not what you secretly yearn for?

Our four characters, in the calendar year 1980, finally confronted the truths that had long shadowed them.

What they did next sets the stage for the end of our story.

Sebastian confronted his tormentor.

Having seen Udo Graf again, he could think of nothing else. The pictures he had taken came back clear and sharp, and when compared to an old photograph the Hunter had acquired, the match was obvious. Despite the years, the *Schutzhaftlagerführer* had not changed much.

But the Hunter had been right. Seeing the devil and capturing him were two different things. Despite numerous calls to American politicians, no one seemed ready to believe that a high-ranking Nazi had found sanctuary in the United States. Sebastian returned to Vienna empty-handed.

He spent months building his case, researching everything he could find on Graf through paperwork the Hunter had collected. He traveled several times back to New York, meeting with various Jewish groups, who were equally stunned to think that former SS officers could be hiding in their country. *How did they get here? Who is harboring them?*

Finally, in early 1980, Sebastian met with a woman whose brother-in-law was a U.S. senator and happened to be Jewish. That senator agreed to meet with Sebastian in his office near the Capitol.

Sebastian was encouraged. If he could convince a high-ranking American politician to pursue Graf, surely the U.S. government could find him.

The night before his meeting, in a hotel room in Washington, D.C., Sebastian finished eating a chicken sandwich from room service. Then, once again, he dialed the number he had for Fannie in California. He had tried it many times, but no one had answered. This time, after several rings, she picked up.

"It's me," Sebastian said.

Fannie seemed surprised. "Where are you? You sound very close."

"I'm in Washington, D.C."

"Why?"

"Graf. From Auschwitz. I'm making progress."

He heard her sigh.

"We're going to find him, Fannie, I swear it."

"I hope you do, Sebastian."

"We will."

"But please."

"What?"

"Be careful."

When she said things like this, it made him feel like she still loved him, even though they had signed divorce papers five years earlier. His tone softened.

"How are you doing?" he asked.

"I'm fine."

"Still working at the diner?"

"I have a new job."

"Where?"

"At a movie studio."

"Wow. Is it going well?"

"Yes. Have you spoken with Tia?"

"Not since I got here. It's expensive. The phone calls. And the time difference."

"You should call her. Tell her you are all right."

"I will."

"Thank you."

"Fannie. Listen. What if, after this was finished, I came to visit you? I've never been to California. I don't know when I'll be this close."

"Washington isn't close to California."

"Yes. I know. But. You know."

"Yes."

"So, yes?"

A pause.

"No."

Udo confronted his past.

There was no denying it now. They were on to him. Although he had returned to Washington, D.C., and resumed his charade—grilled steaks on the barbecue, had drinks with his wife and neighbors—something had changed. His past was not as buried as he believed. The Brother and his screaming Jewish mouth had proved it.

Udo was now on alert. The soldier inside him had been activated.

In the weeks that followed the Chicago rally, he'd made secret calls to two former SS officers who were also living in America, one in Maryland, the other in Florida. He asked if they knew of this Jew named Sebastian Krispis. Neither did. But they had ways of looking into him. Both, however, expressed surprise that Udo would have gone to that rally in the first place.

"What were you thinking?" one of them asked.

"I wanted to see if they were ready."

"They are not us, Udo. They mimic, but they lack conviction."

"They need our leadership."

"Agreed. But on our terms. Not in some circus parade for newspaper reporters. That is not how we do things."

"Agreed."

"Udo?"

"Yes."

"Perhaps we shouldn't be speaking on the phone."

"Why not?"

"The lines. They could be listening now. Use our go-between next time."

"Yes. All right."

Udo hung up, furious at himself. One reckless move after all these careful years? He could have ruined everything. His colleague was right. Caution was demanded.

But. America was a huge country. A hard place to locate one person. He took solace in that. And the Hunter was not as potent as he'd once been. Udo had heard that his money was drying up.

Months passed. No one came looking for him. Udo used the time to dig into the Nazi Hunter's operations. He learned that the Jew Krispis had become a top lieutenant for the old man. Udo's connections in Austria informed him that Krispis was living alone in a Vienna apartment. This was disappointing. A family in the home gives an attacker some leverage. Someone to threaten, or take hostage.

In early 1980, Udo got a message from Austria that Krispis had left Vienna for the United States. No one knew where or what for. Then one morning, Udo drove to Senator Carter's office, and was walking past the security guard in the rotunda of the building. As he flashed his card, he glanced over at the line of visitors waiting for clearance. His blood ran cold.

There he was. *The Jew. Again!* He was wearing a gray suit and approaching the desk. He turned his head in Udo's direction and for a split second they made eye contact, before Udo spun and hurried down the hall. He pushed into a crowded elevator just as the door was closing. He fumbled for the button, pressing it three times. He looked down, away from the people surrounding him.

What the hell is he doing here? What does he know?

Fannie confronted her feelings.

The day she learned that she was getting a promotion, she stayed late at work and missed her normal bus home. As she waited for the next one, she saw an old car exit the rear of the parking lot, and when it stopped at a traffic signal, she felt a catch in her throat.

Him. The man behind the wheel. It looked like *him.* A grown-up version, yes, but Nico. The boy who sat in front of her in school. The boy in the crawl space on Kleisouras Street. The teenager on the Danube, who called her name before she fainted.

Part of her wanted to run up to his car, bang on his window, shout, "It's me, Fannie! What are you doing? Why are you using a different name?"

But she didn't. She needed to be sure. She came back the next night, this time borrowing a vehicle from her former boss at the restaurant. When the old car again exited the parking lot, she followed it to an apartment building near the airport, where the driver parked and went inside. It was dark and Fannie couldn't see much. She returned in the morning. The car was still there. The next day the same. The next day again.

This didn't make sense. Why would a powerful businessman be staying in this poor neighborhood? She began to think she had made a mistake, that her imagination was driving all of this madness, that her unhappiness with Sebastian had somehow made Nico, her first crush, the man who may have saved her life, the answer to everything. It was a foolish distraction. She felt embarrassed, childish.

The next time she drove by the apartment building, she promised herself, would be the last. The car was still there. She rapped her fists on the steering wheel. She thought about Tia. She thought about Sebastian. She should go back home. Stop chasing the wind.

She flicked on her turn signal. Then a figure emerged from the apartment building. She sucked in her breath. *There he is.* He was carrying an old suitcase, dressed in slacks and a white T-shirt. His face was much easier to see in the daylight, and he surely looked like the boy she remembered, except handsome now instead of cute, and weathered a bit around the eyes. His slim body was fit and tanned, and it was hard to believe he would be in his late forties, just a year younger than she was.

He got into his car, and Fannie followed behind him as he drove through the winding streets, then entered a highway and fought traffic for nearly an hour before exiting in a suburban neighborhood. Once again, Fannie wondered if her imagination had overshot reality.

But any doubts disappeared with what happened next.

The car turned into a Jewish cemetery called Home of Peace Memorial Park. The man got out holding a canteen and a bag of rags. He walked slowly up a hill, to a section of older graves, where he got down on his knees and began to clean the tombstones.

Which is when Fannie knew. Tears filled her eyes. She remembered that afternoon in the cemetery in Salonika, when she and Nico and Sebastian had wiped family tombstones in what Lazarre called "a true and loving kindness." And how Nico, of the three of them, had stood up, walked to strangers' graves, and said, "Come on," urging her and Sebastian to join him. It was the first moment she remembered marveling at the gentle purity of the boy they called Chioni. And she realized now it wasn't her mind that had led her on this long and winding chase to find Nico Krispis.

It was her heart.

Nico confronted a familiar smile.

When you lie about everything, you belong to nothing. And Nico, or Nate, or Mr. Guidili, or The Financier, led an unconnected life in California. Unmarried. No children. No relatives. No true friends. He told his associates he preferred formality, addressing them as "Sir" or "Miss" and asking that they do the same.

With no one in his life to trust, his days were filled with useless lies. He told the mailman he could scuba dive. He told a cashier he was an accountant. When a bank teller asked him how his day was going, he said he was off to pick up his kids at school. He even offered their names: Anna and Elisabet.

All this was a manifestation of his condition, which seemed to worsen with age. Nico would enter art galleries claiming to be a dealer. He looked at cheap real estate, then, despite his wealth, said he couldn't afford it. Sometimes he went to German beer halls, claiming to be a recent immigrant.

He never spoke Greek or Ladino, the languages of his youth, but every Saturday morning, Nico took a bus across the city and got off three blocks from an Orthodox synagogue. There he prayed in Hebrew with a tallit over his head, swaying back and forth for an hour, uninterrupted. What he prayed for I shall leave between Nico and God. Some conversations are not our business.

He remained practiced in the art of forgery, although it served little purpose now. He applied for credit cards under false names, then never used them once they arrived. He had three drivers' licenses from three different states. He held passports under four nationalities. There were a dozen banks in which he kept safe-deposit boxes.

He owned an expensive house in a wealthy Hollywood neighborhood, but he mostly slept in a run-down apartment near the airport. He often traveled overseas on short notice, flying in the least expensive seats. He never took more than an old suitcase, the same one he had traveled with when he first arrived in America. He told strangers he was a shoe salesman.

Despite decades of such pathological deception, Nico never sought help. Help meant looking backward, and he wanted no part of that. Instead, he layered more and more sandbags between his past and his present, building a dam high enough to stop even a massive flood of memories.

And then he met his new projectionist.

∞

She had been training with Rodrigo, an older Mexican man who'd had the job for years. Nico liked Rodrigo because he was smart and punctual, rarely asked for anything, and never commented on a film in the screening room. When Rodrigo announced that he needed to retire because of his diabetes, Nico arranged for the top endocrinologist in Los Angeles to visit him at home, every month, and pledged to pay for his long-term care.

Nico's first encounter with the new projectionist was when he screened the film about the German clown. After watching it for a second time that day, he climbed the steps to the projection room. He saw the back of a woman with long dark curls, leaning down to put a canister away.

"Miss?"

The woman halted but did not turn around.

"Why did you say that movie was heartbreaking?"

The woman rose slowly, then turned and smiled. When Nico saw her face, he felt a pang of something even his lies could not describe.

"Because it was, wasn't it?" she said.

Did Nico know it was Fannie?

It was hard to tell, given his reaction. A healthy mind would have blurted out her name, rushed into an embrace. But Nico's mind had not been healthy for a long time. It defaulted to denial, even of the most positive things.

"It's just a movie," he said, looking away.

"Is it a true story?" Fannie asked.

"No."

"It felt true."

285

"That's what movies do."

He allowed himself a quick glance as Fannie bit her lip. All the features were heartbreakingly familiar. The finely shaped face, the Mediterranean complexion, the large, flashing eyes. Even her hair, dark and full and swirling over her shoulders. The teenaged Fannie could be easily found in her adult form.

"To be honest," she admitted, "I haven't seen a lot of films."

"Then why work here?"

"I guess I thought it would be good for me."

"Ah."

He looked at the ground. He looked at the shelves.

"Well, thank you, Miss. See you next week."

He turned to leave.

"Sir?"

"Yes?"

"Don't you want to know my name?"

He locked eyes with her.

"It's not necessary," he said.

Part VI

The Start of the Finish

As the actress Katalin Karády said, there is a price for everything that happens in your life. We will now witness the price our four characters paid—for the truths they told, and the lies they endured. Their final bills came due on the same day, in the same place where our story began.

What brought them all together was an article that ran in Salonika's largest newspaper, the *Makedonia*, in early 1983:

**EVENT TO MARK GREEK JEWISH VICTIMS OF WAR
SET FOR MARCH 15**

It was announced today that a special commemoration march will take place on Tuesday, March 15, beginning at Liberty Square at 2:00 P.M. and continuing on to the old train station. The ceremony will mark the 40th anniversary of the first train to travel from Salonika to the Nazi death camp of Auschwitz. The mayor of Salonika and other dignitaries are expected to attend.

Under other circumstances, this would simply be a calendar note, one of countless events held around the world to mark a war that was fading from memory.

But in our story, it was a siren song.

The Greek march was Sebastian's idea.

He had been pushing it for years. Working with the Nazi Hunter, Sebastian had continuously lamented the lack of attention given to the Greek victims of the Wolf's war. While stories from Poland and Germany were commonplace—books written, movies made—many people seemed unaware that the Nazis had even invaded Greece, or that Salonika, once home to more than fifty thousand Jews, had seen less than two thousand survive.

The Hunter had spoken with members of the Greek government, pressuring them to acknowledge the horrors in their history, many of which were made worse by the complicity of certain Greek officials.

But nations are slow to address their pasts. Finally, promising to attend the event himself, the Hunter was able to convince the authorities to permit a march from the center of Salonika to the old train station, where so many Greek families saw their bonds forever severed.

And where Sebastian last saw his brother.

∞

By this point, you might wonder why Nico still haunted his elder sibling. After all, decades had passed since they'd seen one another. Sebastian was in his midfifties, a grandfather, living in Vienna. And if we're being candid (and what choice do I have?) Sebastian now wore the crown of honesty that Nico once commandeered. His fierce devotion to pursuing the truth filled his days and nights.

But time does not heal all wounds. Some it only rubs deeper. Sebastian had always envied Nico, even as a child. The way he looked. The way he entertained the family. The way Lazarre seemed to favor him. *"Such a beautiful boy."*

Envy between brothers is commonplace; one often feels the other gets all the love. But what truly roiled Sebastian was that when Nico was finally exposed, that love did not die.

Instead, in the crowded train car to Auschwitz, with no food, no water, the air choking with death, Sebastian's mother and father continued to cry for their lost son.

"What will happen to him?" Tanna wailed.

What will happen to him? Sebastian thought. *What about what's happening to us?*

"He'll find a way," Lev encouraged. "He's a clever boy."

Clever? He's a liar! A little liar!

Even Nico's baby sisters were weeping for their brother. Only Fannie, or the idea of Fannie, gave Sebastian comfort. Wherever they were being taken, she would be going, too, and he could try to console her. He could be important to her, the way Nico was seemingly so important to everyone else.

And then the large man pulled that grate off the window, and in an instant, Sebastian made a choice that would break his heart for years. He pushed away the only person who gave him hope. He did it because he loved her.

And years later, she would push him away because she didn't.

∞

Sebastian had not spoken to his ex-wife for a while. She seemed so distant the last few phone calls that he no longer wanted to put himself through the pain. She was in California. He was in Austria. That was that.

He often wondered if she'd found someone new to love. Sebastian had not. Although there were women he found attractive, and several who seemed interested in him, he always defaulted to his work. Nothing felt as compelling as pursuing his tormentors. I suppose it should not surprise us that a boy who felt slighted grew into a man seeking justice.

Still, Sebastian was rightly proud of the event he'd helped create in Salonika, the first official recognition of what had happened there. And if Fannie would not meet him in her new home, perhaps she would do so in their old one.

He sent her the newspaper article and a letter, asking if she would consider attending the march, to honor her father, if nothing else. Perhaps Tia would come, too?

He mailed it off, hoping Fannie had not changed her address.

Fannie read the letter in private.

It had been decades since she'd set foot in Greece. She called her daughter, who said, "If you go, I'll go," and Fannie thought it might be nice if they were all together. Her resentment toward Sebastian had softened over the last five years, partly because they had little to do with one another, and partly because of her rekindled affection for his brother, whom she now saw once a week in a screening room.

Every Wednesday, Nico arrived at 2:00 P.M. to view the films that Fannie had loaded. She observed him while he watched. He was still beautiful, in a mature way. But he rarely spoke. Only after the movies were finished would he walk up to the booth and make polite small talk. He was always kind, asking if the job was suitable, if there was anything she needed. His voice was soft and had a vulnerability that drew her in. And, of course, deep down, she felt intensely connected to him, the way we often feel about those we loved young, even decades later, even after they have changed dramatically.

Did they speak about the past?

No. Fannie waited week after week for a spark of recognition, a moment when it felt right for her to say "Can we talk about what we're not talking about?" But it never came. Instead, they settled into an unspoken complicity. He did not acknowledge who she was because it meant confronting the pain of what he'd done. And she did not push him because his mind was clearly not right. The layers of deception. The meaningless lies. There must be a reason, Fannie thought. She worried her truth might chase him away. The things she wanted to know—*Where had he been? What had he endured? Was he sending great amounts of money to people every year?*—were too much to blurt out. She needed to be patient. She reminded herself that for so long she had no idea if he was even alive. She could wait.

And so, for a while, they exchanged a rare kindness: the kindness of silence. They worked side by side in the present, and let the past sleep undisturbed.

Then, after nearly a year of working together, Fannie brought Nico food for a rare evening screening.

"What is this?" he asked, surprised at the tray of chicken pancakes and stuffed cabbage leaves.

"I just thought, it's so late, and you probably won't get a chance to eat afterward," she said. "I hope it's all right."

He thanked her and she returned to the booth. After the screening, she noticed he had eaten everything.

"It was very good."

"Thank you."

"Where did you learn to cook like that?"

"A Hungarian woman taught me."

He paused.

"So you're Hungarian?"

"No. I just stayed with her for a while."

"When?"

"During the war." She chose her next words carefully. "I was hiding. From the Germans. That Hungarian woman kept me alive until I was captured by the Arrow Cross."

She studied his face, searching for a reaction.

"I went to cooking school in Paris," he said.

He rose from his seat.

"Well, good night, Miss."

∞◦∞

The heart has many routes to love, and compassion is one of them. Fannie used the gap between their weekly meetings to try and understand Nico's affliction. Although she felt uneasy doing it, she sometimes followed him when he left the building. She observed him eating by himself in cheap restaurants, rummaging through bookstores, or disappearing for days at the apartment near the airport.

Every week, on Friday mornings, Nico would drive out to the cemetery and clean the headstones. Fannie would trail behind him. The sight of him bent over those graves touched her deeply. Whatever Nico had suffered, it clearly left him more comfortable with the dead than the living.

Although Fannie had pursued Nico in search of their past, as time went on, she realized she didn't need a past to care about him. With Sebastian, everything had been about the war. They could never escape its shadow.

With Nico, that horror was locked away. Fannie actually preferred that. Perhaps he didn't acknowledge her because he didn't want to dredge up what the war had put her through. She viewed that as kind.

They spent more time together after screenings, talking over coffee that Fannie had brewed. Nico spoke about his love of movies, and what he thought made a good story. Fannie spoke about her daughter living in Israel, how proud she was of her. She never mentioned the girl's father, and Nico never inquired.

Then one night, in early 1983, it was storming outside, and Nico used his umbrella to walk Fannie to her car. The rain was torrential, the wind blowing it sideways. Fannie's shoe suddenly slipped off and she fell into a large puddle before Nico could grab her. Fannie's dress was soaked. She started laughing.

"Are you hurt?" Nico said.

"Oh, no, I'm fine," she said.

"Why are you laughing?"

"Once you're this wet, what's the difference? It's like when we were kids in the summer, remember? If it started raining, we'd just run into the sea with our clothes on?"

"With our clothes on, yeah," Nico said, grinning.

Fannie blinked. "You remember that?"

Nico's expression stiffened.

"All kids do that stuff," he said.

Fannie wiped the rain from her cheeks, then steadied herself with one arm on Nico's shoulder. As she tried to put her shoe on, she lost her balance and fell against him, and when she lifted her eyes, her face was inches away from his, and he had an expression she had never seen before, like a confused, lost boy.

Then, for the second time in her life, she kissed him. She had done this as a child, in an awkward, pubescent rush. But this time was soft and lingering, and her eyes closed and she let herself float in the moment, which felt much longer than it actually was. When she opened her eyes, she saw him staring at her.

"It's all right," she whispered.

He swallowed hard, handed her the umbrella, and ran off into the rain.

Nico learned about the Greek march in a meeting.

A few days after that encounter with Fannie, a director came to his office, seeking money to make a documentary about the famous Nazi Hunter. Nico said he was familiar with the Hunter's work; he had read about the high-profile arrests.

"He would make a great subject," the director insisted. "Imagine a man who refuses to rest until all the escaped Nazis are brought to justice—as well as those who helped them."

"Helped them?" Nico said.

"Yes. The ones who collaborated with the Germans are just as guilty, don't you think?"

Nico shifted in his seat.

"Has the Hunter agreed to be part of your movie?"

"We've exchanged letters. He's considering it. I want to film him next month in Greece. March fifteenth. He's doing a commemoration event there."

Nico looked up.

"March fifteenth?"

"Yes."

"Where?"

"Thessaloniki."

"Salonika?"

The man grinned. "Actually, the Greeks call it Thessaloniki. Anyhow, he's leading a march there to honor all the Greek Jews killed during the war. They'll finish at the old railway station, where the trains took them to the concentration camps. A good spot for an interview, don't you think?"

Nico felt a shiver in his midsection. His muscles tightened. Perspiration formed on his forehead.

He rose quickly.

"Sir?" the director asked. "Did I say something wrong?"

"I'll think about it. Goodbye now."

He hurried out the door, leaving the man alone in his office.

∞

Nico did not sleep that night. He walked the streets of his neighborhood in the dark, then sat in the backseat of his car until the sun rose. He drove to the synagogue and prayed alone for two hours. Then he went to the front steps of Fannie's apartment building and waited until she emerged for work. She smiled upon seeing him.

"I need to tell you something," he blurted out.

"How did you know where I lived?"

"Sit down."

She sat. "What is it?"

"I need to leave."

"When?"

"Soon."

"Where are you going?"

"Away."

"Why?"

"I can't say."

Fannie saw the way his chest was heaving and the sweat on his forehead. She believed this was a form of panic. She herself had felt it many times, alone in her car or in the middle of the night. She reached for his hands.

"Take one deep breath, then another," she urged.

You might think Nico was upset by what the director had said. But he knew all about the Nazi Hunter. In fact, he'd been the man's biggest funder for years, sending anonymous checks that kept the agency going.

Nor was it the idea that the Hunter was looking for Nazi accomplices. Nico knew everything about the man's work, who he had found, who he was chasing.

No, what haunted Nico was something he'd realized the moment the director told him of the march in Greece, something worrisome and dangerous, something Fannie could not know.

"Look at me," she whispered. "You're going to be all right."

Nico's story was bubbling so close to the surface, it forced tears down his cheeks. He placed his hand gently behind Fannie's neck, and for the third time in their lives, and the first time by Nico's initiative, their lips met, softly, lovingly.

And then, right there, on the steps of an apartment building, under the cloudless sky of a California morning, Fannie blurted out what she'd been holding back since the night she first saw him at the traffic light.

"Nico, it's me, Fannie. Talk to me. I know it's you."

Udo circled the date on his calendar.

March 15 in Salonika. He would need a disguise. And a gun.

He took a swig from a bottle of brandy, then capped it and placed it back on the shelf. His father had become an alcoholic in his later years, and Udo was determined not to follow suit. Lately, he'd been denying himself even the glass. Just a taste from the bottle when he wanted one, which was more and more these days.

He plopped down on the unmade bed and looked out the apartment window toward the snowcapped mountains of northern Italy. The ceiling was low and its paint was peeling. A cobweb had formed. Udo crushed it in his palm.

He had been living here for the last three years, ever since everything he'd built in America had come crashing down. Udo had been called into Carter's office. The senator informed him that someone from the old Jew's agency in Vienna was circulating a photo of Udo at a Nazi rally in Chicago, alongside another photo of him during the war wearing an SS uniform. A reporter who recognized the face had already called the office.

"We denied everything, of course," Carter said. "Told him

pictures don't prove anything. Mistaken identity. That kind of stuff."

"Good," Udo said.

"But," Carter said, his voice lowering, "you can't stay here."

"What do you mean?"

"I mean they're close. I mean this could blow up the whole program."

"You want me to leave Washington?"

Carter shook his head.

"Not Washington. The country."

"*What?* When?"

"By morning."

∝∘

And so, for the second time in his life, Udo Graf went on the run. Carrying a single suitcase with all the valuables he could gather overnight, he took a sunrise flight to New York, and connected with a plane to Rome. He never collected the papers from his office. He never said goodbye to his wife. He became a ghost. When authorities came to Carter's office, the senator said they had dismissed the man named George Mecklen a week earlier for personal reasons. All they knew of his past was that he was a Belgian immigrant, and that he'd done reputable work during his time on the staff. His current whereabouts were unknown.

It took four months of Udo hiding in a youth hostel outside Rome for his Italian connections to find him a new identity.

The same underground that had harbored him after the war still had roots in this country, but not as powerful. Udo was eventually sold an Italian passport, but it required a great deal of the money he had scurried out of his safe. His "cover" was a job at a meatpacking plant near the Tyrolean Alps, a job where speaking Italian wasn't necessary. He pushed a broom and kept track of deliveries. It was menial work, and it ate at Udo's soul.

Every day he had to spend in exile was a day he felt he was giving away. In Washington, he'd been building to something. He had money. He had influence. He had Carter under his thumb for the dirty acts he had done for him, and he'd planned to cash in that chip when the moment was right.

Now all that was gone, destroyed by the old Jew from Vienna and the Brother, who were chasing him down like a rat into a sewer hole. Well. A rat can chase as well. And under the right circumstances, it can kill. Udo had been thinking of how to get rid of those two from the moment his plane left Washington.

He looked again at the circled date on his calendar. *March 15.* He had received a letter with a Greek newspaper article, telling of this ceremony for dead Jews in Salonika and those expected to attend. The names of the Nazi Hunter and the Brother were circled in red ink, alongside two hand-written words in German, no doubt from one of his fellow Nazis still in hiding.

The two words were *Beende es.*

"Finish it."

He went to the shelf and grabbed the brandy. Salonika?

How fitting. The city had been the scene of his finest work, and this could be his crowning act. Killing the Nazi Hunter would make it safer for others in hiding. They could re-emerge. Take their proud place in the sunlight.

Udo uncapped the bottle and took another swig. He would need a disguise. He would need a gun. He already had both.

Let Me Count the Ways

If words are a measure of how deeply humans value something, then you must cherish me greatly. Consider how many expressions you have for Truth.

"To tell you the truth," people say. Or "Can I be honest with you?" Or "honestly" or "truthfully" or "no lie" or "the fact is" or "the sad truth" or "the undisputed truth" or "the truth of the matter is . . ."

These are just in English. There's French, *Je dis la verité* ("I'm telling you the truth") or Spanish, *la verdad amarga* ("the bitter truth"). The Germans say *sag mir die wahrheit* ("tell me the truth"), although during the war years, this phrase was an orphan. The Greek word for truth is *Aletheia*, which literally means to "un-forget," a recognition of the fact that I am often obscured.

For what it is worth, of my many verbal references, I am partial to "truth be told." You can imagine a king declaring it. A mother demanding it. The Almighty decreeing it.

Truth be told.

Which brings us back to where our story began, in the city of Salonika, and Liberty Square, where four decades earlier, the Nazis humiliated nine thousand Jewish men on a Sabbath morning by herding them in the hot sun, making them do endless calisthenics, beating those who fell, killing those who resisted.

This time, in that same space, on the afternoon of March 15, a large crowd of citizens gathered to mark the shame of that era. Many carried red carnations to commemorate the dead. Others held white balloons with two Greek words written on them.

Poté Xaná.

"Never again."

Sebastian held a paper on the podium.

As the wind blew his hair across his forehead, he spoke passionately into a microphone about the many ways the Jews of Salonika had suffered in the 1940s. He spoke of the beatings. The humiliations. The random shootings. He spoke of the yellow stars they were forced to wear. The Baron Hirsch ghetto. The barbed wire above the walls and the deadly fate of anyone trying to escape.

He told of how Nazis handed his father's business over to two strangers, then chased him out of his own shop. As he spoke, he wondered if the children of those strangers might be in the crowd, and if they felt even an ounce of shame.

"Our history was destroyed, our community was destroyed, our families were destroyed," Sebastian declared. "But our faith was not. Today we remember. But tomorrow, justice must continue . . ."

Heads nodded. Some people applauded. When Sebastian finished, he stepped aside and let the Hunter speak. When the Hunter concluded by saying, "We will never rest, we will never forget," the crowd began to walk, en masse, in the direction of the old train station.

Sebastian took his place at the front. He breathed in deeply and squinted at the clouds. It was cold for March and felt like it would rain. He dug his hands into his pockets. Although he was happy this event had come together, there was something ill-fitting about it. The people marching were healthy, well-fed, many of them were young, some not even Jewish. They wore fashionable clothes and running shoes. The buildings were different from how Sebastian remembered them. There was a huge new parking structure. A new courthouse. The old Ladadika olive oil market was being renovated into an entertainment zone, with cafés and bars now lining its cobblestone streets.

To Sebastian, it felt too modern and bright for the solemnity of the occasion, as if he were trying to wedge an adult foot into a child's shoe. But then, commemorating something is not the same as living through it.

He thought about those missing from the day. He thought about his mother and baby sisters, how his life with them ended so abruptly. He thought about his father and grandfather, how they had tried to protect him from the horrors of Auschwitz, and how Lazarre insisted, every night, that they recite one good thing that God had provided that day. He wondered if they were all with God now, and if somehow they were watching this march in their memory. He wondered what they thought of such solidarity, forty years too late.

He looked over his shoulder. There were maybe a thousand people—equal to the total number of Jews now left in Salonika. One thousand. Where fifty thousand had once thrived.

Sebastian craned his neck. He knew Fannie and Tia were somewhere in the crowd, but he could not see them. He wondered if the words he'd spoken had shed any light on what he'd done with his life, and why it had taken him away from them for all these years.

Fannie held her daughter's hand.

They moved in step with the other marchers. As they approached the old Baron Hirsch neighborhood, which remained largely desolate, Fannie felt her pulse quicken. She remembered being dragged here as a girl, two women holding her by the elbows, the image of her father's execution still fresh in her mind, gunned down in front of the apothecary, his hand on the doorknob.

"What is it, Mama?" Tia said, seeing Fannie's face.

"Nothing, just memories," Fannie said. She forced her lips into a smile. But her mind was drifting back, to that day, to the raincoat she wore, to the crawl space she hid in. To Nico.

She hadn't seen him since that morning on the steps of her apartment building, when she'd said to him, "I know it's you." His eyes had filled with tears and she was sure he would break through, open up, admit everything. But he hadn't. Instead, he'd risen to his feet and mumbled, "You don't have to come to work anymore, I'll still pay you," before hurrying off to his car.

After that, he was nowhere to be found. Fannie came to work every day for the next three weeks. She went to his house. She went to the apartment. No sign.

The night before she left for Greece, she went once more to the studio, hoping he might somehow be there late. The screening room was empty. His private office was dark. She tried the door. It was unlocked. She hesitated, then let herself in.

She had never entered this room without him in it. She approached his desk. It was mostly clear, just a few scripts piled neatly together. She opened a drawer. Nothing. Another drawer. Empty.

She went to a file cabinet and pulled on the top handle. She saw a half dozen files, with the names of movies she recognized from the screenings. The next drawer down was equally sparse. She wondered, with so little paperwork, if Nico kept track of everything in his head. It was so much information. How could he do it?

She wasn't going to bother with the bottom drawer. But she changed her mind and leaned over to tug the handle. It resisted. She pulled harder. Finally, she squatted down and yanked the drawer loose, and instantly saw why it had been so difficult.

The drawer was stuffed with dozens of files, each of them marked by year, beginning with 1946 and going all the way to the present. She pulled one out, opened it, and felt her breath escape her.

There, inside, was list after list of Jewish names, each with an age and an address—in France, in Israel, in Brazil, in Australia—alongside a numerical notation with a check mark next to it. There were photos and supporting documents, copies of birth and death certificates.

She pulled out a second file. More lists. Another file. The same. Each year, it seemed, the files got thicker. The last one, marked 1983, was so fat, Fannie needed two hands to lift it. When she did, she noticed something tucked in the rear. A large manila envelope, with the word FANNIE written in blue marker. With her hands shaking, she undid its clasp.

Ten minutes later, she raced out of the office. When she reached her car, she fell against it and wept. She wept for all she had lost in her life and the feeling that she had just lost something else. She stared at the envelope and knew that Nico was never coming back. In her insistence on truth versus lies, she had doomed herself to a third alternative: never knowing which was which.

Udo felt the butt of his gun.

It was hidden inside his jacket pocket, and he stroked it as the crowd reached the railroad station. He had thought about killing the Nazi Hunter back at Liberty Square, but he was too far away for a clean shot. Besides, the railroad station was more fitting. It was the site of his best efforts, the cleansing of Jewish filth from this city. *Fifty thousand gone. Soon, two more.*

Salonika had changed greatly since he'd left it, but it was not without memories. As the crowd neared the tracks, Udo, disguised as a participant and carrying a white balloon, thought about the asset he'd put to good use here. Nico Krispis. The boy who never lied.

Udo often wondered what became of him. He had spared the child's life. Over the years, whenever he killed someone, he would remind himself of that single act of mercy and award himself merit. The time they'd spent together in the house on Kleisouras Street was as close as Udo had ever come to being a parent, and he still remembered the night he read Nico a German book, and the time Nico brought Udo a hot towel for his headache. He realized now, in seeing the railroad platform, that his last words to the boy might have been "*You stupid Jew.*" He almost regretted that.

Udo's American wife, Pamela, had discussed starting a family once or twice, but Udo never considered a child with her. Her bloodline included a Lebanese father and a Serbian grandmother. He would not bring a mutt into this world.

He reached up and touched the white-haired wig that covered his head, and the hat sitting atop it. It was itchy and uncomfortable, but necessary, he told himself. He had been recognized twice by the Brother. Only a fool repeats his mistakes.

When they reached the train station, the marchers spread along the platform, awaiting the ceremony. Udo was surprised to see, fifty yards up the tracks, an original wooden cattle car, the kind the Nazis had used to transport Jews to the camps. It had a plaque on its side now, like a museum piece. As Udo stared he recalled its dimensions, how long, how wide, and how many Jews he had estimated to fit inside. Eighty-seven, if memory served, although he proudly crammed in over a hundred.

A microphone and a podium had been set up, and one of the organizers instructed those who were related to the Jewish victims to come forward one at a time, say the names of whom they'd lost, and lay a carnation on the tracks.

An old woman in a gray coat went first.

"On this platform, I lost my husband, Avram Djahon, forty years ago," she said. "He'd sent me to Athens the week before, to protect me. The Nazis took him. I never saw him again. May God watch over his soul."

She dropped a carnation onto the tracks and shuffled from the podium. Next came a thin middle-aged man with a neatly trimmed beard.

"On this platform, I lost my parents, Eliahou and Loucha Houli . . ."

Udo exhaled. Such melodrama. The shaky voices. The tears. Did they have any idea the planning and logistics that went into those trains? The sheer volume of paperwork and manpower?

"On this platform, I lost my great-grandfather . . ."

"On this platform, I lost my three aunts . . ."

Udo shook his head. Where these people saw mourning, he saw honor. Where they saw tragedy, he saw achievement. He was holding a balloon that read "Never again." How ridiculous. He was planning exactly the opposite.

The line of mourners had fully formed, and Udo noted that the Hunter and the Brother had taken their places at the rear of it. When they reached the podium, he told himself, he would kill the first with a shot to the head, then kill the other a few feet away. He slid his way through the crowd, until he found the best angle.

"On this platform, I lost my uncle Morris . . ."

"On this platform, I lost my sister, Vida . . ."

Keep on weeping, Jews, Udo said to himself. He fingered the pistol in his coat pocket. It felt good to touch steel. It felt good to be fighting back. After three years on the run from these Jewish rats, it felt good to be the one chasing.

The Tracks Remember

There are four directions in this world. And four seasons. There are four basic mathematical functions, and four subsystems of the planet. The Bible speaks of four rivers of paradise. Four winds of heaven. There are four suits in a deck of cards. Four wheels on a car. Four legs on a table.

Four is an underpinning. Four is a balance. Four is a complete circle of the bases, until you end where you began, at home.

It is time for us to come home.

Here, then, is the end of our four-cornered story.

Sebastian held a cluster of red carnations.

One flower each for his parents, grandparents, twin sisters, and uncle and aunt. As the line neared its conclusion, he felt a tap on his shoulder. He turned to see Fannie and Tia. Fannie hugged him lightly and wiped a tear from her eye.

"I'm proud of you," she said. "For doing this."

"Me, too," Tia said.

Sebastian felt a choke in his throat.

"Thank you," he whispered.

Fannie held out a carnation. "For your brother."

Sebastian hesitated, then took it.

"Your turn, Papa," Tia said.

The breeze was picking up, and the white balloons whipped with the wind. Sebastian walked across the platform and stopped at the microphone. He glanced skyward to see an unusual sight: snowflakes blowing through the air. Snowflakes? In March? He cocked his head, as if curious, and he felt one land on his nose, cold, small, and wet.

Forty feet away, Udo Graf reached into his jacket.

Finally, a clean shot. He could put an end to this Jewish filth who had ruined his life. *First the Brother, then the old man.* He would barely have to move his arm.

Sebastian opened his mouth to speak, planning to begin the way the others had. The words echoed over the crowd.

"On this platform . . ."

Udo looked up. Sebastian looked up, too. Because it wasn't Sebastian's voice saying those words, but someone else's, a man's voice, blasting through the loudspeakers the Nazis once used to announce their train departures.

"On this platform . . . I told your families a terrible lie!" the voice bellowed. "I told them it was safe! I told them they were going someplace good! I told them they would have jobs, and they would all be together again!

"I'm sorry. It was never true."

The crowd hushed. Heads swiveled. For the first time in their lives, Sebastian, Fannie, and Udo Graf shared the same thought at the same time:

Nico.

"On this platform, I deceived my own people. Everyone I knew. Everyone I loved. I watched them all taken away, still believing what I'd told them.

"But I was lied to, as well. I was told my words were true. I was told my family would be safe."

A pause.

"They weren't."

Sebastian bent forward and back, trying desperately to determine where the voice was coming from. A fury rose inside him as it continued.

"There were many people responsible for the horrors that happened here. But one man more than anyone else. His name was Udo Graf. A Nazi *Schutzhaftlagerführer*. He organized it all."

In the crowd, Udo froze, his hand still gripping the gun in his jacket.

"He put our families in the ghetto. He sent them to Auschwitz. And in Auschwitz, he had them murdered like animals. Shot. Gassed. Their bodies never buried, just burned to ashes."

Udo felt sweat beading under his wig.

"But you should know that justice was served. Udo Graf is dead. He died at the hands of a brave Jew. He died with all his evil dreams denied. *Er starb als Feigling. Er starb allein.* He died a coward. He died alone."

Udo couldn't take any more. He ripped off the hat and wig, let go of the balloon, and whipped out his gun.

"It's a lie!" he screamed. "You're a liar! You lie!"

∞

What happened next took less than nine seconds, yet felt like a long dream. Sebastian saw a white balloon rising, and beneath it, Udo Graf waving a pistol. He heard Fannie's voice screaming his name. He saw the Hunter dive to the ground. Then, just before the sudden pop of gunshots, Sebastian was smothered by a body that knocked him to the platform and sent the carnations flying.

He landed with a thud, blinded by the impact. He tried to find his breath. Lying on his back, feeling the cold concrete beneath his shoulders, he opened his eyes to see a blond-haired man lying on top of him, and a face he would have known forty years earlier, or forty years in the future.

"You!" Sebastian gasped.

"I'm sorry, brother," Nico whispered. "I knew he would be here. I had to draw him out."

"Graf?"

"He's yours now. You can bring him to justice."

In the crowd, three men tackled Udo to the ground. Another man stepped on his arm, freeing the gun, and a police officer pushed through and grabbed it. Tia was on her knees, screaming and holding on to Fannie, who was dragging forward, trying to reach the two men entwined on the platform.

Sebastian, feeling his brother's weight, was almost too

stunned to speak. Udo Graf and Nico? The pair he'd been obsessing over his entire adult life? Finally, he had them both. But not the way he imagined.

"It's really you, then?"

"It's me," Nico grunted.

Sebastian tried to get used to the voice. The last time he'd heard Nico speak, he was a child.

"I hated you, Nico. All these years."

"It doesn't matter, brother."

"It does. The truth matters."

"Which truth?"

"That you lied to us. Why did you do it, Nico? Why did you help them?"

Nico lifted his head.

"To save our family."

Sebastian blinked hard.

"What?"

"Graf said you would all come home. He promised we'd be together again."

"And you believed him? For God's sake, Nico, they were Nazis!"

Nico sighed. "I was a kid."

Sebastian felt the tears welling up, as if decades of misplaced anger were melting behind his eyes.

"Where did you go? How did you live? Where have you been all this time?"

"Atoning," Nico rasped.

He forced a smile, but his breathing was labored. Sebastian

tried to muster a righteous rage, but it was failing. At that moment, he could only hear his father's final request. *Find your brother one day. Tell him he is forgiven.*

"You can stop atoning now," Sebastian finally whispered.

For a moment, they just stared at each other, until the age wrinkles and graying whiskers seemed to melt away. They were back to being two young brothers, resting atop one another, as if they'd just finished wrestling in the bedroom.

"Listen," Nico said, his voice growing thin. "I have Graf's Nazi papers. With fingerprints. They're in my pocket, OK?"

"What?"

"My pocket. Take them."

"You'll give them to me later."

Nico squeezed his eyes shut. "I don't think I will."

As Sebastian shifted, he felt something warm and wet on his chest, and he realized it was blood, a great deal of it. It was sticky, bonding them together.

Nico rolled and flopped backward, his eyes to the sky. He'd taken two of Graf's bullets, and was bleeding badly below the chest. His mouth fell open in a half smile, as if watching something amusing in the clouds.

Suddenly, Fannie was next to him. She leaned over, crying, cupping his face.

"Nico! Nico!"

"Nico!" Sebastian echoed.

At that moment, with his heartbeat slowing, it occurred to Nico how nice it was that the three of them were all together again, like the time they climbed the White Tower by the gulf. And as everything he had done in his life—all the lies, and all the efforts to make amends—came rushing past in a final blur, Nico realized his grandfather had been right about that prisoner, who kept painting and painting until the tower was white enough to cleanse his sins.

A man, to be forgiven, will do anything.

What happened next, as Fannie held Nico's head and Sebastian pressed on his wound, is something I cannot explain.

The old boxcar began to move. It creaked along the tracks, slowly accelerating, ten feet, twenty feet, as if returning from a long journey and pulling into the station. People in the crowd nudged one another until they were all staring, their mouths agape.

Then, as snowflakes rode the winter wind like ashes, the train came to a stop. Its doors slid open. Fannie felt Nico's head lift from her fingers. He stared for a long moment into the boxcar, then smiled, tears running down his cheeks, as if seeing the faces of everyone he'd ever loved and lied to, come to take him home.

He died a moment later, in the arms of the woman who adored him and the hands of the brother who absolved him. It may sound incredible, but that is what happened. Truth be told. Truth be told.

And Let Us Say . . .

Many years have passed since that incident in Salonika. And while perhaps nothing as dramatic as that day is left to share, I am bound to complete the story.

Dead men tell no lies, but their truths must be unearthed. Nico Krispis left behind many layers of discovery. His true identity was never revealed in the Hollywood community, since the only people who knew he was The Financier were Fannie and Sebastian. His studio closed under the same shroud of secrecy with which it had operated, explained in the trades as "the sudden retirement of its reclusive founder." His explicit instructions, found in a manila envelope in a file cabinet, were for his projectionist, a woman named Fannie, to close out his affairs, pay whatever bills were outstanding, and draw down the operations, which she did.

When the moving men were sent to Nico's home, Fannie accompanied them. She stood in his sparsely furnished bedroom, finding only an old leather bag in the closet. When one of the movers asked, "What about the stuff in the basement?"

she followed him down the stairs and entered a dimly lit back room. Once again, she was taken by surprise.

There, in front of a gray curtain, was a movie camera on a tripod, a chair, and a set of lights. On the shelves were rows and rows of blue metal canisters, each bearing a number and containing a reel of film.

"Oh, Nico," Fannie whispered.

That night, in the studio screening room, she threaded the first film through the spools, turned on the projector, and saw Nico's face when he was in his twenties. Looking straight into the lens, his blond hair full and his features still vaguely boyish, he began: "This is how I survived the war . . ."

Fannie stopped the film, and immediately called Sebastian. "When can you come to California?" she said.

In the weeks that followed, the two of them viewed every reel, Nico telling the story of his incredible life. He detailed his various identities, as a German soldier, a Yugoslavian student, a Hungarian musician, a Polish Red Cross worker. He spoke of living with the Romani, learning to forge documents, stealing a uniform, posing as a young Nazi. He explained his relationship with the actress Katalin Karády and credited her with encouraging him to be brave, and teaching him about the movies. When he recalled that night on the Danube, he explained how he'd recognized Fannie, how happy he was to see her alive, and how, after making sure she was spared from the Arrow Cross, he used Katalin's contacts to locate Gizella, the woman who had protected his friend, and sent money to a priest to have her freed.

When Fannie heard that, she burst into tears.

Nico recounted hundreds of conversations. For years, he had told the world nothing but lies, but to the camera he spoke only the truth, as if, having shared it with no one else, he'd preserved every piece meticulously.

In the final reels, he left instructions as to how his fortune should be distributed. Everything he owned—the stolen treasure from a Hungarian church, and every penny he made from his films—was to continue going to the families of survivors listed in his files. He had spent years flying back and forth to Europe to trace as many as he could, starting with children's names scrawled on the walls of a basement in Zakopane, Poland, and continuing to every person on the Nazi manifests of trains out of Salonika.

He insisted that the funds be delivered to the victims' children, and their children's children, every year, on August 10, until it was all gone. He wished for this to be done anonymously, as a *chesed shel emet*, an act of kindness not to be repaid.

In the final reel, recorded just before he left for Greece, he explained how he knew that Udo Graf would be in Salonika, because he'd kept tabs on the man for years, through secret payments to a certain U.S. senator. He'd been notified that the former *Schutzhaftlagerführer* had booked a ticket from Italy to Greece in March. Once Nico learned of Sebastian's ceremony from a film director, and that the Hunter and Sebastian would be there, he knew what Graf was planning. And he had to stop it.

He thanked Fannie for finding him, for making him meals, and for not pushing him to face his own reflection until he was ready, something, he said, he could not have done without her. He also thanked her for letting him "feel what it was like to be loved," even for a little while.

He saved his final story for his brother. He said he knew that Sebastian assumed he had abandoned his family, but in truth, he had spent every day since they parted on the train tracks trying to get to Auschwitz. He explained how, after all that time, they had apparently missed each other by a few minutes on liberation day. But he'd discovered their grandfather, Lazarre, in the infirmary, and although he could not bring himself to tell his Nano the truth, he did come back and stay with him for his final days, posing as a doctor, holding his hand. During that time, whenever the blind man spoke, he always asked for "my brave grandson, Sebastian."

Nico thought his brother would like to hear that.

When Lazarre died, Nico transported the body out of the camp and buried him in a faraway field, because he knew that his grandfather would not wish to be laid to rest in Nazi camp soil. He found a small boulder and used it as a headstone. A year later, using some of his newfound money, Nico went back and purchased the land that held the grave. And every summer, he went there to clean the stone with a rag and some water. He thought maybe Sebastian would like to continue that.

And what became of Udo Graf?

Well. The way our story has gone, you might assume he got what he deserved. But justice is never certain. Its scales can be manipulated.

Udo denied the murder charge, claiming he only shot his gun in the air as protest. He disavowed any connection to the Nazis. Flashing his Italian passport, he claimed to be a nationalist who simply did not believe "the lie of the Holocaust."

Only when Sebastian, during a court hearing, held up a certain piece of Nazi identification his brother had provided and said, "This official document has Udo Graf's fingerprints," did Udo abruptly change his story and admit his true identity. He never knew that those papers, like so many others in Nico's life, were a forgery.

But Udo was not finished with his manipulations. His lawyers insisted upon a trial in his home country. And, difficult as it is to believe, that request was granted, after certain Greek officials, paid by unknown benefactors, agreed that a German court was better equipped to punish a former Nazi than a Greek one. The fact that Udo had privately threatened to reveal the names of his Salonika collaborators from the war years had much to do with his release. Udo kept meticulous diaries. A particular judge, whose father was among the people listed in those pages, ruled in Udo's favor.

The *Schutzhaftlagerführer* was going home.

Sebastian and the Nazi Hunter were livid. They stormed the prosecutors' offices and screamed, "Who's paying you?," but they got no answers. *The Germans will handle it*, they were told.

It took several weeks to extradite Graf. He was set to fly

to Frankfurt, but fearful that a plane could be rerouted and taken to Israel, he requested to go by train. And again, incredibly, his request was granted.

All of this infuriated the many groups who had called for his imprisonment. Editorials were written. Complaints were lodged.

But one person, who had witnessed enough of what this man had done to others, did more than complain. Truth calls for a reckoning, whether immediate or in the distant future. In Udo's case, it took a lifetime. But it came.

When he boarded the train, flanked by two Greek police officers, he was brimming with confidence. Returning to his beloved Deutschland meant he would be treated honorably. Of that he was sure. As the car sped through the countryside, a female attendant offered them drinks from a cart, and Udo asked the police if he could be permitted a glass of red wine. The officers shrugged. Udo privately toasted himself on his survival abilities. He was actually looking forward to his trial. He would get to speak in his native tongue. The voice of the Wolf would be heard again. *Deutschland über alles!*

He drank the wine, down to the last drop, and returned the glass to the attendant, never noticing the white gloves she wore, or her necklace of old red rosary beads, or the fact that two of those beads were missing, having been cracked open and dissolved in his drink.

Two miles from the German border, Udo Graf choked, coughed, slumped in his seat, and closed his eyes forever, the poison in his system denying him his longed-for home-coming.

It was exactly as Nico had said at the train station. He died a coward. He died alone. At the hands of a brave Jew.

Sometimes a lie is merely truth that is yet to happen.

. . . Amen

I told you at the start that Truth was cast out by God. But just as you long to see your loved ones in the hereafter, so do I dream of a heavenly return. An Almighty embrace.

Before that happens, I have a confession to make. Since the beginning of our story, I have omitted one small detail.

I was banished to earth because I was right about mankind. Humans are broken. Susceptible to sin. They were created with minds to explore, but they often choose to explore their own power. They lie. And those lies let them think they are God.

Truth is the only thing that stops them.

And yet. You cannot drown out noise with silence. Truth needs a voice. To share this story, I needed a specific voice. One that listened as Nico confessed his odyssey, one that understood Sebastian in the most personal way, one that was there for every step of Fannie's tortured journey, one that absorbed every word of the posthumously discovered diaries of Udo Graf.

One that could tell you of the horrors the Wolf brought to this earth, from the streets of Salonika to the window of a crowded boxcar to the death camps to the gas chambers to the bloody banks of the Danube River.

One that could explain how hope survived that evil, in the kindness of a seamstress, in the courage of an actress, in the loving protection of a father and a grandfather, in the tender hearts of three children who somehow knew they would see each other again.

A voice that could warn you how a lie told once is easy to expose, but a lie told a thousand times can look like the truth.

And destroy the world.

I am that voice. And to share these words, just like the parable, I donned a colorful robe, and made sure Truth's reckoning was delivered.

I was asked twice in my human existence to "tell the world what happened here," and it has been my lifelong burden to do so, right up to this last moment. I have tried to be a good person, but I am old now, and near death. The others are buried. I am all that remains of the story.

Here then, with my final words, I will finish it.

My name is Fannie Nahmias Krispis.

Wife of Sebastian.
Lover of Nico.
Killer of Udo Graf.

Everything I have told you is the Truth.
And therefore, finally, blessed be the Lord, I am free.

From the Author

This story is a work of fiction, but many brutal truths went into its construction. Because of that, I need to start by thanking everyone brave enough to tell the story of what happened during the Holocaust, from the historians whose books I devoured, to the survivors whose firsthand accounts showed the world what it could barely imagine.

It takes enormous courage to relive the worst things that have happened to you. Without the brave accounts of those who lived through it, we would never know the depth of the evil that took place at the hands of the Nazis, and would have no blueprint to ensure it never happens again.

I tried, in this book, to keep true to the nature of those accounts, and to accurately portray what happened to the Jews of Salonika, or as the Greeks and others call it, Thessaloniki, or Saloniki, or Salonica, reflecting the many influences of such a diverse place. A novel is not a history book, of course, but whenever possible, the events of this story mirror what took place during the late 1930s and '40s in that city.

So why this book at this time? Well. For much of my writing life, I have wanted to set a story during the Holocaust. But I couldn't seem to find one that wasn't already tragically familiar.

On a visit to a museum, more than a decade ago, I saw a video from a survivor recounting how Jews were sometimes used to lie to fellow Jews about where the trains to the concentration camps were going. That perversion of truth, with life and death on the line, stayed with me months and even years later.

The seed of *The Little Liar* began with that image.

Then, a few years ago, I began to read about the Greek experience under the Nazis. I had lived in Greece when I got out of college, as a musician on the island of Crete. During my time there, I came to love the Greek people and their culture.

When, during my research, I discovered that Salonika (as most of the non-Greek world referred to it back then) had the highest percentage Jewish population of all the cities that the Nazis destroyed, I knew I had found a home for my story, and its characters began to rise from those historic streets.

It is my hope that this book, in addition to serving as a warning about what happens when truth is no longer an imperative, will inspire further examination of what Greek Jews had to endure during the war. Their losses and suffering, like the other countless victims of Nazi persecution, can never truly be measured.

∞✧∞

A number of people helped me greatly in this endeavor. I first need to thank the indefatigable Efi Kalampoukidou, who served as my guide, translator, historian, and overall touchstone for life in Salonika over the years. She showed me the city as few could, and I am forever grateful for the large and small details she provided during my writing process. Standing with her as she told stories on the platform of the old train station, I could feel this story rumbling beneath my feet.

Also special thanks to Dr. Drew A. Curtis, PhD, LP, Angelo State University, who patiently explained to me the science behind pathological lying, and how someone like Nico might suffer from it.

Deep appreciation to Rabbi Steven Lindemann, who shared parables, Talmudic references, and Jewish viewpoints on truth and lying, and gave this book an early read. He then produced pages of questions. He did this en route to working with our kids in Haiti, something he does regularly. A true and loving kindness indeed.

It would be impossible to credit all the sources of material that shed light on what took place in the death camps—and in the ghettos, and in Liberty Square, and on the banks of the Danube—or the incredible courage of Katalin Karády. So many personal accounts were researched in the process, and if familiarities are found in some of what Nico, Fannie, and Sebastian go through, I sincerely hope it is perceived as sharing a story that must continually be retold.

Particular thanks go to the Zekelman Holocaust Center, its staff, and its speakers series, as well as Yad Vashem in Jerusalem, a precious and invaluable resource.

My regular team continues to amaze me: Jo-Ann Barnas, who goes to any depth in her meticulous research; Kerri Alexander, who handles all tasks, big and small; Antonella Iannarino, who makes loving sense of the digital universe for me; and Marc "Rosey" Rosenthal, who helps clear the decks of my life so I can give my writing the focus it deserves.

David Black and I have worked together for thirty-five years on a handshake, which has become a symbol of a friendship more than a business. And Karen Rinaldi, who has now edited more of my books than anyone, encouraged me, as I sunk deeper into this story, to never forget the simple beauty that can be found even under life's most impossibly difficult circumstances. The White Tower's inspiration is directly traceable to her.

Thanks to the entire publishing team at HarperCollins, Brian Murray, Jonathan Burnham, Leslie Cohen, Tina Andreadis, Doug Jones, Kirby Sandmeyer, and Milan Bozic, for another inspired cover. And deep appreciation to my foreign publishers, who continue to believe my stories have value in other lands and languages. For that, I have to thank the incomparable Susan Raihofer, who rings the bell for me around the globe.

I grew up knowing older people who wore long sleeves, even in warm weather, to hide the blue tattooed numbers near their wrists. I heard whispers and fragmented stories about a horror that seemed out of a scary movie. Although there are too many to credit, I wish to acknowledge Eva and Solomon Nesser, Joe and Chana Magun, and Rita and Izzy Smilovitz, among many others, for teaching me, through their memories, why the phrase "never again" must be not an expression, but a vow.

Through my readers, old and new, I know the privilege of telling stories. Through my family, immediate and widespread, I know the joy of sharing the world. Through our kids in Haiti, and most recently, little baby Naddie, I get to witness how new life is the cure for old woes. And Mendel is still a bum.

Finally, I could never do what I do without the love of my precious wife, Janine. And neither of us could do anything without the love of God. Truth be told. Truth be told.

Mitch Albom
July 2023